Ptolemaic England

J.C. Pacheco

ISBN: 978-1-7340366-2-6

To my mother, 'S', 'K', and 'S'

CONTENTS

1 LUX AETERNA

Gemma—England—June Wedding

MAYFAIR

Gemma, the daughter of the 8th Baron, sat in the high backed chair at the salon. It was the last week of May, and Poppy had still not selected her wedding dress. The wedding was only three weeks away, and Poppy was undecided. The dress she had originally selected had quickly lost its luster. Poppy wanted something really special. She had waited until forty to get married, so she had had a lot of time to think about her wedding day. You would think this would have made everything easier, but the opposite was true.

Gemma was happy to accompany Poppy on her constant excursions to dress shops across London. Gemma actually enjoyed it.

The dressing room door opened, and the bantam daughter of the 12th Baron stepped into the small mirrored chamber.

The octagonal room in the dress shop in the West End of London had hardwood floors and five mirrors attached to the walls of the salon. There were two doors: one which led to the dressing room and the other to the main room of the dress shop. One wall was a large narrow window that opened on to a private garden. There was an ottoman upholstered in white cashmere wool and two high backed chairs upholstered in the same material. The room was lit by small disc shaped wall lamps which were mounted on the walls around the room. The window also allowed in a lot of natural sunlight, especially on a sunny day in May.

The diminutive Poppy was radiant. The white dress clung to her slim frame perfectly. Poppy's glossy blonde hair had grown out quite a bit in the last

1

few months and rested beautifully on her shoulders. Poppy was not wearing her tiara and veil, so Gemma had to visualize how it would all look together.

'Well, what do you think, Gemmy?' asked Poppy pensively. .

'This one is perfect. I really like it,' replied Gemma happily. 'It's beautiful,' said Gemma as she stood to admire the dress.

'Really, Gem? You like this one the best?'

'Yes.'

Poppy smiled. 'I like this dress most of all. I think it will look fantastic with my tiara and veil.'

Poppy then turned to look at herself in the mirror. She gazed at her reflection. She noticed Gemma standing behind her in her navy blue pencil skirt and white blouse. Gemma was still beautiful.

The two of them had been through so much in the last few months. Poppy felt a shudder race through her. Poppy found herself reflecting on everything. She smiled. They had survived—together. And The Happy Gang of Inseparable Girls was back together.

The door from the main salon opened and Külli entered. She was beautiful. Her glossy brown hair now had blond highlights in it. The approximately six foot tall Külli towered over the two girls in the room. Külli was wearing a charcoal grey skirt, a pale blue open-collared blouse, and a pair of black high heels—which made her even taller than she already was. She was wearing a platinum watch and her mirrored Gentle Monster sunglasses were tilted back and resting on her head.

'You look fantastic, Poppy. I really like this one,' she said, and Külli smiled.

A young salesgirl then came through the door. She smiled and nodded at the women in the room. She stood against the wall and awaited

2

instructions.

'I think this one is perfect, Gula. I think I'll get this one.'

The door then opened again and Violet, the daughter of the 5th Viscount, wearing a pleated slate grey wool skirt with a white blouse, glided into the room. Violet's long blonde hair was tied back with a white ribbon. She was slim, stylish, and attractive. Her blue eyes carefully examined Poppy's wedding dress. Violet smiled.

'Poppy, I love it,' said Violet.

'Really, Vava? I love it too,' said Poppy. Alright then, it's settled. I'm getting this one,' she said and Poppy smiled.

MARBLE ARCH
Külli and Gemma sat in the upstairs office. Külli had taped several fashion illustrations from her coming collection on the walls of her office. Gemma walked around the room examining each drawing very carefully. Külli watched Gemma carefully; she was trying to read her reactions. Gemma smiled as she viewed each illustration.

'I like all of them, G,' said Gemma.

Külli smiled. 'I figured you would say that. Okay, Gem. If you could make any changes to the designs, what would you change?'

Gemma smiled. 'I would put purple piping on the edge of your blazers. I like purple. I would also consider orange piping too. A splash of orange can be nice.'

Külli looked surprised. Gemma was right. Those would be nice additions to Külli's designs.

'Gemmy, you still have a great eye for fashion. You should start your own f   n magazine,' said Külli sincerely.

3

'That's an idea, Gula,' said Gemma and she arched one of her eye brows.

Külli was happy to have Gemma back in her life. Everything was better now. Külli was happy. She was back with Gemma and the girls. Külli woke up every day and happily looked out the windows of her Marble Arch house. Also, Külli had found love.

Daphne had returned to school and unsurprisingly found a boyfriend. Külli had been sad to lose Daphne, but she accepted that it was not meant to be.

Now that she had resolved everything with Gemma, Külli was in the mood for love—and she had found it in the person of a 29 year-old architect. Külli had found love.

OCTAVIA
Külli had met Octavia at a fox hunt a month earlier. Octavia had entered the Victorian era stables to retrieve her mount when she caught Külli's eye. Octavia was wearing a perfectly tailored blue hunt coat, beige jodhpurs, and leather riding boots. Her long hair was worn in a long braid down her back. She looked posh. Külli liked posh girls.

Octavia stood 5'7", had dark brown hair, and blue eyes. Octavia was beautiful.She was slim, and to be entirely honest, yes—she bore a resemblance to Gemma. Only she was taller and over a decade younger then Gemma.

Octavia had also noticed Külli; how could she not? The instant Octavia's gaze met Külli's, Octavia smiled. The attraction was electric—and mutual. Külli smiled.

THE INSEPARABLE GANG OF HAPPY GIRLS
Külli would always love Gemma—that love had remained unchanged and eternal; however, the love she felt had been tempered by understanding. Külli had found peace, and that peace had freed Külli . Gemma and Külli were the closest of friends.

Ever since the gang had reunited, Külli had been amazed at the changes to everyone's lives.

Gemma was not the same person she had known in Sussex or even at Oxford, but Gemma had seemingly recovered from a lot of trauma that she had unfortunately endured. Külli regretted that she had been a big part of that trauma herself. Külli was grateful that fate (and Gemma) had given her a chance to redeem herself and repair the damaged that she had inflicted on the gentle and kind Gemma. Külli doubted she would ever forgive herself for what she had done to Gemma (yes, that's a good way to describe it), but she was determined to try and repair as much of the damage as possible.

Gemma had turned out to be the strongest of the gang. Everyone agreed. Gemma was the strongest. Gemma had endured so much—too much really—and yet, Gemma had survived and now seemed to have regained her bearings. Külli was often brought to tears when she though about it.

Since their reconciliation, Külli had become very protective of Gemma. All the girls had. Külli didn't know what had actually gone on with Grey and Gemma. She knew what she had read in the newspapers and seen on television and what very little Gemma would tell her. The other girls remained completely unwilling to talk about it. Külli didn't force it. She could sense that something really terrible had happened. Külli decided that it was entirely up to Gemma to tell her.

The 'dangerously cute' Poppy had turned out to be stronger than anyone thought possible. Gemma and Poppy had always been close, but the twenty years apart from Külli had brought Gemma and Poppy incredibly close. Külli wasn't jealous. Poppy had been there for Gemma when Külli had not. That abandonment stirred up a lot of remorse in Külli. Gemma had forgiven her; Külli was certain of it. But still, Külli would never forgive herself.

The biggest change had been Violet. Vava's personality had undergone a startling change. She had become warm and kind hearted. She had even hugged Külli when they met for tea that Saturday back in January. The same day that the damaged and brave Gemma had knocked on Külli's front door. Vava had actually started crying when she embraced Gula in her drawing room in Marble Arch that afternoon. Vava also looked different physically. Vava was now quite attractive (to even Gula). The change in heart had led to physical changes in her demeanor and appearance. Vava had become quite alluring. She relaxed completely when she was with the girls and her body had taken on a certain slinkiness it had never had before.

The girls were now in their early forties. Gemma, the oldest by a few weeks or months, was now 41. She was remarkably youthful and still beautiful. In spite of everything Gemma had gone through (and Külli could only guess at the extent of it), Gemma was still beautiful. All the girls had managed to maintain their looks; and all of them had done it through proper diet, skin care, and exercise. Undoubtedly good DNA had also played its part too. Yes, the girls were still quite a striking set.

Gemma— England —Sussex in the Spring

SUSSEX
Freya and Louise found themselves in their room at school on a beautiful spring day studying for their finals. They would soon complete the sixth form and be off to university—separately.

The weather could not have been nicer that year in Sussex. The girls kept the large sash windows to their room open during the day. The leafy green trees shaded them from the Sun and a pleasant spring breeze cooled them constantly. Outside the dormitory **stretched** the wide green lawns of All Saints.

Louise, wearing her blue, red, and purple school tartan skirt and white blouse, sat at her desk. Her strawberry blonde hair had grown to shoulder length. Louise kept her hair tied back with a white ribbon. Louise studied her notes carefully; chemistry was a difficult subject for her, and her exam was next week.

Freya, wearing blue track pants (with three white stripes) and a white t-shirt, was lying in bed. She was on her back and studying notes she had made on a set of index cards. (Yes, some people still use index cards to study.) History was easy for Freya; she enjoyed studying it. It was one of the few

6

classes she did well in. Freya was studying the history of the Crimean War. So many names and dates.

Louise turned around in her chair and looked at Freya.

'Frey, what are you going to wear to the wedding?'

Freya looked up from her index cards. 'I'm not sure. My mother has purchased several dresses for me to select from,' said Freya. She looked at Louise and then smiled. ' Louise, let's go into London this weekend. I'll help you find something.'

Louise looked pensive for a moment. 'Thank you, Freya. Thank you for everything. Thank you for being my friend. You changed my life. And you saved my life, more than once,' she said quietly and reflectively.

Yes, both girls were thinking of that night last January when they had to run for the lives through the forest and evade the two men sent by Grey to kill them. The details had remained scarce. They had only shared the true events of that night with Gemma, Poppy, and Karmen. They were unsure of what had really gone on, but they didn't want to draw attention to Gemma. Everyone had decided to take that event to their graves. But, that being said, none of them could help thinking about what had happened (or had almost happened).

Both girls were now 18 and about to complete the sixth form. They would both enter university in the fall. Both had been traumatized, damaged, and strengthened by the events of that night. Both had been born an only child; both had found a sister, or perhaps, a relationship even stronger. Their bond was holy and pure.

'I'm sure Mummy would be happy to help you find something this weekend. I'll have her take you to Dior,' smiled Freya.

'No, that's alright. I bought something at Zara. It's quite nice. But, thank you, Freya,' she replied and Louise smiled. 'One day I hope I will be able to repay your kindness, somehow, in some way.'

'Being my friend is more than enough, Louise.'

THE CITY

Gemma sat at her desk in The Gherkin. She had been very busy that day arranging files, arranging meetings, and confirming travel arrangements for a seminar in Singapore. Gemma would be going this time. She was excited; she had never been to Asia. Alexa was taking senior staff with her, and that meant Gemma.

She paused for a moment and looked out on London through one of the glass walls which encircled her in the round office. London spread out before her in panorama. She had a lot to do before the wedding. A wave of relief moved through her like a breeze. Gemma was free. She had survived a lifetime of reversals, and she was now moving forward. She wanted to cry; instead she chose to smile.

'Gemma,' asked the slim young man with a red and blue tartan neck tie, 'What time is the meeting with Mr Lee?'

'Eleven in the morning,' replied Gemma.

'Thank you,' he replied. 'Oh, a package arrived for you this morning via courier; did you get it?'

'No,' she replied. 'Where is it?'

'It was left at the front desk for you. I'm surprised you weren't informed this morning.'

'Thank you. I'll go and get it now.'

Gemma stood up and walked across the large office past desks, computer monitors, and ringing telephones. She was wearing a light grey pleated pencil skirt and a white blouse. She stopped in front of the semi-circle front desk near the elevator and asked if she had a package. She did. The apologetic receptionist handed her the small cardboard box wrapped in plastic and covered in address tags and bar code stickers. She looked at the label: JERSEY.

She walked back to her desk. She would open it later. Right now, she had a lot of work to do.

MARBLE ARCH

Külli stood on the treadmill and tapped on the digital screen in front of her. She was wearing blue Adidas track pants (with three white stripes) and a white t-shirt. The treadmill started to move. She tapped on the screen of the machine and it started to speed up. Okay, now this was a good rate. Külli's slim and athletic form moved steadily. She was physically fit, and her body responded immediately to each adjustment.

Külli didn't have a care in the world.

The last few months had been transformative. She was at peace with herself and her friendships with the girls had been restored. She had her dress for the wedding upstairs in her closet and had already selected wedding presents for Poppy and Brian.

She had had lunch at a Hungarian restaurant in the City with Vava—of all people—and enjoyed steak and riotous conversation with her. Vava had truly changed, for whatever reason; she had become a better person. The disconnected Violet was gone, and a warm and friendly Vava had replaced her. Vava's wit had remained as sharp as ever. Külli liked that.

They had invited Gemma to lunch with them at the last moment (the whole luncheon had been a spur of the moment event), but Gemma was unable to make it. Poppy also had a lunch commitment. Vava was happy to have lunch alone with Gula; after all it had been *yonks* since they had been alone. Perhaps it was better; the two of them had not been alone together since the rapprochement.

THE HUNGARIAN RESTAURANT

Vava's long glossy blond hair rested on both of her shoulders. She was wearing a white Egyptian cotton blouse with a large collar and faded denim blue jeans. She was also wearing brown leather Chelsea boots and carrying a blue suede clutch. Vava absolutely glowed. At 41, she looked at least a decade younger. She was slim and shapely. No one would have guessed that she a daughter who was about to enter university. Violet could barely believe it herself.

'It's dreadful, G. Freya did so poorly in school that she is going to attend uni in the Midlands. The Midlands,' she said and Violet shook her head.

9

'Louise is attending school in London—at a really good university—so Freya won't be able to room with her. They are best friends. Louise is the kindest little thing. I adore her,' said Violet.

'Yes, Louise is very sweet. The girls are lucky to have found each other. We were lucky too,' replied Külli and she smiled.

'Yes. Sussex was such a *hoot*,' replied Violet happily. She sighed. 'I only wish Freya had enjoyed it. I doubt she will send any of her offspring to be educated there. It's *too* sad really. I would liked to have kept the tradition going. My grandmother and mother both attended.'

'You never know. Freya just might surprise you. She seems the type to do just that,' replied Külli.

Külli smiled; she was positively overjoyed to be reminiscing with Violet about their school days. Külli couldn't believe it. Everything in the Universe was as it should be now.

ESTONIA

Külli looked around the restaurant. Its red walls were decorated with 19th century Hungarian hussar tunics and old photographs. Above the entrance to the small private outside seating area were crossed sabres. Külli's grandfather had been in a hussar regiment. When she thought of her relatives in Estonia, she only felt sadness.

After the fall of the Iron Curtain, her father had attempted to discover the fate of his parents and grandparents to no avail. The family estate had been taken over by the Soviet army and had served as an officer club for the Red Army after World War Two. In 1997, after a lengthy legal battle, Külli 's family had recovered the main house and a few acres of land around it. The house was in a terrible state of disrepair; Russian soldiers had vandalized the house just before they departed the Baltics and returned to Russia.

Külli's father had paid to have basic repairs done, but he died before the house could be fully restored. Külli had continued to pay for its upkeep. Sitting in the restaurant, at that very moment, Külli resolved to fully restore the family home.

'You know, Va, I plan to visit Estonia this summer. I'm going to oversee the renovation of my family's house.'

'Is that the house you showed me photos of when we were in Sussex?'

'Yes'.

'How *completely thrilling*. I remember. It's quite an impressive family pile.'

'We only have a few acres around it. The house used to be a country estate, now it is surrounded by abandoned factories and Soviet style apartment blocks. It's all *rather* depressing. The area has become a Bohemian area of the city. The local government wanted to lease it from me so that they could turn it into an art school. I refused. I suppose I'm being selfish, but I feel that restoring it to a private home is what my father would have wanted.'

'Not selfish at all, G, said Violet. 'A person has a right to do what they want with their own property.'

'So, when am I going to meet Octavia?' asked Violet with a smile.

Külli blushed. Violet noticed and laughed.

'Gula. I never thought I'd see the day that you blushed about anything.'

Külli smiled. She didn't know why she had blushed, but perhaps it was because of the remarkable resemblance that Octavia bore to Gemma. Yes, everyone would notice and comment privately. Gemma would notice too, but Külli knew she would never say anything about it.

Yes, Külli had finally found a love beyond Gemma. Though Külli loved Gemma as much as ever, Külli's reconciliation with Gemma had freed her and fate had led her to Octavia.

Octavia. The mere thought of her filled her with happiness—a happiness that Külli hadn't thought possible just a few months before. It wasn't too late to find love. Now Külli realized that. She prayed that Gemma would find love too. Yes, she wanted Gemma to find someone too.

'Octavia is busier than I am these days. Don't fret, Vava. You'll meet her soon enough,' she replied and Külli smiled. Violet smiled as well—but in a mischievous and knowing way. Violet had known the caresses of girls too.

'Well, do bring her around one day soon. I'm sure everyone wants to meet her. We could have lunch here. Poppy's loves this place. So do I,' said Violet and she smiled. Violet's smile was illuminating. Külli was still adjusting to the new and improved Vava. Yes, Violet had gone through a profound change for the better. So had everyone.

The Hungarian cuisine was fantastic. Poppy was right: this small restaurant served some of the best fare in London. Both girls ate heartily (unusual for Violet) and enjoyed Bakonyi pecsenye (beef tenderloin which is served on a wooden board), **Toltott paprika (stuffed bell peppers), and Csontleves (bone broth).**

The restaurant's atmosphere was usually subdued at lunch time, but at night, when the restaurant filled with Hungarian migrant workers and their families, the place became electric.

THE RAPPROCHEMENT
Violet, Gemma, Poppy, and Külli all had their first dinner together at this very restaurant back in January. That first night was a bit awkward for everyone; the twenty year absence had remained unexplained, but everyone was happy that Gemma and Külli had reconciled. And it was decided (without any conversation) that whatever had transpired between the two was a private matter that they both wanted to stay private. It was accepted by all.

The gang had reunited, but the group was (unbeknownst to its members by varying degrees) enveloped in secrets. Violet had never learned (and Gemma didn't want her to know) what Grey had done to her. Violet was

12

also completely unaware of Poppy's involvement in Grey's death. Külli didn't know Grey had ever met Gemma, and the group wondered if Külli was even aware of his existence. Poppy and Violet were still in the dark as to what had happened between Gemma and Külli. The only person who was aware of everything was Gemma, and she wasn't talking, nor would she ever.

The girls all had very different memories of that Saturday night in January.

VAVA
Violet was happy to see everyone back together. Vava missed Gula more than she had realized. When Külli telephoned her and invited over for tea that afternoon, Vava had burst into tears and spoken to Gula in incoherent sobs. Gula had responded in kind. Vava summoned her driver and had him take her directly to Gula's house. Violet had arrived at Külli's front door in Marble Arch wearing faded denim jeans and a pale blue cashmere jumper. Gula welcomed her with a hug.

POPPY
Poppy had been asleep when Gula telephoned her a few minutes later. She was mentally and physically exhausted.

Poppy didn't regret what she had done; she felt it was the only way to save Gemma's life. Gemma was Poppy's absolute *brick*; and Poppy hers. Poppy didn't feel she had done anything wrong, and neither did Gemma. Gemma only felt gratitude. Gemma's sincere gratitude had further convinced Poppy that she was in the right. There was no need to feel guilty at all.

Not a day had gone by since Grey's death that Poppy didn't look at the sterling silver engraved ring her father had given and recited aloud in Latin: *Bonis nocet quiquis pepercerit malis* (In all things, whoever spares the bad injuries the good). Poppy had done what had to be done in order to save Gemma's life; and that was it. Poppy's conscience was clear.

Poppy was worried about the police investigation. And here is where it would later become interesting. Brian's classmate from Harrow had been assigned to the case. Brian knew that Gemma had been briefly engaged to

Grey, but he never spoke of it to anyone, not even to his classmate at Scotland Yard. While the Old Harrovian police detective never discussed the details of the case with Brian, he did pass on privately that the police had no idea who had killed Grey. They assumed that he had an endless list of enemies. The trail had gone cold and The Yard had little inclination to pursue the case any longer. The police had all reached the same conclusion: the world was a better place without Grey.

Brian had no idea the role Poppy had played in Grey's death. He did, however, inadvertently calm her nerves considerably when he told her what he had learned of the case. Poppy, when alone, could only sigh heavily in relief.

Külli had been mired in misery for the last two decades. She had desperately wanted to contact Gemma, but the mere thought of doing so after all *Gula had done* proved too daunting. Külli was too ashamed to approach Gemma. Gemma's appearance at her front door and completely blindsided her.

GEMMA
Gemma was an angel. Gemma had handled the rapprochement with kindness and forgiveness. It had been almost otherworldly. Gemma had healed Külli and forgiven her. Really, it was Külli who needed forgiveness, understanding, and kindness. Only Gemma was capable of healing her, and she had done so—miraculously.

Külli would always be grateful to Gemma for her understanding. And Külli loved her as much as she ever had. And, most importantly, Gemma loved Külli and Gemma had also been healed. Külli was also overjoyed to have Gemma back as her friend. She had missed their conversations and closeness. Gemma's friendship was now enough. And, Gemma loved Gula, truly.

Gemma, for her part, felt she had finally broken away from the event horizon she had been bouncing along and escaped an impossible situation. Five months ago, Gemma had been staring into the abyss. If it were not for the love and bravery of friends like Poppy and relative strangers like Winter,

Gemma would have perished, for sure. Gemma had been given a new lease on life, a second chance, and she was extremely grateful to everyone who had helped her get this chance. Gemma was going to make the most of it. Gemma felt that she had momentum. Gemma was happy to have reconciled with Külli . Gemma was happy that Violet had undergone a sea change. And Gemma was grateful for the loyalty of her loved ones. Gemma had a lot of emotions swirling through her mind. She still needed time to process everything.

Gemma also worried about Poppy. Undoubtedly, the events of the last few years had taken a heavy toll on Poppy too. They had never discussed the details about what had happened that morning in January; all that mattered was that Grey was gone. Gemma worried about Poppy's wellbeing. Poppy had turned out to the strongest of the group; and the most decisive.

Gemma had spent the last few months recovering from, well, everything. Poppy seemed to be alright, but Gemma couldn't help but worry. For now, everyone was excited about Poppy's forthcoming wedding. There was still so much to do.

BRIAN
Poppy refused to sell her small semi-detached house in Covent Garden; it was a symbol of her independence and success. Poppy had purchased the small Edwardian house with the money she had made in banking and finance.

Brian owned three properties in London, including his current residence. His house, in Marylebone, was much larger then her semi-detached, but Poppy insisted that they live in Covent Garden. Brian agreed—kind of. He would keep the house in Marylebone, but live in Convent Garden. They would keep some of their clothing at both houses, and hopefully divide their time between the two.

Brian loved the terraced Georgian townhouse in Marylebone. It had been in the family since the 1800's. It had been constructed of brick and had a Bath stone facade. It was three stories high, but rather narrow. It was a relatively small house, but by modern London standards, it was palatial. The glossy black door with its silver door handle seemed to almost welcome Brian home from work every day. He felt an immediate wave of relief every time he crossed the threshold. This house was Brian's refuge from the chaotic world outside.

The white walls were, for the most part, kept bare. Brian liked that. The white walls reflected the sunlight which streamed in through the large windows of the house. The creaky hardwood floors were made of oak and were all original.

The fireplace in the drawing room was made of Bath stone. A portrait of one of his ancestors in full military dress uniform hung above it. The ancestor had been killed leading a cavalry charge at Waterloo. His visage was not one of sternness, but, perhaps ironically, of kindness. Brian often reflected on the short life of this illustrious ancestor who had been killed in battle at the age of 32. He had left behind a wife and four small children. The youngest of which was his maternal great-great grandmother.

When he had inherited the house, it had been unoccupied since the early 1980s. Brian had had the electrical wiring and plumbing upgraded. He had also had central air installed. The kitchen, a relic of the Victorian Era, was fitted with a new cast iron Aga stove and modern stainless steel appliances.

His parents had given him some Persian rugs and a bear skin that his great uncle had brought back with him from Canada in the 1920s.

The house was unfurnished when Brian first acquired it, which actually pleased Brian as it would allow him to furnish it anyway he wanted. Brian, by that time, operating under budgetary constraints, furnished the house with new furniture, not antiques. Brian didn't mind, he really didn't want to live in a museum. He purchased furniture from a variety of sources.

The drawing room furniture was bespoke and made of cherry, walnut, and there was even a cabinet with sterling silver handles made from polished antique hemlock. A large red and blue Persian rug covered the floor of the room.

There were several accent and console tables made of Savoy olive ash burl. On each of the tables were silver picture frames containing cherished photographs from Brian's life: his mother holding him when he was a baby; Brian at Harrow; Brian during his first year at Oxford wearing his blue boating blazer (which was trimmed in gray); a teenage Brian on horseback at a fox hunt, and Brian with his parents the day he graduated from Oxford.

Of all of these photos, there was one that Brian cherished the most: a photo taken at the banking conference in London the day he had met Poppy. A friend had snapped the picture of them together talking immediately after Poppy's presentation on gold ETFs. Brian's friend and co-worker had unwittingly taken this amazing photo on a lark. He had had no idea that the two people talking to each other next to the conference table had fallen for each other just minutes before.

When the co-worker showed Brian the photo on his phone, Brian immediately asked for it to be emailed to him. Brian then had a hundred glossy copies of the photo printed in varying sizes. He had carried a small sized one in his wallet ever since. He had presented one to Poppy in a small silver frame from Asprey. He had also sent one to his parents. And one he placed in a silver frame and placed on the bookshelf in the drawing room of his residence.

Brian's love and affection for Poppy had never dimmed—not in the slightest. Every time he looked at this photo, he smiled.

The bedrooms had minimal amounts of furniture; Brian preferred space over clutter. Brian's room had a queen sized bed with a polished olive ash burl wood headboard. The white walls were left bare. There were small nightstands on either side of the bed, each with a small modern lamp. There was also a large walnut and olive ash burl bespoke wardrobe. Brian had had it made because the Georgian townhouse lacked built in closets. Brian kept his clothes in it along with some of Poppy's.

There were three other bedrooms. All three were as sparsely furnished as Brian's room. His parents would stay in one of them whenever they visited London.

The Georgian house had an almost modern vibe to it now.

Brian had spent the last three years sitting in the drawing room and imagining Poppy and their small children playing in this room while he watched over them. Brian wanted children with Poppy. Both were now in their early 40s, but Brian was not worried. He was confident that love would see them all through.

THE RESTAURANT

'I love the clothing and kit your outfitter produces, Gula. It's the finest in England. I bought Freya's first riding outfit from you. She was only eleven, or was it twelve? Well, she looked *marvellous*. Unfortunately Freya doesn't like fox hunting. It's dreadful, G.'

'I'm glad you like it. That means a lot to me, Violet. You've always had a great sense of style, Vava. I have to be honest with you: I saw every order you placed with us. *Every single one*. I made sure everything was done perfectly; I checked to make sure. I always personally boxed and wrapped each outfit sent to you. I wanted everything to be perfect—better than perfect. I even saw the special order you had made last December for the cape. I missed you. I wanted to drop a note in the box every time I sent something off to you, but I couldn't bring myself to do it. I regret it,' said Külli quietly.

'Let's not waste any more time on regrets, Gula,' said Violet. 'As Gemma used to say in Sussex, "All is well. We are together" and that is all that matters now,' replied Violet. She reached over and held Külli's soft and toned hand. 'I love you, G.'

Külli was deeply moved, and, at the same time, more than a little surprised by Violet's heartfelt affection. This new Vava still took some getting used to; but Külli was happy that Violet had changed.

'You have been a loyal client, Vava. Thank you. You are my greatest advertisement. I noticed you sporting my clothes in *Tatler* more than once,' said Külli and she smiled.

'I remember you sitting at your desk at school, Gula. You were always making drawings of cartridge belts and jodhpurs. I remember you modelling the leather cartridge belt from Holland and Holland around the alcove. I knew you would make it, G.'

Külli smiled. 'Yes, I remember everything like it was yesterday,' said Külli reflectively.

'I can't wait for the wedding,' said Violet. 'It will be nice to see Poppy finally getting married. She has waited for so long, and Brian is adorable and sweet. I'm so happy for her. And besides, it's been *yonks* since Poppy has had a chance to wear her tiara.'

And the girls both laughed.

Gemma—England—The Package

THE GHERKIN
Gemma looked at the blue digital LED aluminum clock on her desk: 5:30. The day was over. Gemma exhaled. Time to go home. Gemma smiled.

She shutdown her computer and put away the files that had accumulated on her desk. Gemma then took off her tortoise shell reading glasses and put them in their case. She put the case in one of her desk drawers. She stood up, adjusted her slate grey pleated skirt and white blouse, and walked across the large circular glass walled office.

'Good night, Gemma,' said one of her co-workers as she passed her. Virtually everyone in the office had already left.

'Good night, Allegra.'

Allegra entered the elevator with another member of the staff and the doors closed. The office was now deserted save Gemma and Alexa.

Gemma knocked on Alexa's office door.

'Come in,' Alexa replied.

Gemma entered the office. A large glass wall curved behind Alexa's desk. Alexa, wearing a dark blue jacket and charcoal grey pencil skirt, looked up at Gemma from her desk. She smiled.

'How are you, Gem?'

'*Marvellous,*' answered Gemma in her flawless Sloane accent. 'All the files for the Singapore conference are ready, including the Power Point presentation that Jemima prepared. I have hard copy and digital files of everything. Oh, and the hotel confirmed our reservations this afternoon.'

'Thank you, Gemmy. I really appreciate all of your hard work.'

Gemma smiled.

'Do you have any weekend plans?' asked Alexa.

'Yes. I'm going to meet Poppy, Brian, and Mars for dinner tonight.'

'Mars? Really? I used to see him all the time when I lived in Singapore. He was always nice to me whenever I visited Hong Kong. He was extremely insightful and resourceful back then, before, well, everything happened,' said Alexa as her voice trailed off.

Alexa leaned back in her chair. She sighed. Gemma was a friend, a confidant. She knew she could speak freely with her, and her conversations were secure. She looked at Gemma standing before her desk then motioned for her to close the office door. Gemma complied.

'Please have a seat, Gemma,' said Alexa.

Gemma pulled one of the chairs out and sat down.

Alexa was now 41 years old. She was not as slim as she had once been. She exercised and was careful about what she ate, but time and motherhood were slowly taking their toll on her. Alexa was still fairly attractive. She now kept her blonde hair shoulder length and her nails were always perfectly manicured. The fashionable Alexa could still hold her own against The Inseparables.

Alexa marvelled at Gemma's appearance. Gemma's skin had remained flawless and glowing. Her brown hair was shiny and glossy. Gemma had kept her bangs. Alexa couldn't remember a time when Gemma had not had them. She wasn't jealous. Gemma had always been beautiful. But what good had Gemma's looks ever done for her? Alexa privately felt that Gemma's appearance had always worked against her.

Alexa was the mother of two daughters; the eldest daughter, Aurelia, was entering a second tier university in August. Her younger daughter, Sarah, the academic one, was hoping to enter Oxford next year. Alexa knew how Violet must have felt about Freya failing to enter Oxford, or for that matter, a decent university. And, as fate would have it, Aurelia was entering the same second tier *uni* as Louise.

Aurelia had grown up in Singapore and attended exclusive schools there. Aurelia, though not particularly academic, had several advantages going for her; one being her ability to speak Mandarin Chinese like a native. She was also blonde and athletic. Aurelia had taken up Kendo and had done well competing in tournaments across Asia. She was rather plain looking, but made up for it by having an outgoing and kind personality. And Alexa loved Aurelia. She might not be that academic, but, like Freya, she was intelligent and had a lot of common sense; something that a lot of young people these days lacked.

But today she had decided she wanted to talk privately to Gemma about something really important.

'Gemma. Do you know who Enoch Tara is?'

'Yes. Well, I did. A long time ago. His family is from Somerset. Why do you ask?'

'Enoch Tara is a venture capitalist that I would like to do business with. He is a rather mysterious figure in finance. No one seems to know that much about him. He keeps a low profile. How do you know him, Gemma?'

'He was at Oxford with me. He went to Christ Church. We acted in a play together the year before I graduated. I was Cleopatra. Violet had played the part in Sussex; do you remember?' Gemma asked.

'How could I forget? Vava was perfect. She's naturally imperious,' replied Alexa and she smiled. 'Yes, Vava was a great actress.'

'Vava was having a hard time with her studies at that time; she was the one that had encouraged me to audition for the part. I did, and I got it. I really enjoyed acting. I had even considered pursuing it, but I was offered a position at the magazine.'

Gemma smiled; memories started to return to her of undergraduate days at Oxford—mostly happy ones (barring the situation with Gula).

'He was a good actor. He played Ptolemy, Cleopatra's brother. He had a *rather* small role. He was quite fun actually. I remember everyone going out together after rehearsals; he would often sit next to me. I remember him being really cute. He only talked about acting. He was so excited about a future on the stage. He was really sweet—*terribly* innocent really.'

'You've had no contact with him since?'

'None.'

Alexa looked out through the glass wall of her office and watched the heavy London traffic on the streets below.

'Gemma. I saw Enoch Tara at a meeting last week. He mentioned to me that he knew you. He had heard you were working for me. He asked how you were doing.'

'How did he know I was working for you?'

'Gemma; everyone knows you are working for me,' answered Alexa, and she smiled. 'You are notorious to some, and loved by others. Enoch Tara seems to be sincerely concerned about your welfare. Otherwise, why would he have asked me about you?'

'I don't know. I'm sure he has heard all about what happened. Most of the people from my past avoid me now. It's nice that he asked about me.'

Alexa sat quietly for a moment. She really wanted to bring Enoch Tara into her financial orbit, or perhaps, it would be better to say, enter his. Gemma was the way. She hated to use Gemma, but this was probably the only way Alexa had into his world. Tara was extremely secretive. And he was definitely interested in Gemma.

'Gemma,' said Alexa pensively. She hesitated. No. It wasn't right. Forget it. 'Gemma. Have a nice weekend. Please tell Mars I said hello.'

Gemma smiled. 'I'll be happy to. Have a nice weekend, Alexa.'

THE CITY
Gemma took the Underground home that evening. She made her way slowly up the steps of the station near her apartment. She was really tired. It wasn't until she was half way home that she realized that she had left the unopened parcel from Jersey in her desk drawer. Oh, well. She could open it on Monday.

Gemma—England—A House in the Country

THE APARTMENT
Gemma showered and changed into her favorite dinner party finery—well at least what she enjoyed wearing when she had dinner at Poppy's: faded blue jeans and a white semi-fitted cotton dress shirt.

Dinner with *The Honourable* Poppy was usually informal and relaxed. Both girls preferred that these days.

Hons Gemma and Poppy had a lifetime of formal dinner parties behind them: printed invitations, name cards, seating charts, sterling silver trays, black tie and sometimes even white tie affairs, white gloved servants, and a vast array of crystal, linens, porcelain, and sterling and sometimes even Britannic silverware.

Traditional French meals meant thirteen courses; in London formal dinners could mean twenty-one, ten, six, or at a minimum, four courses being served. The more courses served, the smaller the portions. And at formal dinner parties, guests never served themselves; uniformed staff served and cleared plates from the left side while new plates were simultaneously slid into place.

Table runners, plates, and cutlery were placed according to exacting specifications; flower arrangements were at eye level and candelabras were so that everyone could make eye contact.

Baroness Gemma had, in her heyday, been one of London's most popular and stylish hostesses; that is, until it had all fallen apart. Now Gemma was persona non grata among most of the London Set; she was an outcast, a pariah.

Truth be told, Gemma had loved all of the dinner parties she had ever given or attended. She enjoyed everything about them, right down to the minutest details. But those halcyon days were behind her now, and most likely, would never return.

Gemma had been so stunned by the turn of events in her life four years ago, the loss of social status was the least of her worries. Gemma had never been a snob. She had always been kind to everyone. And she had never turned away a friend regardless of what others might think or say. Gemma was loyal. She used to miss some of her supposed friends. She had been shocked by how instantly she had been dropped by most of them. Gemma realized how superficial these friendships had really been. Now that only thing she regretted about her former friends was that she hadn't seen them for what they really were much earlier.

Gemma bought Poppy a potted aloe vera plant. The terracotta pot was what had attracted Gemma to the plant. The terracotta pot was shaped like the head of a Medusa; the Aloe vera stems were its snakes. Gemma loved it. She bought two of them: one for her flat and the other as a gift for Poppy. It now sat in a cardboard box on the kitchen table/desk.

She adjusted her shirt in the mirror. Yes, the wide shirt collar looked nice. Yes, quite casual and comfortable. Gemma was glad to be wearing comfortable clothes again.

Gemma then froze and stared into the mirror. Gemma had noticed a flash of something: a few silver and white strands of hair. Yes, Gemma was getting older. She tilted her head to one side, and then the other. The silver strands seemed to almost glint in the florescent light that emanated from the lamps on either side of the bathroom mirror. Gemma sighed. And then, upon reflection, she smiled. She was alive; she was happy; and she was moving forward.

Gemma exited the tiny white-tiled bathroom and walked back into the main room. She put on a pair of brown suede Chelsea boots and grabbed her blue quilted Burberry jacket. The nights were still cold in May. She put the jacket on and exited her apartment. Gemma was running late.

COVENT GARDEN
Gemma enjoyed the cool night air as she made her way down the pavement in Covent Garden.

Enoch Tara. This was someone she had practically forgotten. Enoch, however, had not forgotten her. Gemma wondered why he had entered the world of finance and not the theatre. Then again, life rarely seems to turn out as one hopes. Gemma knew that only too well.

On the way over, while taking the Underground, Gemma had searched the Internet on her smartphone for any information she could find on him; there wasn't much beyond his financial dealings. No recent photos of him seemed to exist (at least online); only a few of the angelic looking Enoch while he was as Oxford. Yes, Enoch had been really cute. There was nothing on his private life at all. All Gemma could discover was that he was a highly successful financier. Even his net wealth remained a mystery.

POPPY'S SEMI-DETACHED

Gemma approached the front door of Poppy's house. So many memories were here. Most of them were terrible and sad. Poppy had taken her in at the lowest points in her life (and there were several). Poppy, her truest friend, had saved her life many times. Gemma would always be indebted to her. Please God, let me one day be able to repay her loyalty, kindness, and bravery. Somehow let it be possible.

Poppy answered the front door with a smile and hugged Gemma tightly. Poppy was positively beaming with happiness. Gemma smiled. But tonight, the smile was Gemma's Sussex one. The smile she had before fate had hurled so much misery at her. Poppy noticed immediately, smiled, and hugged Gemma once more. 'Come in, Gemmy. Everyone's here.'

Poppy was wearing faded denim blue jeans and a beige cashmere top over a white collared cotton blouse. Her engagement ring's diamond flashed and sparkled every time Poppy moved her hand.

Gemma entered the small Edwardian house. She presented Poppy with the potted aloe vera plant. 'Thank you, Gem. It's beautiful.' Poppy led Gemma into the front room.

Brian and Mars stood as she entered. Brian was wearing a pair of blue jeans and a pale blue button down oxford dress shirt. He was slim and handsome. He smiled when she saw Gemma.

It's good to see you, Gemma.'

Mars was wearing a pair of grey trousers, a white dress shirt with a St James collar, and an Omega watch. He looked every inch the hedge fund manager he once was. Mars wasn't very good at dressing informally. It didn't seem to come easily to him. Mars' hair was brown but with touches of white, silver, and grey.

Mars was attractive in a way. Mostly, Mars was kind and thoughtful. Yes, Gemma felt somewhat attracted to him, but not because of his appearance, but because of the life experiences that were so similar to her own. Mars understood her. Mars smiled and nodded as she entered the room.

'How are you, Gemmy?'

'I'm doing well, Mars,' replied Gemma, and she smiled.

The friends enjoyed Gemma's favorite: steak. Silverware clinked and the conversation was mixed with heavy doses of laughter. The meal was excellent. Afterwards everyone helped clear the table and then sat down in the front room. Poppy and Gemma went into the small kitchen to make coffee while Brian and Mars talked in the front room.

The girls returned and Poppy happily played hostess serving everyone coffee. The conversation continued in front of the small fireplace. Later Poppy went into the kitchen and Brian followed her. Mars and Gemma were left alone.

'The developer I work for has purchased some property in the Lake District near Poppy's family pile. It's an unusual collection of buildings, Gem. The group has purchased an old Royal Air Force station from the Second World War. It was used as some kind of training center for pilots. It sits on nine acres. There are several brick buildings: a couple of barracks, a depot, a mess, a main office, and a training center. The land is going to be parcelled up and sold to other developers.'

Mars then took a tablet computer out of a soft leather case and turned it on. He tapped on the screen and photos started to come up. He showed Gemma photos of the old base. It was what Gemma had expected: a collection of derelict looking buildings. The grounds were unkempt; tall grass and even taller trees obscured the buildings. Then Mars waved his hand and more photos came up. He showed Gemma photos of the interiors of the buildings. The interiors were in surprisingly good shape.

27

'Yes, the previous owner maintained the buildings extremely well. None of the roofs leak and the structures are all sound. He turned the training center into a workshop. He built bespoke furniture. He purchased the air station back in the 1970s. He retired and his daughter moved the business into a new facility closer to London, and the client base. So, he sold the buildings to us.'

Mars handed Gemma the tablet and Gemma carefully scanned through the photos. She stopped and using her manicured hands enlarged several of the photos.

'How much is this building, Mars?'

Mars looked at the photo.

'That's the old classroom building. It's being sold along with a hectare of land. Why do you ask?'

'How much, Mars?'

'Thirty thousand pounds.'

'Sold!' responded Gemma excitedly.

Mars looked at Gemma. 'Are you serious?'

'Yes.'

'What on earth would do with it?'

'I think it would make a great country house,' replied Gemma happily.

'Gemma, it doesn't even have a shower or a kitchen. It will need a lot of work to convert it into a house, Gemmy.'

'It has a large restroom for the student pilots. I can convert it into a bathroom. And look here, the two offices at the end could be made into bedrooms. And the main classroom, a drawing room. And the front office, a kitchen, you see?'

Mars looked perplexed. Gemma *was* serious.

'Gemma. I mean, you would be there all alone in the middle of nowhere.'

'Yes. And it's not nowhere; it's the Lake District,' she said and Gemma smiled.

Poppy and Brian then entered the front room. They sat down on the two leather chairs opposite the sofa were Mars and Gemma were seated.

Gemma then explained (while showing Poppy and Brian the photos on the tablet) about her plans to buy the former RAF classroom building. Brian looked as perplexed as Mars had, but Poppy nodded in agreement and smiled.

'And it's only twenty minutes away from the family pile, Gemmy,' said Poppy happily. 'We'll be neighbours,' she said excitedly.

'Mars, please let the office know that I'd like to buy the classroom building. Okay?'

'Sure. I email them tonight,' responded Mars and he shook his head.

'Thank you, Mars. You are wonderful!' said Gemma. She then got up and hugged him while he was still seated and tapping on his smartphone.

Gemma was on the brink of homeownership once more.

THE CITY

Mars drove Gemma to her apartment later that night. Her escorted her to the front door. Gemma was exhilarated. She couldn't believe her luck. She had found a place to call her own. A million home decor ideas flooded through her mind.

'Thank you, Mars. This means so much to me.'

'I'm glad I could help, Gemma,' replied Mars. 'Do you really plan to live there?'

'Not exactly. It will be my country retreat. I'll keep my flat here and stay at the house in my free time. It's only a three hour train trip from London. I just want a place to call my own, Mars.'

'I understand, Gemmy. I do. I'm happy I could help you.'

'I plan to install book shelves in the drawing room. I'm also going to buy the Art Deco furniture I mentioned to you last winter. Also, I'm going to have the wooden floors resurfaced. I think a Persian rug would look nice in the drawing room too. The high ceiling is a nice touch. Also, a clawed bath tub for the bathroom.'

'Gem, may I ask how you will pay for all of this?'

'I will pay for it little by little. I have it all planned out in my head.'

Gemma smiled. Yes, her smiled bordered on the supernatural. Gemma stood in the doorway illuminated by the lamps which adorned each side of the double door entrance. She was beautiful. And tonight she appeared to have the youthful glow of the Sussex school girl he had first met back in the early 90s. Yes, Gemma had found her way again. Mars smiled.

'Good night, Gemma.'

'Good night, Mars.'

THE APARTMENT
Gemma unlocked the front door of her flat and entered the small apartment. She was too excited to sleep. Tomorrow would be a busy day. She had a lot to do. She had to map out her building plans and then come up with some kind of budget. Gemma would soon have a country house. Well, not exactly what most would think of as a country house, but to

Gemma it was everything. She never thought she would own anything again. Now fate, something that had for so long been so cruel to Gemma, had delivered a home to her. Gemma had not given up; God had not given up on her.

Gemma—England—Cleopatra and Ptolemy

THE APARTMENT
Gemma came home exhausted on Monday night. It had been an eventful weekend: she had found a house in the country and spent the rest of the weekend sitting in the library reading through interior design books to get ideas on how to renovate and redecorate her new country retreat.

Gemma was more excited about buying this dilapidated building in a relatively isolated part of the country than when she had purchased her luxurious home in Notting Hill with George in 1999. This small building was hers, all hers. She would finally have a place to keep her belongings (well, what was left of them), and she could enjoy fresh country air. Also, she would be able to visit Poppy and her family at their ancestral home, which was close by.

The excitement had kept Gemma wide awake nearly all weekend. She arrived at work happy, but rather tired. She had left exhausted. But, this time she had remembered to bring the package that had been sitting in her desk drawer all weekend.

THE PACKAGE
The cardboard box had arrived in a plastic airfreight pouch covered in postal and overnight air freight stickers. The address on it: Jersey—one of the Channel Islands. Gemma paused; who did she know in the Channel Islands? No one.

She carefully tore open the plastic shipping pouch and removed the cardboard box; a large sticker had been placed across it which read: FRAGILE. She carefully opened one end of the box. Inside was another cardboard box, but this box was quite old and faded looking. It was a small white hat box and it had been sealed on all four edges with clear tape.

Gemma used a butter knife to gently cut each piece of tape on all four corners of the white box. She then put the box on the kitchen table in her tiny London flat. She lifted the top of the box off and placed the lid on the table top. Inside was something wrapped in white tissue paper. She carefully folded back the paper. Gemma gasped when she saw what was inside.

THE PSCHENT
A Pschent was a double crown—one the White Hedjet Crown of Lower Egypt, the other the Red Deshret Crown of Upper Egypt—worn by the pharaohs of ancient Egypt. The ancients usually referred to it as sekhemty (the Two Powerful Ones). It also bore two emblems on its front which protruded out of it like small antennas: a uraeus (an Egyptian cobra) and a vulture.

This particular version was far from ancient; well, unless you consider 1998 to be ancient. This double crown was made of cardboard, red and white felt, and small pieces of papier-mâché which had been painted with gold paint.
This was the crown that Gemma had worn in the play at Oxford University. She was stunned to now be holding it in her hands after more than two decades. It was very fragile. It had broken twice during the performances; each time the prop girl quickly repaired the damage between scenes. Gemma examined it carefully. She smiled. She was happy to have it back.

She had wanted to keep it, but had forgotten to ask for it in all of the excitement of the closing night's performance. (George had come to see the play on closing night.) After the final curtain call (there had been two), she rushed backstage to change. Now, it had been returned to her. She was elated.

She looked in the larger postal box and a white envelope fell out. She picked it up. Hand written in blue ink on the envelope was her name. She opened the envelope and read the letter.

Dear Gemma,

I have kept and carefully protected this crown ever since I found it in your dressing room the day after the final performance. I don't know if it means that much to you, but it has always meant a lot to me. I think you should have the crown back. It is, after all, yours.

With affection,

Enoch (Ptolemy)

Gemma couldn't believe it. Enoch? He had kept this small cardboard prop all these years, and now he was returning it. Why now? Why had he kept it? Gemma thought about it carefully and decided that it was the artist, the thespian part of Enoch's soul, which had compelled him to preserve it.

Gemma wanted to thank Enoch, but she had no way of contacting him. Jersey? Jersey was a financial services center that was bursting with secret bank accounts and laundered money. Perhaps Enoch was headquartered there? She would ask Alexa about it tomorrow. But now, after a long day, Gemma was tired.

She carefully returned the cardboard pharaonic crown to its box and placed it inside a drawer in her small closet.

How sweet. The middle aged Enoch still had the youthful heart of a thespian. She would have to write and thank him for his kind and thoughtful gesture.

Gemma undressed sleepily and then entered the small white tiled shower. She showered quickly. After stepping out of the shower, she dried off in front of the kitchen table.

The plastic shipping pouch was still sitting on the table. Gemma looked at the label closely. There was a return address: a post office box in Jersey. She would write him tomorrow. Gemma took the label off the plastic pouch and placed it inside her soft black leather brief case. Yes, tomorrow she would write him, but now, it was time to go to bed.

THE GHERKIN

Gemma sat at her desk and wrote out a short thank you card for Enoch in her florid handwriting on Tuesday morning.

Dear Enoch,

You have no idea how happy I was to have my pharaonic crown returned to me after all these years. I never thought I would see it again. How lovely. How sweet of you, my dear Enoch. You are still the same good-hearted soul I remember from Oxford. Thank you so much. So many memories came flooding back to me with that small cardboard hat that I had forgotten in haste. Thank you with all my heart.

Yours truly,

Gemma

Gemma then sealed the envelope and wrote the Jersey address on it. She stood up and walked over to the reception desk.

'Helen? Have you taken the mail downstairs yet?'

'No, ma'am.'

'Oh, good. Please post this letter for me. It's going to Jersey.'

'Yes, Ma'am. I'll be happy to.'

'Thank you, Helen.'

Gemma turned was about to walk back to hear desk when someone said, 'I don't think that will be necessary.'

Gemma stopped and then turned around. Standing a few feet away was another ghost of Oxford: Enoch. Gemma froze and stared. It was him.

Gemma—England—The Mysterious Mr Tara

THE GHERKIN

Gemma stared at Enoch for a moment. Enoch must have been around 40. Gemma remembered him being a year behind her at Oxford. The Enoch Tara that stood before her now was still slim and attractive. He must have stood around 5'9"—at best. (Why is it that virtually all the men in Gemma's life were fairly short?) His hair was light brown and he had it cut like a City banker. He was clean shaven. He was wearing a charcoal grey suit, a white dress shirt, and a blue and grey wool tartan necktie. Enoch had aged very well. Or, to be more exact, he really hadn't aged much at all. He looked quite smart in his suit and tie. He had an air of sophistication about him that he had lacked completely at Oxford.

Enoch's blue eyes met Gemma's. He felt a rush of emotions surge through him; Gemma was older, but still beautiful. She was still shapely and her glossy brown hair was styled in the way he remembered it: shoulder length and with bangs that touched the top of her eyebrows. Gemma smiled in the way only she could. Enoch couldn't believe this moment had finally arrived; he was standing before Gemma after an absence of 21 years. He was suddenly speechless.

'Hello, Enoch. How are you?' said Gemma. She smiled. Enoch just stared at her. 'It's good to see you,' said Gemma. Gemma took a few steps forward and stood in front of Enoch. 'You know, Enoch; I'm starting to think you've forgotten my name.' Gemma then smiled—her Sussex schoolgirl smile—and the natural sunlight flooding into the 12th floor of The Gherkin seemed to become a few shades brighter.

Enoch smiled. 'I'm sorry, Gemma. I...I...can't believe I'm here. With you.'

'Well, I'm glad you are,' replied Gemma. She smiled again.

'Hello, Mr Tara. Welcome to Millennium Investments,' said a young woman's voice from behind them. The flaxen haired Jemima walked up to Enoch and smiled. 'Are you here to meet someone?'

Jemima was in her mid-twenties and her star was in ascendancy. The slim and blonde Jemima was from a prominent family of bankers, much like

Poppy. She was also a graduate of the London School of Economics. Alexa had discovered her toiling away at a bank branch in the midlands—of all places.

'I...was...just in the neighborhood and...I got lost and found myself...on the 12th floor of The Gherkin. Yes. That's what happened,' replied Enoch. And he stared at the young Jemima.

'Would you like some tea, sir?' asked Jemima politely.

'Yes. I would like that. Thank you.'

Gemma smiled.

MILLENNIUM INVESTMENTS

Enoch Tara sat in the conference room with Gemma and Alexa. The long modern conference table stretched nearly the entire length of the room. It was made of aluminum and glass. The table was bespoke and quite expensive. One side of the room was the curved glass wall of The Gherkin, and the other side of the conference room was an intricate wall of patterned glass that served to obscure the goings on in the room.

Alexa sat on one side of the table with Gemma, and Enoch sat on the other. Alexa was elated. Enoch Tara was in her conference room. Thank you, Gemmy.

One of the secretaries entered with a silver tray. She placed the chrome tea pot and three white bone china tea cups and saucers on the table. She then poured tea into each cup and served the tea to each person at the table starting with Mr Tara, then Alexa, and finally Gemma. She smiled and quietly left.

Enoch lifted his cup and drank some tea. He smiled nervously.

Everyone sat in silence. While the young woman had served tea, everyone had been thinking of what they would say. No one had any ideas.

'It's nice to see you again, Alexa. I would like to work with Millennium in the future.'

Alexa smiled. Got him. 'Let me get a prospectus for you, Enoch,' said Alexa. She knew that this would be a good moment to leave the two of them alone. She stood up and made her way out the room. Gemma and Enoch were finally alone.

Enoch suddenly recovered his bravery and spoke. 'I missed you, Gemma. I mean. I know we didn't know each other that well, but you made quite…the impression on me.'

Enoch's eyes searched around the room and then he looked at Gemma. Behind her was the curved glass wall of The Gherkin; beyond the glass was the London skyline and an ocean of blue interspersed with white clouds. Gemma seemed to floating before him.

'Thank you for sending me the crown, Enoch. It means a lot to me,' said Gemma quietly. She then pushed the envelope containing her card forward across the glass tabletop. 'For you,' she said.

'May I read it now?' asked Enoch.

'Yes; if you like,' replied Gemma.

Enoch took the card out of the envelope and read it. He then read it again. And once more after that. He looked at Gemma and smiled.

'I kept the crown, but only because I thought you had discarded it. I thought, perhaps, maybe, it didn't mean that much to you. It meant a lot to me. I saw it in the dressing room the next morning when I came back to the theatre. When I saw it sitting on the side table, I decided that if no one else wanted it, I would keep it.'

Gemma looked at him carefully; she was studying his expressions. What was Enoch really trying to say? Gemma didn't want to rush to any conclusions. All of this had come as a complete surprise. She had liked the young Enoch, but she had barely known him.

'Enoch. What would you like to say to me?' asked Gemma quietly. She looked at him. He looked nervous. Was this person really the mysterious Mr Tara that everyone in the world of finance was in awe of?

Enoch paused; he was building up his courage. He had waited 21 years to tell Gemma what he was about to tell her now. Finally.

'Gemma,' he said softly in a barely audible whisper. 'I have always…'

'Here we are, Enoch. Our prospectus,' said Alexa as she re-entered the conference room. Alexa placed the file on the table in front of Enoch and smiled. Enoch looked at the file. He looked up at Gemma. He stood up and picked up the file. Suddenly, his nerve broke. No. Gemma wouldn't want to hear this. She barely knew him. What had he been thinking?

'Thank you, Alexa,' said Enoch. 'I will read through it and contact you soon. Thank you for your time. I really appreciate it.'

He then turned towards Gemma and said, 'It was good to see you again, Gemma. I'm glad you like the crown.'

Oh, Enoch; why did you say that? Enoch was panicking. He turned and looked at Alexa and then turned back and looked at Gemma who was now standing a few feet away from him. And, then, like an army in retreat, he left the room.

THE ELEVATOR
Enoch pushed the button and waited for the elevator. He hated himself. He was a coward. He had always been a coward, and now—once again—she was slipping away from him. He wanted to cry.

The elevator doors opened and Enoch stepped into the elevator. They started to close and then the doors encountered an obstacle: Gemma's soft leather Montblanc briefcase; the same case that Brian had given her for Christmas a few months earlier.

The diminutive Gemma stepped into the elevator and smiled. 'The least I could do is buy you lunch, Enoch. I really like that crown. I'm actually glad you kept it. I would no doubt have lost it along with my house and household belongings.'

The elevator doors closed and the elevator began its rapid descent. Enoch was floating. Floating and descending with the elevator down The Gherkin.

And Gemma was with him.

Gemma—England—Ptolemaic Oxford

THE GHERKIN
Gemma and Enoch stood in the lobby of The Gherkin. She looked at Enoch and smiled. Enoch was transfixed. Gemma was beautiful. Enoch suddenly realized something: that even if Gemma had aged beyond recognition, he would feel exactly the same about her. People didn't love Gemma for her physical appearance, but for the beauty of her soul. At that moment of realization, a ray of morning light fell upon Gemma's face and illuminated it. She was angelic, pure. Gemma smiled.

'Do you still like Japanese ramen? I remember you eating that a lot when we were at Oxford,' said Gemma.

'Oh, you remember. Um, that was more a combination of convenience and…a lack of funds,' Enoch replied and then he smiled. Enoch had the cutest smile. Yes, Enoch was much older now, but he retained a lot of cuteness—just like Poppy had.

'Well, where would you like to go for lunch?' asked Gemma.

'Could we go for a walk? That would give me a chance to think about it.'

'Sure.'

THE CITY
The two of them left the lobby of The Gherkin and walked outside onto

the pavement. They turned right and started walking in the direction of the Underground station.

While walking through the City, Enoch noticed several more things about Gemma: She was still quite fashionable, in a very conservative way. She was remarkably youthful, and in many ways she seemed to be the same person he had rehearsed scenes with in the theatre at Oxford all those years ago. But, in another unidentifiable way, Gemma had changed. How she had changed was beyond him to explain, but Gemma had changed, for sure, for sure.

They pair walked without speaking for several minutes. They crossed the street and continued to walk in silence; perhaps contemplation would be a better word.

Gemma didn't know how to feel. She wanted to have someone in her life, but, to be honest; she had never even considered Enoch. When they met at Oxford, Gemma was in love with George, and, even deeper in love with Gula; and she had left her and broken her heart.

Gemma had auditioned for the play as a way to distract herself from the trauma of losing Külli. That was the real reason. Gemma felt completely lost after losing Gula.

She had never told George about Külli. George had been completely unaware of Külli's existence—as well as Gemma's affection for her. Enoch, though sweet and thoughtful, hadn't made much of an impression on her. In a way, he couldn't have; Gemma had been consumed with thoughts of Gula and their shattered friendship.

OXFORD 1998

The Oxford Playhouse, a Regency style building with a grey stone facade in Oxford, England, had seen a galaxy of young hopefuls perform on its stage. Gemma and Enoch had been part of that galaxy.

It was here on a chilly autumn evening in late October that Gemma found herself on stage before a packed house. Gemma was playing Cleopatra, the last Ptolemaic ruler of ancient Egypt. She wondered the stage that night dressed in her golden costume and wearing an Egyptian double crown.

Gemma radiated beauty and youth. The wooden framed canvas backdrop was of ancient Egyptian hieroglyphics.

In the final scene of the play, Cleopatra was dreaming. In the dream, her long dead brother, Ptolemy, appeared before her.

Enoch, wearing a golden shirt of scale armour, a blue fabric pteruges skirt, and a blue Khepresh—the Blue Crown; otherwise known as a War Crown in Ancient Egypt—walked on to the stage. He was young and beautiful. His lithe body glided across the stage and stopped. He turned and faced the audience and began to speak.

THE SCRIPT
Act 5 Scene 3: The Dream

(Ptolemy enters stage right. He walks to the centre of the stage and faces the audience.)

PTOLEMY: *Cleopatra, did you ever love our sister Arsinoë?*

CLEOPATRA: (Speaking coldly) *I did.*

PTOLEMY: *If you loved her, as you say you did, then why did you allow the Romans to take her away to Rome and parade her in chains in a humiliating triumph? Why?*

CLEOPATRA: (Speaking haughtily, coldly, and imperiously) *Arsinoë defied me! Arsinoë led a rebellion against me! She tried to destroy me! I had to destroy her before she destroyed me!*

PTOLEMY: *But you still say you loved her?*

CLEOPATRA: (Speaking coldly) *I did.*

PTOLEMY: *Then why, dear sister, did you have her brutally murdered in the Temple of Artemis in Ephesus? She was just a young girl. She cried out your name as they killed her.*

(Ptolemy begins to cry).

CLEOPATRA: *I did what was necessary in order to secure my rule. No more, no less.*

PTOLEMY: *Dear sister, was it really necessary to kill her? Do you ever question what you did to her? Do you ever regret what you did to our sister Arsinoë?*

CLEOPATRA: (Speaking coldly and imperiously) *Regrets? I have none. I am a queen. A queen cannot allow emotions to cloud her judgment. Regrets are weakness. I would do it all again.*

PTOLEMY: *Then you are truly lost, dear sister. Good bye. Forever.* (Ptolemy exits stage left)

(Cleopatra looks at the audience and then walks to the centre of the stage. She stops and then turns to face the audience. She speaks in cold and imperious tone of voice.)

CLEOPATRA: *You would have done the same.*

(Cleopatra exits stage right)

THE OXFORD PLAYHOUSE 1998

The final night's performance saw many of Gemma's friends in attendance. Most of them had also attended opening night the week before. For George, it was his first. He had been *terribly* busy on opening night.

The play had been a brilliant success. The reviews had been glowing. Gemma's performance had been highly praised. One reviewer wrote, 'Never have I seen Cleopatra played with such majesty and by so beautiful a young actress.'

Gemma collected all of the reviews she could find. She bought two or three copies of every newspaper or magazine. One copy she kept; another she sent to her grandparents, and the third was often given to Poppy (who still had them) or to George (who secretly threw them away immediately without even bothering to read them). Gemma had cherished those reviews for years. She kept them in her desk at her house in Notting Hill. She would often take them out and reread them. They made her happy. The bailiffs had taken them all away when they seized her furniture for George's unpaid debts.

Every performance of the play had sold out. Each night had been a triumph. And after every night's performance, the cast would go out together and celebrate.

On that final night, Poppy, Violet, Gerald, and George were all seated in the front row. Gemma had made all of the arrangements. There was another person there that final night too. Unbeknownst to Gemma or any of the other Inseparables, Külli was also in attendance. However, she was seated up in the balcony in the last row of seats. She attended alone.

Gemma was performing flawlessly that night. All was well, that is until the final scene. And then, inexplicably, something happened. The scene was not performed as it should have been.

ACT 5 SCENE 4: THE DREAM
Enoch entered stage right. The energy in the theatre was electric. Everything was going perfectly. He walked on stage in his golden armour, blue fabric skirt, and Blue Crown. His eyes had been painted with kohl. Enoch's gold armour shimmered in the theatre lights. His lithe movements propelled him to centre stage.

Gemma stood off to one side of the stage. She wore her Egyptian dress and double crown regally; Gemma was every inch a queen.

Enoch stopped and turned to the audience. *'Cleopatra, did you ever love our sister Arsinoë?'* asked Enoch.

Gemma, speaking in a cold and disconnected tone of voice replied, '*I did.*'

'If you loved her, as you say you did, then why did you allow the Romans to take her away to Rome and parade her in chains in a humiliating triumph? Why?' asked Enoch.

And then Gemma fell into the grip of emotions beyond her control. She was supposed to answer in a haughty and imperious tone of voice bereft of grief, but this time was different. Gemma wasn't thinking of Arsinoë; she was thinking of Gula. Gemma, her voice trembling with emotion, began to speak. The script had called for her to shout her lines, but this time she said them in a quiet and remorseful tone of voice, like someone on trial attempting to justify their misdeeds.

'Arsinoë defied me. Arsinoë led a rebellion against me. She tried to destroy me. I had to

destroy her before she destroyed me,' responded Gemma softly.

Enoch looked at her; the surprise in his eyes was evident to everyone seated in the front rows of the theatre that night. Those in attendance for the second time knew something was definitely amiss.

Enoch continued, *'But you still say you loved her?'*

'I did,' replied Gemma quietly.

'Then why, dear sister, did you have her brutally murdered in the Temple of Artemis in Ephesus? She was just a young girl. She cried out your name as they killed her,' replied Enoch, and he began cry on stage.

'I did what was necessary in order to secure my rule. No more, no less,' replied Gemma softly.

Gemma seemed lost in her own world. She stared into the audience, or at least in their direction. The audience could not be seen very well by the actors; the stage lights blinded them. The audience appeared from the stage to be a black ocean.

Enoch could feel the sadness emanating from Gemma. It was real. Enoch continued, but this time with genuine emotion.

'Dear sister, was it really necessary to kill her? Do you ever question what you did to her? Do you ever regret what you did to our sister Arsinoë?' asked Enoch. Tears were beginning to well up in his eyes.

Gemma paused for a moment. She looked into space pensively. She recited her lines word for word, but with the opposite of the intended intonation and feeling. While the script called for an imperious detachment, Gemma's response was choked with emotion.

'Regrets? I have none. I am a queen. A queen cannot allow emotions to cloud her judgment. Regrets are weakness. I would do it all again,' replied Gemma quietly.

Enoch, on a wave of emotion, gave his final reply. *'Then you are truly lost, dear sister. Good bye. Forever.'*

Enoch started to cry, really cry. He turned away from Gemma and walked

44

off the stage. The audience was on edge; they knew this was no ordinary performance. The audience held its breath as Gemma walked to centre stage to deliver the final line of the play. When she turned to the audience, everyone could see that she was crying.

'You would have done the same,' said Gemma softly.

She then turned and slowly exited stage right. The scene ended. The house lights went dark, and for a moment there was not a sound in the theatre.

All was darkness and silence. And then, just before the lights came back up, the audience burst into wild applause accompanied by shouts and hoots. The audience stared at the large curtain. The audience stood—a standing ovation. The applause grew louder and louder.

BACK STAGE
The playwright, an American from Northern Virginia, had watched the final scene of *his play* from the wings. The young Southerner stopped Gemma as she exited the stage.

'Gemma; are you alright?' asked the playwright in his Virginian drawl.

'I'm fine. I'm sorry; I know I didn't perform the scene as you intended. Something came over me. I don't know what. But, I can't believe that Cleopatra was entirely without regrets or remorse,' said Gemma quietly.

The young Southerner smiled and then he reached over and held Gemma's hand. 'It worked, Gemma. It worked. You captured the audience. And me.' He smiled once more. 'Now, go back out there and take the applause. They are calling for you.'

Gemma hugged the young American. She wanted to say more, but overcome with emotion, she could not. The rest of the cast had been standing in the wings quietly observing what was going on when Gemma turned to them and said, 'Come on, everyone. They are calling for us.'

The actors burst into applause and smiles; they then ventured out onto the stage. The cast was given a standing ovation. The applause was rapturous.

In the front row, George and Gerald stood and clapped. Poppy and Violet were also standing and clapping, but both of them were openly crying. They knew what emotions and memories had propelled Gemma's performance that night.

Upstairs, on the balcony, and in the last row of seats, stood Külli. She hadn't clapped. She had only cried. Overcome with emotion, she had viewed Gemma's final scene through tears. Still shrouded in darkness, Külli made her way out of the theatre and down the stairs to the lobby. She didn't want to risk running into any of the girls, her former friends.

Gemma—England—Gemma and the Hussars

THE RESTAURANT

Gemma and Enoch continued to walk in silence until they found themselves standing in front of one of Poppy's favorite restaurants. The small building with its grey Portland stone facade was wedged between a used book store and a florist's. The wooden double doors seem to almost beckon them.

Gemma looked at Enoch and asked, 'Have ever had Hungarian food?'

'No,' replied Enoch. 'Have you?'

'Yes, and it's *marvellous*,' cooed Gemma in her posh accent, and she smiled.

Enoch smiled. That voice. That accent. That smile. Gemma.

'Alright. Let's have lunch here then. It's only 11:30, so we should be able to get a good table.'

The two of them entered the restaurant and were greeted by a young Hungarian girl with dark brown hair. She smiled and asked them to please come with her in accented English.

Gemma and Enoch walked through the deserted red walled restaurant towards the back of the restaurant. Enoch looked carefully at the photographs and paintings of the Magyar Hussars which adorned the walls.

The waitress seated them at a table near a large window which looked out on the enclosed restaurant garden. Sunlight poured in through the window and seemed to reflect off of the white table cloth and silverware.

Framed on the wall above the table was a painting of Colonel Ottmar Muhr, the Austro-Hungarian war hero of 1914. He wore the dark blue hussar tunic of the Nadasdy Hussar Regiment. Gemma thought the portrait was really quite haunting. Gemma knew the story of this brave hussar officer. He had been killed leading a counter attack against the Russians in the early stages of the war.

Gemma sat opposite Enoch at the small table. She looked at the menu. Enoch looked at her.

'What do you recommend, Gemmy?'

'Well, I always get the steak. Well, the Magyar version of it,' replied Gemma.

'Alright. I'll have that, too.'

The waitress returned and took their orders. She quickly departed and headed for the kitchen. They were alone at the table near the window. It would be at least another 15 minutes before the lunch time crowd flooded in.

'So, Enoch, what have you been doing for the last 20 years?' asked Gemma. But before Enoch could answer, Gemma sighed and said, 'I won't pretend that you don't know what I have been up to.' She was obviously referring to her well publicized scandalous past. She felt it was best not to pretend Enoch was unaware of it.

Enoch looked at Gemma. Of course, he knew all about it. He had wanted to reach out to Gemma (like so many others), but he hadn't. And he really couldn't answer why he hadn't.

Enoch had found himself sitting in his Jersey offices reading about Baroness Gemma, 'the toxic wife' of Lord George, in the newspapers and watching the news reports on television like most others. Enoch knew that the way the press had presented Gemma was completely untrue. Gemma simply wasn't like what the press was portraying her. He also knew that

Gemma had been left socially ostracized by most of The London Set. It was way beyond being just unfair and unjust; it was cruel.

However, at the time, he didn't know what to do. So, like most others, he did nothing. He would never forgive himself for that. Enoch suddenly looked downcast. Gemma recognized that and decided to lighten the mood.

'How is life on Jersey? I've never been there.'

Enoch looked up. 'It's quite nice, Gemmy. If you like, I can arrange for you to visit.'

Gemma smiled. 'Well, I'll keep that in mind, Enoch.'

There was a long awkward silence that followed for several minutes. Each sat staring at the other trying to think of something to say. Gemma wanted Enoch to finishing telling her what he had been about to say in the conference room when Alexa burst back in, but she didn't think he would. At least not here.

The lunch time crowd started to fill up the restaurant. A group of Hungarian builders sat down at the table next to them. Gemma smiled. Yes, Poppy was right. It was fun to watch City bankers sitting next to burly migrant workmen.

Soon their food was served and the both were relieved that the food gave them an excuse not to say much.

Gemma would often look up from her meal of Bakonyi pecsenye and smile at him. He was so shy. Gemma couldn't put any of it together. The sensitive and sweet young actor from Oxford wasn't really apparent; neither was the venture capitalist that so many talked about in glowing superlatives. Where was Enoch in all of this?

'I am curious; what have you been doing these last two decades? Why didn't you pursue acting? You were easily one of the most talented actors in the theatre. And, well, you were in that final scene with me. You didn't stop. You went with it; *you went with me.* You were perfect, Enoch—my perfect Ptolemy,' said Gemma, her voice about to break.

Enoch suddenly felt himself being pulled back to that night on stage when he stood opposite the most beautiful soul he had ever encountered. That night had changed everything for Enoch. Gemma had touched his heart in a way no one else ever had. It was at that moment that Enoch knew; he knew. He also knew that Gemma had already given her heart away to someone else. He knew at that moment Gemma would never be his, and it broke his heart. It wasn't difficult to cry on stage that night; it would have been difficult for him not to.

'Thank you for making that night possible, Enoch. I couldn't have done it without you. I know that. I have always known that,' continued Gemma, who by that time had become quite emotional.

Enoch looked down at the white table cloth for a moment, and then he looked back up and stared at Gemma. He had *so much he wanted to say*. And, at precisely that moment, he realized that he could say everything he wanted to say with just a few words.

'I love you, Gemma.'

Gemma froze. She stared at him for a few moments and said nothing. How could she speak? She had also stop breathing. Perhaps her heart had stopped beating at that moment too.

Enoch was scared. How would Gemma react? He had been wanting to tell her this for 20 years; now he had. Part of him wished he hadn't, but the rest of him was overjoyed that he had. He felt as if an enormous weight had been lifted off of him. Now, he was Prometheus unbound; freed from his chains. He felt himself sprinting away from that desolate place that had held him for so long.

Gemma didn't know what to think. What should she do? More importantly, how did she feel about what Enoch just told her? No one spoke. Enoch's declaration seemed to hang in mid air. Someone would have to say something.

'Gemmy!' exclaimed Poppy happily. 'It's so nice to see you!' Poppy, dressed in a slate grey pencil skirt, pale blue blouse, and a matching grey jacket, was standing next to the table with Brian. Brian smiled.

Enoch stood up politely and nodded.

'Poppy; it's so good to see you here. Please, join us,' replied Gemma.

'Oh, we'd loved to Gem, but we are meeting Brian's parents for lunch today. They are curious what this place is like. I talk about it all the time,' she said and Poppy laughed.

Enoch smiled. He was secretly happy they would be unable to join them for lunch.

'Poppy, I would like to introduce you to my former castmate, Enoch. He played Ptolemy in the play at Oxford. Do you remember?'

Poppy's expression became one of inward recall and then she smiled. She looked at Enoch and said, 'You were amazing. What a truly great actor you are. Gemma talked about your performance for weeks afterwards.'

Poppy looked at him carefully for a moment. 'You look very different without your heavy kohl eyeliner and blue crown. But, you are still quite handsome,' said Poppy.

Enoch smiled again. 'Thank you, Poppy. It means a lot to me that you remember that night so well.'

'I'll never forget it. Oh, Enoch, this is my fiancé Brian Atherton.'

Brian then extended his hand and Enoch extended his and the two men shook hands.

'Enoch Tara. It's nice to meet you.'

Brian's eyes widened a little—just enough that everyone noticed—and then he smiled. 'It's nice to meet you too,' said Brian in an almost shaky voice.

Poppy eyes flickered with recognition. Yes. *The* Enoch Tara was standing before her. She smiled. 'Well,' said Poppy a little flustered, 'I hope you two enjoy your lunch.' Poppy and Brian then politely nodded and made their way through the lunch time crowd towards their table. Enoch took his seat.

'They were really nice. I'm amazed Poppy remembered me,' said a surprised

Enoch.

'She was in the front row that night. And, she's right; I talked about you for weeks afterwards.'

'I didn't know that I had had that kind of impact on you, Gemma,' said Enoch; his voice seemed to be almost trembling.

'Enoch. I don't think this is the right place to talk about…this,' said Gemma. She looked around the now packed restaurant. Gemma thought for a moment.

'Enoch, what are doing after lunch?' asked Gemma.

'Me? Oh, um…I'm not sure. I mean, I will probably just go back to my office in the City. I guess you'll be heading back to The Gherkin.'

'Actually, I have the rest of the day off. Alexa decided I deserved the rest of the day off after all the work I've done for the upcoming conference in Singapore.'

'Really?'

'Yes.'

'Gemma, would you like to spend the day with me?'

'Yes,' replied Gemma.

Gemma—Sequel—The Day Spent in the City

THE RESTAURANT

Gemma and Enoch enjoyed their lunches and the atmosphere of the Hungarian restaurant at lunch time. Enoch glowed with happiness. He had finally told Gemma what he had wanted to tell her for so long, and she seemingly accepted it. He wondered what she was thinking. He ate his steak, and with the exception of commenting on how much he liked the food, he said nothing else.

Gemma didn't know how to feel. She was still processing what had happened. That morning Gemma had awoken to another day at the office. Well, not exactly, Gemma loved her job and the people she worked with. She was happy.

Alexa had given Gemma the chance to have her own flat and make real money again. She had also pledged to invest in her private kindergarten. She now had a future; at least a chance at one. Gemma still dreamed of marriage and a nice home life. She wanted to have someone to come home to every night. She wanted to know the simple joys of marriage again. Hopefully, this time with someone who truly loved her.

Was Enoch Tara 'The One'. Hmmmm. Gemma didn't know. With everything that had been going on for the last four years, she had practically forgotten him. The memory of their time together had always been a happy one; but those happy memories had almost drowned completely in the misery that had been Gemma's life. As cute as Enoch had been at Oxford, she had never had any romantic feelings for him. How could she have? Her heart had belonged to George—and Gula. Enoch was something of an unknown quantity. A near stranger from the distant past who had declared their love for Gemma. What was she supposed to make of it?

Gemma paid for lunch at the register, and the two of them left the restaurant.

'Thank you for treating me to lunch, Gemma. It was really good, and I enjoyed the atmosphere there. I'll definitely come back.'

THE CITY
It was a nice sunny day in May. There was a light breeze. A few white clouds floated serenely across the sky. The street in front of the restaurant was bustling with people. Gemma looked around.

'Where to?' asked Gemma.

'Anywhere you like,' replied Enoch.

Gemma turned around and looked behind her: ST GEORGE USED BOOKS. Ah, a used book store. Gemma smiled. She loved used books stores.

Gemma had once had a large collection of books; alas the bailiffs had taken them all away to pay George's debts. However, now that Gemma once again owned a home, she would have a place to keep books. Gemma decided that today was a good day to rebuild her collection.

She looked at Enoch. He looked rather smart in his charcoal grey suit and tartan tie. He was still cute. He was physically attractive, but there was more to a relationship than looks. Gemma had learned that lesson with George.

'Do you like books, Enoch?'

'Yes,' he replied with a smile. At that moment, Enoch would have consented to tour the London sewers with her.

'Follow me, Ptolemy,' said Gemma in her smooth posh accent, and she flashed her Sussex school girl smile.

The pair walked into the book shop. The door was painted a glossy blue. The sign which hung over the large paned glass window spelled out the name of the shop and included a hand painted image of St George in medieval armor fighting with a dragon. The background of the sign was the white and red Cross of St George.

The interior of the shop was made up of wooden bookshelves which were packed with used books. The shelves which sectioned off each section had a small white sign nailed above each shelf and hand painted the type of books in black paint.

The store was empty save for the young woman behind the counter and two customers; both wore grey suits with pale blue dress shirts, ties, and black leather dress shoes—City bankers.

A young blonde woman, wearing a white blouse and wearing black framed eye glasses, smiled as they entered the shop.

'Good afternoon. My name is Jane. May I help you?'

'Yes,' replied Gemma politely. 'Could you point us in the direction of your history books, please?'

The young woman smiled and then came around the counter and said, 'Right this way, please.' She was wearing faded denim jeans and brown suede shoes with bright blue soles.

She walked down between shelves of books and turned right; Gemma and Enoch followed. She motioned with her right hand and said, 'Here you are. This entire section is nothing but history. Please let me know if I can be of any other assistance.'

'Thank you, Jane,' replied Gemma.

Jane smiled and made her way back to the front of the book store.

Gemma approached the shelves and started scanning through the titles. Enoch went to a different shelf and started looking through them. Gemma knew exactly which books she wanted to buy; Enoch had no idea what books he wanted, if any. He was just happy to be spending the day with Gemma.

Gemma took one book off the shelf and looked through it. She smiled. This was exactly what she wanted. Did they have another copy? Ah, they did. She took that one too. She then made her way down the long book shelf. She was looking for something else.

'Here you are,' Gemma said out loud. She pulled the book out of the shelf and opened it. She slowly looked through the pages. Yes, this was a good book. Gemma walked back to the front of the store and returned with a wicker basket. She placed the three books in it and then continued to explore the corner of the store for more paper bound troves of knowledge. She was happy.

Enoch only pretended to look for books. He was focused completely on Gemma and the possibilities that this day offered. He had almost let her slip away from him. It was Gemma that had chased him to the elevator. He sighed. 'You almost lost her again, Enoch,' he thought to himself.

Gemma wondered around the store for another half an hour. She then made her way over to Enoch carrying her wicker basket of books. She smiled.

'Find anything interesting?'

'Yes. No. I mean…what did you find, Gem?' asked Enoch.

'A basket of surprises,' said Gemma. 'Shall we go? I'll show them to you later.'

Gemma paid for the books, and the two of them walked back out onto the street. Gemma looked at Enoch and said, 'I know a nice tea shop nearby. How about we go there?'

'I'd like that. But only if you let me buy the tea.'

Gemma smiled. 'Okay. But, I warn you. I drink a lot of tea.'

Enoch smiled.

THE TEA SHOP
The tea shop was in a narrow building sandwiched between a Royal Mail post office and a store that sold a wide variety of cardboard boxes. The store front was a large window and a wooden door painted with white and blue tea cups.

They sat at a small wooden table after ordering two cups of tea. The small tea shop only seated around a dozen people, and Gemma and Enoch had managed to get the last table available.

Gemma placed her cloth shopping bag on the empty chair next to them. She took out one book from her bag and placed it on the table.

Gemma lifted the book up so that Enoch could see its title: The Ptolemies.

'They had two copies. I bought both of them,' said Gemma happily. Gemma then took a silver pen out of her black leather briefcase. She opened the book and started writing on the front page. When she finished she closed the book and, with both hands, handed it to Enoch.

Enoch accepted the book with both hands and a smile. He opened the book to the front page and read what Gemma had written on the first page.

To my favorite Ptolemy and the one who saved my crown. I will never forget that night on stage. You made it possible.

Love,

Gemma

Enoch smiled. He looked up from the book and said, 'Thank you, Gemma. This means a lot to me.'

'The crown and that night on stage meant a lot to me, Enoch.'

Enoch brushed his hand gently over Gemma's beautiful florid handwriting. She wrote like Jane Austen. Really, the same penmanship used by Jane Austen. Enoch wondered how Gemma had learned to write like that. This used history book had suddenly become Enoch's most cherished possession. It was an almost cosmic exchange. The cardboard, felt, and papier-mâché crown had become one of Gemma's most cherished possessions as well.

'What other books did you buy?'

Gemma pulled the other two books out of the cloth bag. One was a copy of the Ptolemaic history book she had given Enoch; the other was a book on Medieval England. Gemma opened up the book and searched through the pages. When she found the page she was looking for she turned the book around and showed Enoch.

'Here; my family fought in this battle. You see. He was one of my ancestors.' Gemma then pointed to a medieval painting on one of the pages. It was of a knight in armor carrying sword and shield. She then turned a few more pages and then stopped. She turned the book around to show Enoch the page.

'Here. The Taras of Somerset. A Saxon family. Is this your family castle?' asked Gemma.

'Yes. It was. Now it's a ruin owned by the National Trust,' replied Enoch. He read over the pages. The book was interesting. He looked up at Gemma. So, did we fight on the same side?'

'Yes. Well, usually,' replied Gemma, and she smiled.

Gemma and Enoch sipped their tea from delicate blue and white ceramic tea cups. The tea was a nice refreshment to have on a cool breezy day. The white walls of the tea shop were decorated with old posters advertising products from companies based in India during the British Raj that had faded away with the British Empire.

Enoch had never been happier; not in his wildest dreams did he think this day would ever come. Had he won Gemma's heart? Probably not. But he had finally told her what he had been wanting to for so long. And Gemma had not runaway. Not yet.

Gemma liked Enoch; she always had; but she was struggling with the idea of having a romantic relationship with him. Gemma wished that he had not told her that he loved her. Of course, she had suspected it while they were seated in the conference room, but now that he had confirmed it, she wished he hadn't.

The Enoch she knew at Oxford had the gentle soul of an artist, an actor.

He had been very sweet and innocent. Gemma had been innocent too. She would have never guessed that he had loved her at Oxford. Gemma had nothing but questions for Enoch.

'Enoch, why didn't you pursue an acting career?'

Enoch's facial expression changed immediately. He looked around the tea room pensively. He said nothing for couple of minutes. He was deep in thought. Then he looked at Gemma and responded.

'I continued to act while at Oxford until I graduated. I was on stage for two years, acting at small theatres across England. I auditioned for several roles at theatres in London, but never seemed to get the parts I had hoped for. Then, one day, when I was 24, a stage director told me that I should pursue another field of employment. He told me I wasn't good enough to be a professional actor. He said I lacked true ability. He was a prominent director. That conversation crushed me. He told me I would never be given anything but minor roles. I was devastated,' said Enoch; his voice breaking with emotion.

Gemma stared at Enoch wide eyed. 'Enoch, that's horrible. And the director was wrong. You are an outstanding actor. I can't believe anyone would ever say that to an actor, especially one so young as you were. That's cruel. Enoch, you are a great actor. I know that,' replied Gemma with more than a little emotion in her voice. She then reached over and held Enoch's hand. 'I'm sorry you had to go through that. This is heart breaking. I'm so sorry that happened to you.'

Enoch gently grasped Gemma's small, soft, manicured hand. 'Thank you for saying that, Gem; but I think he was right.'

Gemma felt fury building up inside her. This was not an emotion she was used to. Gemma was gentle and kind. But what had happened to Enoch was shockingly cruel and unfair.

'Enoch, please believe me when I tell you, you are a great actor. That director was wrong. This makes me so angry. You didn't deserve that. It's not true. It's not true. I swear on my soul, it's not true,' said Gemma, she starting to cry. She then took her other hand and gently brushed Enoch's cheek. 'Enoch, I would never have been able to perform that scene without you. You made it possible that night, and proved to me what a talented actor you are.'

Enoch started to tremble. He could feel the warmth of Gemma's hands: one on his right hand, the other on his cheek. He had chosen not to deal with these memories for almost twenty years. He hadn't forgotten; not a day passed that he didn't remember the words of the director at the theatre in London. It had remained an open wound. His confidence had been shattered that day. And now, with Gemma holding his hand, he felt that wound healing. Gemma had sworn on her soul that she believed him to be a great actor. Enoch knew—everyone at Oxford had known—that Gemma was a truly great actress. If Gemma believed he was too, then that was enough for Enoch. He was free. Suddenly, he was free.

'Thank you, Gemmy. You have no idea how much your words mean to me. Thank you so much,' said Enoch, and with that, tears started to roll down his face.

Gemma picked up a paper napkin and dabbed his tears. 'Now, now, Enoch. Everything will be better now.'

'I'm sorry, Gemma.'

'Don't worry about that. I have cried oceans of tears in the last four years. I was lucky to have people there for me. I'm glad I could be here for you.'

Enoch looked around the tea shop. Yes, some people were staring. But, he wasn't embarrassed. His confidence in his acting abilities had been completely restored. Not that he had any plans to return to the stage. He didn't. But this hole in his side had been healed. Enoch smiled.

'Gemma. Could I buy you dinner tonight? Please say yes.'

'No. I'm having a dinner party at my flat tonight. Brian and Poppy will be there, along with my friends Violet and Külli. I would like you to meet Violet and Külli. All of us have been friends since boarding school in Sussex.'

'I don't want to intrude, Gemma.'

'You won't be. And besides, I think Violet would be thrilled to finally meet Ptolemy,' replied Gemma, and she smiled.

2 POTLUCK

Gemma—England—The Dinner Party

MARBLE ARCH

Külli sat at her polished wooden desk in the office upstairs in her house in Marble Arch. She had a lot of paperwork to do, but tonight she had other things to worry about. Gemma had invited everyone to a dinner party at her tiny flat in the City. Külli had been looking forward to spending time with her friends, but something had come up: Octavia.

Everyone wanted to meet her; they were curious about Külli's new love interest. Külli hesitated to introduce her. Octavia's resemblance to Gemma was something that everyone would notice—including Octavia. How would Octavia feel about that? Gemma had invited Külli to bring her to the get together.

It was to be, in accordance with Gemma's wishes, a small and informal get together. Jeans were recommended. Gemma's dinner party would take place around her kitchen table/desk. It was to be a potluck. Everyone had been asked to bring one dish. Everyone was expecting it to be a lot of fun. Külli was filled with trepidation.

Gemma wanted the first dinner party at her flat to be with her closest friends. Everyone had been invited to bring their significant other with them. For Poppy this meant her fiancé Brian. For Violet it meant her husband Hugh; only Hugh couldn't attend because he was in Borneo or some such place supervising a mining operation. Gemma didn't have anyone. Külli had Octavia.

Külli had decided that it would be a good opportunity to introduce Octavia to the group; after all, she had to do it eventually; why not now?

Octavia was excited—and nervous. She wanted to make a good impression on everyone. Octavia wanted to be part of Külli's life forever.

Octavia still addressed her as Külli, not her Sussex school girl name Gula. Only the girls from the alcove at All Saints called her by that name. Külli's father—a bootmaker—had given her the nickname of Caligula was she was very young. By the time she had arrived at the boarding school in Sussex, it had been shortened to 'Gula.' Everyone else called her Külli. Even Octavia.

Külli was wearing a pair of faded blue jeans and a white cotton blouse with a large collar. Her shirt was a product of her own equestrian outfitters brand: Külli Vahtra. The company her father founded in the 1950s had started out manufacturing riding and hunting boots and leather shoes. It had expanded into hunting and riding outfits and leather kit in the 1990s thanks to Külli's influence.

After a brief and highly successful modelling career, Külli returned to England and took control of the company from her aged and ailing father. She then expanded the label into regular clothing, much of it bespoke. The family firm had been growing ever since. Külli had turned Külli Vahtra into a exclusive and much in demand high-end luxury brand. The company's coffers overflowed. She had done it: Külli was a brilliant success. Her father would have been proud of her. Sadly, he had passed away before Külli's innovative designs and marketing abilities had made the company the brand it was today.

Külli was wearing her soft white slippers. She didn't like to wear shoes in the house. She looked at her platinum watch: 8:17pm. They had better get going. She got up and the nearly six-foot tall Külli walked through the doorway and down the white walled hallway. She knocked on one of the bedroom doors.

'Octavia? Are you dressed?'

The glossy white door to the bedroom opened and the physical fit Octavia answered.

She was wearing faded denim blue jeans, a white open collared blouse, and a beige suede jacket. Her long glossy brown hair had been cut earlier that day. Octavia peered out at her from under her brown bangs—she had always styled it like Gemma. Octavia had never met Gemma, and she knew nothing of Külli's unrequited love for her—no one beyond Gemma and Külli knew anything of it. Octavia had quite innocently shared the same hairstyle with Gemma. The resemblance bordered on the uncanny. Külli masked her emotions as she smiled at Octavia, but inside she was starting to panic.

Would the rest of The Inseparables put two and two together and see what had really transpired between Külli and Gemma? Külli hoped not, but what could she really do about it? She wasn't about to break up with Octavia over her resemblance to Gemma. Privately, Gula wondered to herself if she had fallen in love with Octavia because of the uncanny resemblance Octavia bore to Gemma.

'I'm ready,' said Octavia happily. Octavia usually carried herself with a sophisticated air , much the same as Külli. But the patrician Octavia, for all of her posh upbringing, and Oxford education, was actually quite sweet, much the way Gemma was. Külli loved her for those qualities more than anything else. Yes, Külli loved Octavia.

Külli adjusted Octavia's jacket for her. 'There,' she said, 'perfect.'

'Thank you, K,' replied Octavia.

'We'll take the Porsche tonight,' said Külli.

THE APARTMENT
Gemma liked faded blue jeans. They were comfortable and she thought them stylish. She stood in front of the large mirror in her flat and looked at herself. Yes, the white blouse was perfect. She put on her brown leather belt. Her waist was still slim. Gemma smiled.

She had cooked a dozen steaks. Some of them well done, others medium well, and a couple rare. They were now all under a silver cloche on the kitchen table. That and some fresh sliced bread and salad were Gemma's contribution to the potluck.

'A potluck', how American, Gemma', Vava had said laughingly. ' But, I think it's a fantastic idea. I wonder what I'll bring?'

Yes, potlucks were relatively new to England, but Gemma loved the very idea. She had never hosted one, and she thought an informal dinner party at her tiny apartment in the City would be ideal.

Gemma had covered the long wooden kitchen table/ desk/ dining room table with a white table cloth. She had purchased new silverware just for tonight. She placed the inexpensive white ceramic plates on the table. She measured the distance between each plate with a plastic ruler. Yes, old aristocratic habits die hard.

She placed the silver dish of steaks on the table and covered it with the silver cloche. She then placed a white ceramic salad bowl and two different white ceramic plates with sliced bread at each end of the table.

Gemma then carefully and expertly folded the white cloth napkins and placed one on each plate.

She placed metal folding chairs around the table, one for each guest. She had purchased four extra chairs the weekend before just for this occasion. The aluminum metal chairs were perfect. When not in use, they could be folded and neatly stacked along the back wall. She would use them again; Gemma had decided that this would not be her last dinner party.

She stood back and looked at the table. 'Not bad, Gemma,' she thought to herself. Gemma smiled.

VIOLET
Vava spent over an hour soaking in a hot bath. She then carefully applied skin cream. She looked at her long shiny blonde hair. She decided to have the Hungarian maid braid it into a single braid down her back. Yes, that looked quite nice.

She put on a pair of faded denim blue jeans, a pale blue blouse (that matched the color of her eyes), a pair of black leather Chelsea boots, and her black Dior sunglasses and headed down the stairs.

The sun was setting and the orange and magenta rays of twilight were shooting directly into the main entry hall of her house in Marylebone.

She nodded at the French chauffeur who was waiting for her in the marble tiled foyer. Violet told him the address of Gemma's apartment and they both walked out the door to the waiting gleaming blue Range Rover.

A burly bodyguard, an ex-Para, sat in the front seat. Vava's husband, The Honourable Hugh ('Hughie'), had insisted she have one. London was no longer safe, and being the wife of a wealthy mining CEO could invite trouble. It was for the best. Vava agreed.

The chauffeur opened the passenger door for her, and she got into the backseat. The chauffeur had already placed two covered dishes in a wicker picnic basket in the backseat of the SUV. Vava opened the basket and inspected the contents. She smiled. 'Alright, Henri, please take me to the City,' said Violet.

The Range Rover then sped away into London traffic; the ex-Para carefully scanned the area ahead for any possible trouble.

Behind them, a silver BMW sedan followed with two other bodyguards (both former Paras).

Vava would never be allowed to go unprotected in London again.

POPPY
'You look nice, Brian,' said Poppy when she saw Brian walking down the stairs of her small Edwardian house in Covent Garden.

Brian was wearing faded blue jeans and a grey, white and blue tattersall dress shirt. He was slim and his brown hair was cut like a British army officer's. Poppy loved Brian; that he was handsome was an extra. Poppy smiled.

Poppy was wearing a pair of faded blue jeans and a white Egyptian cotton blouse with a high collar. She looked at her silver Asprey wrist watch:

8:10pm. They would be the last to arrive at Gemma's, for sure.

'Well take the hatchback,' said Poppy and she waved the keys to her silver Citroen.

'Wait. We almost forgot the dish,' she said.

Brian went into the kitchen and returned carrying a covered white ceramic bowl. He smiled.

'Okay,' said Poppy, 'Let's go.'

ENOCH
Enoch sat in the backseat of the silver Volvo sedan. His driver was maneuvering through traffic when his smartphone pinged.

He looked at the screen: a text from Gemma. He smiled and tapped on the screen.

Hi Enoch. How do you like your steak?

Enoch tapped out a reply: **Medium well. Thank you, Gemma.**

Enoch was wearing faded blue jeans; something he rarely did anymore. He had found this pair in his closet at his house in Marble Arch. He hadn't worn them in years. They still fit. He put on a white cotton button Oxford dress shirt and his silver Omega watch.

Oh, and he didn't forget to bring a covered a dish that his housekeeper had made for him at the last minute: dishes of Yorkshire pudding, mash, and a large bowl of gravy she placed in a cardboard box to make it easier for him to carry. It was still piping hot when she handed it to him in the kitchen just before he had departed for Gemma's.

'It's smells great, Mrs Glasse. Thank you.'

Enoch was both excited and nervous. He wanted to make a good impression on everyone. The guests at tonight's dinner party were all Gemma's closest friends. He would have to win them over too.

Gemma—England—Octavia and Enoch

THE APARTMENT

Gemma looked at her silver Cartier watch: 8:45pm. Twilight in London. Everyone was running late tonight. Gemma smiled. No worries. As long as everyone showed up she would be happy.

Gemma looked around her small studio flat. She loved it. This flat represented independence. Tonight, with seven people seated around her kitchen table in folding chairs, the apartment would be crowded. But, Gemma didn't mind that either. She was happy that her dearest friends in the world had finally reunited after a twenty year separation.

This was to be Gemma's first dinner party since her divorce from George. The former Baroness Gemma, had once been one of London's most popular hostesses. The last dinner party she hosted at their Notting Hill house was for fourteen guests. George invited several of his former classmates from Eton and Oxford; among them were two barons and a future duke of the realm. Poppy was there with an ex-boyfriend (an Honourable) and so were Vava and Hughie (both Honourables). All but one of the attendees was in Burke's Peerage, and she had a double barreled surname.

The dinner party had been sumptuous, the food excellent. Dinner had been served on gilt-edged white bone china and the guests had no less than seven sterling silver utensils. Gemma had worn a white beaded dress from Givenchy and a platinum and diamond tiara from Cartier. She was radiantly beautiful. The dinner party was one of the highlights of the social season that year. And then it all fell apart.

Tonight, Gemma was hosting an informal dinner party served on a long wooden table surrounded by seven folding aluminum chairs.

The table was covered in a brand new white table cloth she had purchased on sale at Zara. The silverware looked nice, but it was stainless steel; still, it looked beautiful. The plates, glasses, and silverware had been placed perfectly on the table. The silver cloche and tray were sterling silver, an item the bailiffs missed because she had loaned it to Poppy for one of her dinner parties.

The attire for tonight's dinner party: informal: jeans.

The menu: potluck. Potluck could some up Gemma's life: a series of surprises and the unexpected.

Gemma sighed.

She had fallen far, but now she was slowly recovering. Gemma had loved her previous life with George, **but she didn't miss it**. Her new life felt pure. Most of the friends she had in her previous life had abandoned her. The friends attending her dinner party tonight were her true friends. They mattered.

THE FIRST GUEST ARRIVES—LATE
The buzzer rang: someone was downstairs at the front door.

Gemma walked over to the intercom and looked at the CCTV screen. It was Vava and two tall dark suited hard looking men—her bodyguards. One of the men was carrying a wicker picnic basket with silver handles.

Gemma pushed a button and the door downstairs clicked open.

She walked to the front door of her flat and opened it. She left the white metal door open and walked down the white walled hallway. The overhead lighting reflected off of the polished hardwood floors. She stopped at the elevator and waited. The stainless steel elevator doors opened and Violet and her two bodyguards exited onto the landing.

'Gemma! It's so good to see you!' said Violet happily. She hugged her and said, 'You look beautiful.' This new warm and outgoing Vava was still something Gemma was getting used to, but she was happy about Vava's transformation.

'It's great to see you, Vava. You look fantastic!'

Gemma looked at the muscular bodyguard carrying the picnic basket and extended her hand. 'May I please have the basket? I'll carry it in.'

The man held the basket up and Gemma took it. 'Thank you,' she said and then she smiled at both of the men. Gemma looked at Violet and said, 'Welcome to my home, Vava.'

'Thank you for inviting me, Gemmy. I've never looked forward to a dinner party more in my entire life.'

Violet looked at one of the bodyguards and said, 'Stewart, please order some take away for you and the others. I don't want you starving downstairs while we are feasting the night away,' said Violet. 'Have Henri put it on the household credit card. And please get whatever you and the others like.'

'Thank you, ma'am,' replied the smartly dressed Stewart.

The two women then walked down the hallway and entered the small apartment. The men both turned and one of them pushed the elevator button. They would wait downstairs in the cars with the others.

THE APARTMENT

Violet entered the small studio apartment. The flat consisted of one relatively large room with a tiny white tiled bathroom. The kitchen was at far end of the apartment. A small stainless steel stove, kitchen sink and counter top were along the wall. Next to the counter was a silver SMEG refrigerator.

One side of the apartment had a row of windows. The bottom portion of each window was made of frosted glass. Gemma had installed long white curtains for additional privacy when she wanted it. The walls of the apartment were all painted white.

Gemma's twin bed was in the corner next to the door. The high thread count white pillows, sheets, and duvet were expertly made.

Violet marveled at Gemma's domestic abilities. Violet hadn't made her bed since leaving Oxford. Well, since leaving All Saints boarding school in Sussex. She had never made her bed while attending Oxford.

Violet walked over the dinner table and paused. The table had been set perfectly; the staff at Windsor Castle couldn't have done it better. The steaks smelled delicious. Violet turned around and looked at Gemma. 'You remain the greatest hostess in London.'

Gemma smiled, 'You are too kind, Vava, but thank you.' Gemma placed the wicker basket on the counter. She looked at Violet and asked, 'What did you bring us, Vava?'

Violet walked over to the counter and opened the basket. Inside were two covered dishes. The aroma was fantastic. 'I brought lasagna and Confit Potatoes. Elizabeth made them for us,' said Violet. 'Oh, and she asked me to say "hello" for her.'

Gemma smiled and said, 'Perfect, Vava. I haven't had either in *yonks*. Please tell Elizabeth that I miss her and her kind smile.'

Gemma uncovered the dish of lasagna and placed it on the table. Violet placed the dish of Confit Potatoes on the table next to the lasagna.

The front buzzer rang again. Gemma and Violet walked over to the intercom and looked at the CCTV screen. It was Brian and Poppy. Gemma smiled and buzzed them in.

BRIAN AND POPPY

Gemma greeted them at the elevator landing and escorted them into her apartment. Brian and Poppy were carrying a cardboard box with a covered dish inside.

'Poppy! Brian! It's so good to see you!' said Violet as they entered. Poppy looked at Violet. Violet looked youthful and beautiful. How did she do it? Poppy noticed Violet's hairstyle; it looked really nice.

'Good to see you, Vava. How have you been?' Poppy walked over to Violet and hugged her. Brian smiled and nodded in acknowledgment.

'*Marvellous*,' replied Violet. 'It's so good to see the two of you together.'

Brian placed the cardboard box containing their covered dish on the kitchen counter; he then turned and joined Poppy who was standing in front of the long kitchen table. They were both impressed. 'How sumptuous, Gemma. I'm *terribly* impressed,' said Poppy.

'Thank you, Poppy. I'm glad you like it.'

'Gemma, Brian and I thought everyone would enjoy beef ravioli. I made it myself. I think it turned out quite well.'

'I'm sure everyone will.'

The front door buzzer rang again. It was Enoch. Gemma buzzed him in. She greeted him at the elevator landing.

'Welcome to my lair, Enoch. No one knows you're attending. You're my surprise guest.'

'Thank you for inviting me, Gemma. This really means a lot to me.'

Gemma—England—Surprise Guest

THE CITY
Külli shifted and the silver Porsche Caymen slowed in the heavy London traffic. Octavia sat next to her. She had a cardboard box in her lap. Inside was a raspberry pie that Ivika had made for the potluck.

Octavia was nervous.She wanted to make a good impression on everyone. She had to. These were Külli's friends She wanted to be accepted. Külli had assured her that everyone was really nice and accepting. And if Külli liked her, then he friends would too.

The orange rays of twilight reflected off of the silver car as it moved adeptly through London traffic. Külli shifted again and the German engine revved; the Porsche moved forward. The bright orange sun grew dimmer by the minute. Going. Going. Gone. Külli switched on the headlights. The beams cut a path through the darkness ahead.

THE APARTMENT

It was dark when Enoch entered the apartment. Poppy, Violet, and Brian were all standing next to the dining room table when he walked in. Enoch was carrying the cardboard box his housekeeper had given him.

Brian and Poppy, both City bankers, were well aware of who Enoch Tara was. Well, at least they knew *of him*. The sight of *the* Enoch Tara clad in faded blue jeans seemed to almost startle them. Yes, Enoch Tara was standing before them in faded blue jeans and a white Oxford button down dress shirt. Holding a cardboard box with a potluck dish inside. The world suddenly seemed to be a much stranger place than usual. Enoch looked at the small group and smiled, perhaps nervously. It was difficult to tell.

Enoch was attractive. He was slim and had a rather youthful complexion and appearance. His light brown hair was cut like a City banker's. His blue eyes were kind and thoughtful.

Poppy and Violet found themselves both remembering that night some twenty years ago when the young and lithe Enoch, wearing pharaonic attire and heavy kohl eyeliner, stood next to Gemma and both of them gave the greatest stage performances of their lives. It had brought the entire audience to tears—and silence. The silent pause was followed by rapturous applause. Yes. Enoch had made Gemma's performance that night possible. Without him, it would have never worked. Enoch went with the wave of emotion and both actors and audience were richly awarded for it.

'Hello,' said Enoch. And Enoch smiled.

'Hello, Enoch,' replied Poppy. 'It's nice to see you again.' Poppy smiled.

Brian smiled and nodded slightly in acknowledgement. He was too nervous to speak.

'Enoch,' said Gemma. I would like you to meet Violet. She is one of my dearest friends.'

Enoch smiled and bowed slightly. 'It's nice to meet you, Violet. Gemma has told me a lot about you.'

'It's nice to finally meet Ptolemy. I watched your performance on stage that night. It was amazing. Truly. I have never seen anyone perform as well as you two on the stage that night at Oxford.'

Enoch smiled. 'Thank you. However. It was Gemma. Gemma made it all possible. She was the one that changed the tone that night. I don't know what came over her. But the energy around her was incredible. It was almost audible. I became part of it. I was happy to be part of it.'

'Well, Enoch. You complemented each other perfectly. I will never forget it,' answered Violet.

Gemma held out her hands. 'That box looks heavy. I think it would look better on the counter over there,' said Gemma, and she smiled. Enoch smiled and walked the short distance to the counter. He placed the box on it and turned around. As he did, the door buzzed. Someone else was downstairs.

OCTAVIA
Gemma walked over the metal panel near the door and looked at the small screen. She froze. Külli was standing in the doorway. Next to her was **Gemma**. Well, a younger version of her. Was this Octavia? She was beautiful. And Gemma eyes scanned the digital image that flickered before her on the screen.

Okay. Let's get this over with. Yes. The others would notice the resemblance immediately. Gemma hoped that no one would mention it or stare too much. Gemma shook her head slightly. Very slightly. This should be interesting.

Külli and Octavia stood together in the elevator. Okay. So everyone will notice the resemblance immediately. And then what? Külli hoped that no one would remark on it. They probably wouldn't. But what of Octavia? She would notice too. What would she make of it? Okay, Gula. Be calm.

The elevator doors opened and they stepped out onto the landing. Gemma glided down the hallway to greet them. When she saw them she smiled. Octavia glanced at her and almost dropped the cardboard box she was holding. Külli caught it.

Gemma and Octavia stood and stared at each other. Gemma and Octavia, meet your reflection. Gemma smiled. She had been better prepared, albeit just slightly. Octavia had been caught completely off guard.

Külli, now holding the cardboard box, smiled. 'Hi Gemma. Thank you for inviting us. I'd like to introduce you to Octavia. Octavia; this is Gemma.'

Octavia stared for a moment and then regained her composure. She smiled. 'Hello, Gemma. It's nice to meet you. I have heard so much about you from Külli.'

'Welcome to my home. Please come in. Oh, Gula. Please. Let me have the box. I'll put it on the counter.' Gemma smiled and Külli handed her the dessert. Gemma led the way down the hall and through the doorway of her small flat.

Gemma entered first followed by Külli. Everyone exchanged greetings. And then Octavia entered. She looked like a deer in headlights. She was still reeling from the shock of Gemma's appearance. Külli was near panic though her visage remained as still and smooth as marble.

'Everyone, please allow me to introduce you to Octavia,' said Külli . Her voice was clear, concise, and unwavering. She smiled.

Of course everyone noticed. Even Enoch noticed. Octavia was a younger version of Gemma. She was beautiful. She had Gemma's hair color, hair length, and even her bangs. Octavia had a nice smile too.

And everyone smiled.

Gemma—England—End of Term

ALL SAINTS SCHOOL
June 2019
It was a beautiful day in June in Sussex, a glorious English summer day. Hundreds of family members had shown up for the End of Term (the final one for Freya and Louise) on that sunny, breezy day.

All Saints, a posh and exclusive (read: rather expensive) all-girl Anglican boarding school, had been founded in 1837; the same year Queen Victoria had ascended the British Throne. The school had been started by a wealthy English noble family with the mission of educating the daughters of the English nobility. The school had always been exclusive, and being small and well funded, had managed to maintain its status as one of the country's premier all-girl boarding schools.

The number of students was limited: a maximum of 350 students attended at any given time. Most of the girls who enrolled were the children of past graduates; around 70% of the girls were the daughters of All Saints alumni. The small number of available openings at the school had made entry into the school formidable. While academic qualifications mattered, one's social connections mattered more.

Gemma and Poppy were daughters of the nobility, 'Honourables' or 'Hons' that had both come from ancient aristocratic English families. Violet was also a 'Hon' and her grandmother and mother had both graduated from All Saints. The girls had all been accepted immediately upon application.

There was also the 'Ten Percent'. These were the students who were academically gifted, but lacked noble pedigrees and were not the daughters of alumni. Allowances had to be made for modernity. Allowing a few commoners in was one such allowance. The *Ten Percenters* were usually the offspring of very wealthy parents. Külli and Louise were two such students. Külli's father had owned a highly profitable outfitters, and Louise's father was a former Coldstream Guards officer who was also a rather wealthy and successful farmer in East Anglia.

The school's main building, built in the 1790s, was a Palladian revival structure with a Portland stone facade. The large three storey building still housed the schools' classrooms, library, and administrative offices. The building's main entrance was a large set of glossy black double doors with sterling silver handles that were polished every day by the staff.

Behind the school was a row of seven two-storey red brick buildings that housed the students. Each 'House' had its own name. Each house had been named after an Anglican Saint. Some girls lived in Saint Albans. Others lived in Saint George. While the houses had seen modern conveniences installed in them like air conditioning and Internet access, the houses had not been redecorated since the 1920s. The stairways were carpeted with Persian rugs and the polished wood panelled walls gleamed.

Large oak, maple, and willow trees shaded the buildings and lush and well maintained green lawns surrounded them. There was a large bell tower behind the houses.

To the left of the main building was the school's Anglican chapel. The Portland stone structure was quite impressive. The interior floors were a combination of stone and black and white tile. The chapel, a Victorian structure, had been featured several times in magazines and on television. The school choir gave public performances at Christmas and Easter and often toured the country.

To the right of the main building was the school theatre. The Art Deco Portland stone structure, which had been built in the 1920s, while not very big, was quite beautiful. It had witnessed numerous performances over the years, and, on occasion, was also used to show films. The theatre also hosted school assemblies and ceremonies.

Behind the theatre was the school's great hall. This is where the students had their meals and where school clubs often held their meetings. The great hall was a Portland stone building lined with large windows and panelled with polished burl wood. The food served was excellent. The students enjoyed sumptuous meals in Edwardian surroundings. What else could one ask for?

At the other end of the row of student houses was the school gymnasium. It was here that Külli had led the school's volleyball team to victory after victory. It was here that The Inseparable Gang of Happy Girls had cheered her on.

All Saints was an excellent school by any measure. Most of its students went on to Oxford or Cambridge.

The original Inseparables had all attended and graduated from Oxford University. The two newest members of the gang, Freya and Louise, would not. Louise would attend a second tier university in London; Freya, plagued with school discipline problems and poor grades, would be attending a third tier university in the Midlands.

At first, Freya's mother, Violet, had been deeply upset, but the new year had brought with it a sea change in Vava's character. Now Violet was happy to have a daughter who she loved and who loved her. Now Violet was proud of her daughter despite her lack of interest in hunting and poor academic performance. Vava was proud that Freya had been made of stronger stuff. She was proud that Freya was fiercely loyal to her family and friends; Freya was someone of character. Freya was her joy.

Louise, alas, gentle, kind Louise, remained abandoned by her family. Louise had spent her first two years at All Saints adrift and totally alone. Alone, that is, until fate had seen her room with Freya. Freya, isolated and widely disliked because of her spirited defense of her godmother Gemma, had found a true friend in Louise. The girls connected immediately and their friendship had allowed both of them to heal and blossom.

Gemma and Poppy were the first Inseparables to take Louise under their wings; it had been love at first sight. Vava followed, and then Külli would welcome both girls into the ranks of the Inseparables. Yes, Louise had found a new family.

While Gemma, Külli, Poppy, and Violet had loved their time at All Saints, Freya had largely hated it. Louise, lonely her first two years, loved her time in Sussex because she had met Freya. Freya happily admitted that she too was glad she had attended All Saints because she had met Louise and couldn't imagine life without her.

Now Freya's five years in Sussex were coming to an end. Her parents and grandparents would be attending The End of Term. Poppy and Külli were also set to attend. Freya's godmother Gemma would not. Gemma, left a social pariah by her divorce and the scandals which surrounded it, did not want to cause any disruptions on Freya's last day of school.

END OF TERM
The school theatre was filled to capacity with friends and family. The atmosphere was electric. People chatted happily and many in the audience snapped photo after photo with their smartphones. The ceremony soon began.

Freya and Louise sat with their classmates and listened to speaker after speaker. Well, not exactly. Freya and Louise were both lost deep in thought.

All Saints had been part of their transformation. As unpleasant as it had been, it had played a large part in shaping their characters. And now, like everything else, it was coming to an end. Neither would miss school in Sussex. They were both relieved that it was over. For both girls, life loomed ahead of them. And, sadly, their lives were about to diverge. They would soon be separated. Next year they would room with strangers at different universities.

Louise, sitting in a folding wooden chair next to Freya, reached over and grabbed Freya's hand. Freya turned her head slightly and looked at Louise. Freya smiled. Louise looked at Freya, but she couldn't bring herself to smile.

Louise found herself on her last day at All Saints without any family present. She had called her father and invited him, but he had replied coldly that he wouldn't be able to attend. He had offered no reason why. He told her that he had paid her university school fees for the coming year and that he would be doubling her monthly allowance to (a paltry) two hundred pounds a month. Louise thanked her father and before she could say anything else he hung up.

Louise was scared.

The pomp filled ceremony seemed to conclude rather quickly. Or maybe that was emotion speeding everything up? After a brief speech by the headmistress, the girls all stood and sang the school song. Most of the girls stood and openly wept as they sang it. By the end of the song, there was barely a dry eye in the theatre.

ALL SAINTS ALUMNI
Freya and Louise made their way through the crowded theatre to the main entrance and walked outside and down the steps of the Art Deco stone structure. At the base of the stairs, waiting at the pre-arranged place, were Freya's parents, both sets of grandparents, Poppy, Brian, Külli, Karmen, and *Gemma*.

'Gemma!' shouted Freya as she descended the stone steps. Freya couldn't believe it. Gemma was here. She had attended the End of Term at All Saints.

'Godmother! You're here! In Sussex! Thank you! This means so much to me, Gemmy.'

Gemma, wearing a blue and white polka dot cotton dress, smiled. Freya and Gemma embraced.

'I love you, Godmother', whispered Freya into Gemma's ear.

'I love you, too,' replied Gemma.

Freya then realized that she should have greeted her grandparents first. She turned and smiled. She hugged each of her grandparents in turn and thanked each one for attending. Each one of them told Freya how proud they were of her and smiled.

Violet's father, the 5th Viscount and his wife the Viscountess, told Freya how proud they were of her and invited her to attend a fox hunt later that year. Freya smiled and thanked them for their invitation (while at the same time rehearsing excuses inwardly as to why she would be unable to attend).

Poppy, wearing a pleated navy blue skirt and white blouse, made her way to Louise and hugged her. Poppy was privately upset and deeply saddened that Louise's father had not attended Louise's final day of school. Poppy couldn't understand how her father could be so cruel and indifferent. Poppy was determined that Louise would know that she was loved and not alone in the world.

'I'm very proud of you, Louise. You've worked very hard,' said Poppy as she hugged Louise.

'Thank you, Aunt Poppy. Thank you for being so kind to me. I really liked the letters you wrote me and the biscuits you and Gemma made for us. You are really nice.' Louise looked as if she were about to cry.

'You're a good person, Louise. I'm glad I met you. You are a very welcome addition to our gang,' said Poppy and she smiled.

Louise smiled and the two bantam girls embraced.

'Louise, don't forget about me,' said a posh voice. Louise looked up. It was Külli. The six foot tall Külli. She was wearing a pleated grey cotton skirt and a white blouse. Her black sunglasses were propped back and resting on her head. The beautiful Külli flashed her healthy white smile.

'Thank you for attending, Külli. It's nice to see you here today.' Louise then hugged Külli.

'When you are in London, you will have to come by my house in Marble Arch for dinner. Or lunch. Or tea. I expect to see you often, Louise,' said Külli.

'I would like that, Külli. Thank you,' replied the diminutive Louise.

Louise's strawberry blonde hair was now shoulder length. She had tied it back with a pale blue ribbon. Louise's brown eyes glowed with happiness. She smiled.

'I'm so proud of you, Freya,' beamed Violet. 'I'm rather sad this day has finally come. I will miss being able to visit you at All Saints.'

'Don't worry, Mummy. You'll be able to visit your granddaughter here one day,' replied Freya, and Freya smiled.

'Freya! I'm so happy to hear that!' said Vava excitedly. 'I was worried that you would never send your daughter here. The family tradition will continue then.'

'Yes,' replied Freya happily.

Freya's father, the towering and athletic Hugh (Hughie to his friends and family) smiled. 'My Freya has graduated from All Saints and is now heading off to uni. It seems like just yesterday you were playing in the nursery with Karmen and Gemma.'

Freya hugged her father. He had always been kind and attentive to her. She loved him. Hughie's position as the head of the family's mining company had forced him to spend most of Freya's childhood overseas and away from her. But still, when home, he was a good father to her.

Karmen, the Croat nanny, was wearing a navy blue dress with a white collar. Karmen, at 44, was still quite slim and attractive. Her light brown hair was kept shoulder length and was streaked with white and grey hair. She smiled as Freya approached her.

She had raised Freya along with Gemma, and truth be told, Freya was much closer to Karmen and Gemma than her mother Violet. Violet knew it, but she was grateful to Karmen and Gemma for their kindness and loyalty to Freya.

Karmen had never married. Instead, she had dedicated her life to the 4th Baron and his family. Karmen had spent the last 18 years in service to the family. She was now raising the children of the 4th Baron's only daughter.

Karmen usually wore a brown uniform when performing her duties, but today she was attending the End of Term as Freya's honoured guest and wearing her regular clothing. Karmen was quite fashionable.

Freya smiled and embraced Karmen. They spoke in Croatian; the language that Karmen had taught Freya while raising her.

'Nanny, thank you for everything,' Freya said in Croatian as she embraced her. Thank you for always being sweet to me. You have always been kind to me. I remember everything. You will always be special to me. I love you, Karmen. And I will always be here for you. Please never forget that,' said Freya in Croatian.

Karmen started to cry. 'Freya, my little Freya. I am so happy I had the chance to raise you. You will always be my little Freya,' replied Karmen in Croatian. Karmen then paused. She held Freya and then said quietly, her voice breaking with emotion, 'I love you, too, Freya.'

The group of friends and family continued to congratulate and hug each other for several more minutes. Afterwards the group walked around the school and reminisced about All Saints for over an hour. For Gemma, Poppy, Külli, and Vava, the memories were happy ones, much less so for the Freya and Louise.

None of the other attendees said anything to Gemma, which was a relief to everyone.

When the bell tower came into view, Freya took Gemma by the hand and led her across the lush green lawn away from the main group. Freya wanted to speak with Gemma privately.

'Godmother. I didn't think you would attend today. Thank you,' said Freya.

Gemma stopped walking. She reached over and held one of Freya's hands. 'You are so brave, Freya. You defended me from your classmates and you paid a high price for that. I know that. And I'm sorry that happened. I wish it hadn't,' said Gemma sadly.

Gemma then lowered her voice and said, 'You were also brave that night,' said Gemma, alluding to the events that transpired in January when Grey had sent men to harm her. It had been a harrowing experience for both Freya and Louise. Only Gemma, Poppy, Karmen, and the two girls knew what had really happened. Gemma shuddered every time she thought about what could have happened that night. Winter had warned her to get the girls out of Sussex. He had been right. Winter had saved their lives.

'If you are brave enough to overcome all of this, *then I can find the courage* to attend the End of Term at All Saints,' said Gemma quietly. 'I've always been proud of you, Freya.'

The group then started walking towards the parking lot. The girls had already loaded their suit cases, books, bedding, and other belongings into Vava's blue Range Rover. Henri, the driver, had helped.

Parked next to the Range Rover was Poppy's silver Citroën. Next to that was Violet's in-law's dark blue Audi. Kulli's silver Porsche Cayman sat gleaming in the parking lot too. Next to it was a silver BMW with two bodyguards standing beside it. They both nodded slightly as the group approached.

Goodbyes were said, more hugs exchanged, and the group then started to separate and drive away in different cars.

The 4th Baron, his Rhodesian wife the baroness, and Karmen made their way to a dark blue Audi. They waved goodbye and then drove away.

Vava and Hughie stood next to the Range Rover and chatted with the driver.

Gemma, Poppy, Külli, Freya, Louise, and Brian stood next to Poppy's silver hatchback and spoke to each other.

'Alright,' said Külli. 'I'll see everyone next weekend at the wedding.' Kulli then looked at Freya and Louise and said, 'Octavia will attend the wedding with me. You'll finally get to meet her.'

'I'd like that,' said Freya. The 5'9" Freya then hugged Külli.

'Yes, I've heard a lot about her. She sounds *marvellous*,' said Louise in her attempt at a Sloane accent, and Louise smiled. All the girls started laughing happily.

'We'll make a Sloane Ranger out of you soon enough,' said Poppy and she smiled.

'I'm excited about your wedding, Aunt Poppy,' said Louise. 'I expect it to be quite *smart*.'

Poppy smiled. She loved that Louise was adopting Sloane language. Louise wanted to be part of the group, to be accepted. She was alone, and she wanted to part of something, a substitute family. Poppy understood that. Gemma understood Louise completely.

Brian smiled at both girls and said, 'I'm happy you are both coming to the wedding too. I'd like you both to meet my family. My parents and sister have heard all about you.'

Freya and Louise smiled and hugged Brian. Brian seemed a little embarrassed by that, but his shyness was considered endearing by the girls.

Gemma hugged Louise and said, 'See you next week. I'll be coming by the house in Mayfair to see everyone.'

Louise was spending the summer with Freya. She would be alternating between the family homes in Mayfair and Marylebone. Freya and Louise planned to spend the summer travelling around England and relaxing at home in London. The girls both wanted to spend every minute possible with each other before they went off to separate universities.

Louise was awaiting her dormitory room assignment for next year at her *uni* in London. Freya was awaiting her room assignment as well. University filled both of them with apprehension.

The girls walked over to the waiting glossy Range Rover and waved goodbye to everyone. They both climbed in and the dark blue SUV sped away.

Poppy and Brian said their goodbyes to Gemma and Külli and drove off as well.

It was just Gemma and Külli left standing in the parking lot next to Külli's silver sports car.

People were still walking through the parking lot and getting into their cars. Many tears were still being shed along with smiles of happiness. Yes, today was not only the end of term, but the last day at All Saints for many of the girls. So much had happened to everyone. Their futures now lay ahead of them all.

Külli leaned up against her car. She put her dark sunglasses back on and let the cool summer breeze wash over her. She stared at Gemma.

'What are you thinking about, Gemmy?'

Gemma, adjusting the slender white patent leather belt around her blue and white polka dot dress turned around. She propped her dark sunglasses back on her head and looked at Külli.

'I'm thinking about us, G. Our days here in Sussex. I was so happy. It seems almost like it was all a dream.'

Gemma gazed at Külli pensively and then turned back to look at the school. 'It hasn't changed a bit, Gula. It looks exactly the same; only everything is different, isn't it?'

Külli stood up straight and then slowly walked over to Gemma. She took off her sunglasses and held them in her right hand. She stood in front the 5'3" Gemma and met Gemma's gaze.

'Well, I guess that's how it always is, isn't it? I mean, life changes and we change with it.' Külli then looked at the direction of the school buildings and said, 'I wish I could go back and relive those days again too. Just one more time. It was idyllic. Yes, I miss those days too. We were young and filled with hope.' Külli smiled gently. 'Life has been difficult for you, Gem. I know that. I should have been there for you. I'm sorry. Life hasn't been fair. You didn't deserve all that has happened to you.'

Another summer breeze cooled the girls as Külli spoke. Now Külli was the pensive one. She spoke softly, in gentle tones. She wanted to say this correctly. 'Gemma. You have always been our guiding light. You have always set a good example. Everyone has always loved you for it. I know I contributed a lot to your sadness; I know that. I know it's supposed to be behind us, but I can't help but thinking about what I did. I caused you so much harm.'

Gemma shook her head and responded quietly, gently, 'That's in the past, G. I don't hold anything against you for it. I never have.'

'I know,' replied Külli. 'You're an angel, Gemmy. But, I want to make amends. Please let me help you.'

Gemma turned on the heels of her white patent leather flats and grasped Külli's hand. 'Gula, being my friend is enough.' And Gemma smiled. And then Gemma hugged Külli tightly. Külli hugged her back even tighter. When they separated, both girls were crying.

'Gemma, I will always regret everything I did to you. I know we have moved on in many ways, but I know that I caused you a lot of heart break.'

Gemma looked down and spoke quietly. 'Gula, thank you for those words. I've waited a long time for people to apologize to me for many things. But, I don't want you to carry this guilt with you for the rest of your life. I don't want revenge against you. You didn't hurt me on purpose. You didn't want to; it just happened because of the circumstances. I'm grateful that we are back together. I still consider you to be one of my closest friends. I love you, Gula. I always will.'

Gemma wiped her eyes and then continued. 'Yes, I have to admit that your acknowledgement of what happened is important to me. We were both very young and emotional. And emotions often carry people away. It's part of being human, Gula. I'm not perfect either. I have made mistakes too.'

'Oh, I don't know, Gemmy. I think you're as close to perfect as I've ever met,' said Külli in barely above a whisper.

'My broken heart has been healed. We are friends again, that is what matters the most,' said Gemma softly.

Gemma then held Külli's soft manicured hand. Gemma smiled. 'I'm glad you found Octavia. She's beautiful. She's sweet. I really like her. I want you to be happy, G.'

Külli tried to smile; her face was still wet with tears. 'I hope you find happiness too, Gemma. I won't be truly happy until you find someone worthy of you.'

'I think there may be someone,' replied Gemma with a smile.

'Enoch?' replied Külli.

'Maybe, G. I don't know. Enoch is so kind and innocent. I do have feelings for him, but I don't know. The last four years have been really difficult for me. I don't want to rush into anything. I have to be cautious.'

Gemma's acknowledgement of her true and uncertain feelings for Enoch was incredibly reassuring for Kulli. Gemma was confiding in her again. Gemma trusted her again. Külli then looked at Gemma. She had been wanting to talk to Gemma about this since the dinner party the week before.

'Gemma. About Octavia. What do you think of her appearance?' asked Külli nervously.

'Oh, that,' replied Gemma mischievously. 'Well, she is incredibly beautiful. And...there is a certain something about her...hmmm.' Gemma's smile grew into a broad grin and then she started laughing. 'Gula, I think Octavia is *your type.*'

'Gemmy!' said Külli laughingly. 'Okay. I admit it. She does bare some resemblance to you. Just a little.'

'Just a little, G?' replied Gemma. 'She could be my younger sister!'

Both of them laughed.

Külli then put her dark sunglasses back on and took out her car keys from her beige leather clutch.

'Come on, Gemmy. Let's drive back to London. Please have dinner with me tonight in Marble Arch. Octavia won't return from Iceland until next week. I telephoned Ivika and asked her to make steak for both of us tonight. She's also going to make us Raspberry Mannavaht. It's an Estonia dessert which I'm sure you will love.'

'For sure, G. I haven't had Raspberry Mannavaht in *yonks*,' said Gemma happily.

And both girls laughed.

Gemma—Sequel—Singapore

CHANGI AIRPORT
Gemma walked down the gangway wearing faded blue jeans, a white blouse, and brown suede Chelsea boots. She had her laptop in a leather shoulder bag slung over one shoulder and a small grey leather handbag over the other. She was exhausted. She had been unable to get much sleep on the flight from London to Singapore.

Blinding sunshine poured through the windows of the sky bridge leading from the British Airways airliner. Gemma opened her handbag as she was walking down the passage and found her black sunglasses. She put them on. Much better.

Gemma continued down the gangway until she entered the massive airport terminal. It had high ceilings and the walls of the terminal were intricate layers of glass. Everything in the terminal seemed to gleam with cleanliness and modernity. Robots moved quietly around the terminal and there were white kiosks with glowing touch screens everywhere. Gemma had never seen anything like it. The furniture inside the terminal alternated between Scandinavian postmodern to some rather bizarre and uncomfortable looking circular chairs.

Gemma followed the other passengers and made her way down the futuristic concourse. Gemma entered the fully automated border-control kiosk, facial and fingerprints scans verified her identity as she made her way through the control gate. A CT camera scanned her as Gemma picked up her suitcase from an automated kiosk. When she arrived at the glass exit she looked at her silver Cartier watch: the entire process had taken only fifteen minutes.

THE HOTEL
Gemma took the MRT—the Singaporean subway— to the five star hotel where the conference was to be held. Alexa had reserved rooms for everyone on her team. Gemma entered the gleaming and sterile hotel lobby. Another architectural marvel enveloped her. Yes, Singapore was the stuff of techno dreams.

She checked in and took the elevator up to her room. The elevator was empty and as it quickly ascended Gemma noticed that it was moving in complete silence.

She got off the on the 11th floor. Another sterile and futuristic hallway appeared. Gemma, exhausted, hid behind her black sunglasses as she dragged herself down the hall towards her room pulling her wheeled aluminium suitcase behind her.

When she arrived, she waved her card over the door lock and tapped in the code that was printed on a white card that front desk had printed out for her. The door unlocked with a barely audible click. As she entered the room, the lights came on and the air conditioning system engaged. It reminded her of the security system in Grey's Primrose Hill house.

Gemma closed the door behind her; the electronic lock engaged. Gemma turned and locked the additional door bolt with her small soft manicured hand. Okay. She felt better.

One wall of the room was made almost entirely of glass. The window looked out on futuristic Singapore.

The large king sized bed was covered in a beautiful white duvet that was so perfect it reminded her of Cartier's white gift wrap.

She left her suitcase were she stood.

She placed her laptop case and hand bag on the desk in the room.

Gemma walked slowly towards the bed and stopped at its edge. She turned around and then fell backwards into the soft bedding fully dressed. She was asleep in a matter of seconds.

3 THE CHERWELL

Gemma —England—Wedding Day

COVENT GARDEN
Gemma stood behind Poppy as they both looked into the large mirror in Poppy's bedroom. Poppy was wearing her wedding dress. It was a simple design of ivory white satin. It was stunning in its simplicity and quality. Poppy was also wearing a white veil and a glittering diamond and platinum tiara. However, something was not quite right.

Külli, wearing a white, minimalist, satin dress, stood off to one side. Actually, Külli really wasn't wearing the satin dress; she had been positively poured into it. The tall and fit Külli had lost none of her looks, even at 41. She looked into the mirror at Poppy's reflection. Yes, something about the fit was off.

The bedroom door opened and Violet entered the room wearing a pleated, tea-length, white satin dress. 'Poppy, you're going to be late for your own wedding,' said the flaxen haired Violet.

'Sorry, Violet. I'm having a bit of a problem with the dress,' replied Poppy as she was attempting to adjust it.

Gemma, radiant in an ivory white satin dress of simple design, arched an eyebrow. 'Poppy, is it just my eyes deceiving me, or have you gained weight?'

Poppy froze and then blushed into the mirror. Everyone suddenly looked at Poppy. Poppy turned around and said, 'Why, yes, Gem. A little.' And then Poppy flashed her impish smile.

The Inseparable Gang of Happy Girls, a mixture of smiles and laughter, all moved forward, encircled Poppy, and hugged her.

ST ALBANS
The stone Victorian Anglican church gleamed in the June sunshine of another beautiful English summer. The lush grass lawn in front of the church was shaded by large leafy green trees.

The guests had already taken their seats. The women all wore dresses. They were conservatively attired in combinations of colors and shades of the same. The men wore black morning coats, waist coats, striped trousers, and black leather shoes.

Mars, the 13th Baron, wore a black morning coat and a dove grey waist coat. He looked quite handsome. Poppy's brother James and the 12th Baron had donned black morning coats, white waistcoats, and striped trousers for the occasion. Both men cut dashing figures.

Helen wore a sky blue midi dress dabbled with small Cotswold lavenders in purple and green beads, and the 12th Baron's slender wife wore a lavender and blue floral print satin dress and white gloves.

Violet's father-in-law, the 4th Baron, was attired a black morning coat, white waistcoat, striped trousers, and black leather Balmoral boots. The 6'4" baron stood out like a dark obelisk as he sat in one of the Victorian box pews. His white haired and svelte Rhodesian wife, the baroness, wearing an elegant blue dress with a white collar and white gloves, sat next to him. They made for a striking couple.

Next to them sat Hugh and Violet. Hugh wore a black morning coat and a beige waist coat. Violet, her long, glossy blonde hair contrasting sharply with her white satin dress, looked positively beautiful. Her blue eyes glowed with happiness.

Freya, in a chirimen Hepburn swing dress (the dress was a stylish collection of stripes of varying shades of blue and sky blue) and Louise, in a bluish-violet periwinkle (with a white collar) tunic dress, sat in the pew behind Violet and The Honourable Hugh. Freya and Louise were both so excited they could barely contain themselves.

The 4th Baron's tall blonde daughter, her career naval officer husband, and their two young blonde daughters, sat with them.

Across the aisle in another ornate box pew sat Gemma and Enoch. Enoch, as stylish as ever, wore a black morning coat, a white waist coat, cashmere stripe trousers, and black leather shoes. Enoch was slim and quite attractive. More cute then handsome, he cut a sharp and contrasting figure next to Gemma, who, clad in ivory white satin, radiated beauty and happiness.

Gemma was serene. Just six months earlier, her life seemed to be near its end, and now this. This sunny and warm moment in St Albans surrounded by the ones she loved most in the world. And seated next to her, in the Victorian box pew, was Enoch. What to make of him, Gemma didn't know. He was kind and vulnerable. He had revealed so much about himself to her. He had declared his love for her. Did Gemma love Enoch? Gemma really couldn't say she did. Not yet. But today it didn't matter. Gemma had reclaimed her life, found direction, and hope for a bright future, and, perhaps, just perhaps, love.

Mixed in with the wedding guests were Alexa (Poppy's former All Saints crush) and her sharply attired husband.

Seated next to Gemma was Külli —'Gula' to the former alcove gang—and Octavia. Yes, the couple were together. The slender Octavia was quite fetching in her blue and light blue patterned tea-length dress. Her brown hair had been pleated into a long braid down her back. Octavia was grateful to have received a wedding invitation. She had only recently entered Külli's life, and the invitation, printed on thin white cardboard, was more like a ticket into the inner circle than a mere wedding ceremony. For Octavia, the invitation meant acceptance. At least that is what she hoped.

Külli was happy. Yes, after decades of anguish and regret, she had reconnected with her dearest friends. Gemma, of course, was back in her life. Külli was completely at peace with their relationship. All was well. Külli glanced at Gemma. She was next to Enoch. Gemma occasionally leaned slightly towards him and smiled. Külli had found love. She hoped Gemma would too. And this time was someone who was worthy of her.

The small church had been built with donations from British colonists in India in the late 1800s. The symbols of the Raj had been removed from the front doors and walls. They had been placed in storage, somewhere, and forgotten. The church was beautiful. Its ceiling was ornate in a very Victorian way. Bright summer sunshine flooded into the church and filled the vaulted chamber with natural light and warmth.

Brian, dressed in black morning coat, a white waistcoat, striped trousers, and black leather shoes, stood ramrod straight at the altar. Brian was truly handsome. And most importantly, Brian was kind, good-hearted, and loved Poppy with every bit of his heart and soul. His dark brown hair already had a few white and silver hairs in it. He had waited until 41 to marry. He had searched for true love, refusing to accept anything less. And now, on this sunny day in June, his search had finally ended. Brian smiled.

Next to him was his closest friend, a morning coat clad classmate from Harrow

Brian glanced at his parents and younger sister one last time before Poppy was set to enter. His mother's gaze met his and tears filled her eyes. Finally, Brian, her son, would marry. Brian's father nodded slightly in acknowledgement. Yes, it had all been worth it. The sacrifices made and the hard work. Brian's parents had always trusted him to make the right decisions in all things. Brian always had. And this, the most important decision of his life, had been no different.

It began with one note from the Victorian organ, and then another. Music. The wedding march began and Poppy, dreamily beautiful, blonde, draped in white satin and hidden behind a gauzy white veil held in place with a diamond tiara that reflected the bright sunshine, appeared at the entrance of the stone church, a surviving remnant of the formerly mighty British Empire, on a perfect sunny day in June in the heart of London.

Gemma—England—On the Cherwell

OXFORD

Enoch untied *the painter* (a rather posh way of saying the rope) while standing at the end of the weathered wooden punt. He then let the end of the long wooden metal tipped pole drop vertically to the bottom of the river. Enoch leaned the pole forward, and with a gentle push, the wooden punt moved forward across the water.

It was a warm summer day in June. A rare sunny day. A slight breeze cooled them both as the punt glided slowly down the Cherwell.

Gemma leaned back against the blue cushion and looked up at Enoch from under her wide brimmed straw hat, which was adorned with a white ribbon. Gemma, clad in a white cotton open neck blouse, a pair of navy blue narrow leg cotton trousers, and a pair of brown leather shoes with clear rubber soles, gazed at Enoch through a pair of herringbone sunglasses. Gemma's shoulder length glossy brown hair rested against the weathered wooden hull of the punt. Gemma looked rather sultry in her abandoned languid pose.

Enoch looked *quite* nice himself. He was wearing a white button down Oxford dress shirt, dark brown cotton trousers, and a pair of rubber soled dark brown leather shoes. He was also wearing a straw boater hat with a blue and red ribbon. He was slim and attractive. He also radiated gentleness.

Enoch had an innocence about him that Gemma liked. Enoch was kind and sensitive. Gemma's forensic gaze had failed to detect any trace of the awe inspiring investment banker in Enoch that was spoken off in superlatives in the City. Enoch remained an unusually somewhat mysterious individual. Only Enoch did not seem enigmatic at all. Gemma didn't know what to make of him. No one did.

Gemma had reunited with Enoch only three and a half weeks earlier. In that short interval, he had attended Gemma's first dinner party and Poppy's wedding. It was as if she had been reunited with a long lost love. Only he wasn't. Enoch had known Gemma for only a brief spell at Oxford over twenty years ago. What to make of it? Gemma didn't know. She knew, Gemma knew, that there was nothing sinister about him. She could sense that Enoch was good-hearted. And that he loved her. She knew why. Enoch had glimpsed the true Gemma. Not the physically beautiful one, the beautiful soul that resided within her.

As Enoch piloted the small wooden punt down the placid River Cherwell, Gemma would occasionally look from side to side. The willow trees swayed in the breeze along the lush green of either side of the river. Sometimes geese would glide alongside the punt. Yes, today was a beautiful, idyllic day on the river.

Gemma trailed her fingers in the silky waters of the Cherwell. The water was cold. It felt good against the summer warmth. The contrast in temperature was quite nice.

Gemma exhaled. Gemma was completely at ease. Relaxed. She felt safe. A languid morning. Only the wildlife was stirring.

Gemma closed her eyes. She could feel the summer warmth, the cool breeze, and the cold water against her hand as she rested against the cushion. Every other minute or so, a slight jolt would raced through her as Enoch adjusted the long wooded pole and gave it another push. The sounds of geese, the wind in the trees, and the splash of water caressed Gemma's senses. It was heavenly.

THE WEDDING BREAKFAST
After the wedding, everyone had driven to a hotel in Mayfair for the reception. It was quite posh. There were toasts, brilliant sunshine which flooded through the large windows and open double doors of the white walled hotel ballroom, and plenty of conversation. It was a joyous occasion.

It was at the reception that Enoch had suggested visiting Oxford. Yes. Oxford. Gemma hadn't been there in *yonks*. Not since her downfall almost four years earlier.

Yes, that was the moment that her life seemed to pivot on. Only now it no longer did. Gemma's life had restarted on January 10th, 2019, the day Grey had been killed. Well, technically, it had been the early morning hours of the 11th. And it was on Saturday that Gemma had approached Gula's glossy black door in Marble Arch. A cosmic whirlwind had enveloped the Inseparable Gang of Happy Girls and reunited them. Gemma had found peace, as had the others. Now on this sunny day in June, Gemma's future was unfurling before her. Gemma smiled.

'I'd love to go, Enoch. When are you free?'

'Now,' smiled Enoch.

Gemma looked at Enoch. He was seated next to her at the large round table which was covered with a white table cloth which was covered with glittering silverware, white bone china, and crystal wine glasses and champagne flutes. He looked *terribly* dashing in his blacking morning coat and white waist coat. He was attractive, more cute then handsome. No. Enoch was handsome. Gemma determined at that moment that Enoch was handsome, and so he was. He looked quite handsome in his black morning coat, white waist coat, grey and white striped trousers, and black leather shoes. Perhaps it was the way the sunlight highlighted his silky light brown hair? Or maybe it was the way Enoch smiled? Or maybe, just maybe, it was because Gemma knew that Enoch's love for her was pure?

Gemma studied him carefully as he talked. Her expression softened each time he smiled or spoke. Yes. Gemma was developing feelings for Enoch. Was it love? No. Not yet. Would she ever love him? Gemma didn't know. But at that moment, she really didn't care. Gemma abandoned herself to the moment.

If one were lucky, one could experience a few moments of happiness. If one were truly lucky, one would still be able to find happiness after suffering long intervals of misery. Gemma had almost given up hope of ever experiencing happiness again. Almost.

The hotel ballroom was an ocean of black morning coats, striped pants, beige, blue, bluish grey, sky blue, purple, and lavender satin dresses, waist coats, and the white jackets and gloves of waiters. The white walls reflected the sunshine off of the silverware which glittered on tables covered with white table cloths.

The reception lasted quite a while, much longer than usual. Towards the end, Gemma and Enoch slipped away unnoticed.

OXFORD

Gemma and Enoch got into Gemma's white Peugeot hatchback and motored their way through London and onto the M40. From there, Gemma piloted her hatchback down the motorway, eventually making her way onto a lush country backroad. The car decelerated and Gemma relaxed. Gemma enjoyed driving, but not driving fast.

Enoch and Gemma were still dressed in their wedding finery. That was alright. Enoch liked dressing up and Gemma looked really nice.

Sitting next to Gemma in the car allowed Enoch to observe her in a new environment. Yes, Gemma was a good driver. She wore her shoulder belt and always used her turn signal. Gemma played by the rules.

Enoch listened attentively as Gemma talked about her days at Somerville. She smiled and laughed as she talked about Violet's Japanese roommate, Akiko. Poor Akiko. But, in the end, Akiko had benefited from sharing rooms with the wild, unpredictable, and ultra posh Violet. Akiko graduated from Oxford with a degree in Modern Languages and a posh accent and manner which had served her well in international finance.

Enoch liked the sound of Gemma's voice, her posh intonation, and Sloaney language and manner. He liked how Gemma laughed and the way she sometimes dipped her head down slightly when she smiled. He loved Gemma. Enoch knew that Gemma didn't love him. Not yet anyway. But, he hoped that one day soon she would.

Enoch knew that Gemma had had an extremely difficult time in the last few years. He didn't know most of the details; he didn't think he wanted to know. Enoch couldn't bear the idea of Gemma suffering. It hurt him to even think of what she must have gone through. And more than that, Enoch had remained quiet on one of the Channel Islands watching Gemma being destroyed and doing nothing to help her in her hour of need. Enoch would never forgive himself for that. It was at those moments that his chest would tighten.

Enoch had decided that if Gemma rejected him, he would still be her friend and try to protect her. For the rest of his life, he would be there for her. Yes. He would be there for her.

The small white car slowed as it entered Oxford. It was late, twilight, when they arrived. Gemma turned on the headlights and the car slowly made its way over the cobblestone and narrow streets of Oxford.

THE HOTEL

The hotel was on Beaumont Street and at the corner of Magdalen Street, which was across the street from the Ashmolean Museum and a short distance from the Oxford playhouse. Enoch insisted they stay there. He privately wanted to be close to the playhouse. That was, after all, were they had first met. Gemma suspected as much, but said nothing.

As they slowly made their way through the now dark streets, Enoch happily informed Gemma that he had already reserved two rooms for them at the Randolph. Gemma parked her car near the hotel and they both walked to the hotel together.

It was a cool, almost cold night. The elegantly dressed couple walked to the end of the street and stopped. Enoch looked in the direction of the playhouse.

'Just think, Gemma. We met for the first time in 1998 just a couple blocks away from where we are standing now.'

'Yes. It seems like a lifetime; or perhaps, another life all together. It's surreal to be back here with you on a cool night in June.'

Enoch became lost in thought for a moment. He had dreamed of being reunited with Gemma for so long, and now, they had been. Enoch did not know what to expect from their reunion. He had no idea. All he knew for sure was that he truly loved Gemma, and he had to tell her how he felt. How she would react, he didn't know. When he told her, she didn't balk; she just listened in silence. Enoch's declaration had freed him.

Now, what would he do next? What happened next was entirely up to Gemma. Gemma had been pursued her whole life. Gemma had suffered so much. She deserved better. She had always deserved better. Was Enoch good enough? Was he worthy of Gemma? He had not come to her aid when she needed it most. Had he forfeited ever earning her love and trust? That weighed on him constantly. To love and be loved means being worthy of it. Was he?

'Enoch, we have nothing to wear tomorrow. I hadn't even thought about that. Today has been so exhilarating and wonderful; the thought hadn't even crossed my mind. Not even while I was driving to Oxford.' Gemma burst out laughing. 'The affect you have on me, Enoch. What am I to do?' And Gemma started laughing again.

'There are plenty of stores in Oxford. I'm sure we will find something.'

'Enoch. We are going to go shopping dressed like this tomorrow.'

'I know. Won't that be a lot of fun,' replied Enoch happily.

And Enoch and Gemma both smiled.

THE HOTEL ROOM
Gemma's room was rather nice: white walls and a huge bed with white cotton sheets, several large white pillows, and a purple, pink, and blue tartan wool bedspread. There was a desk and chair, and a coffee machine. Or did

it make espresso? Gemma wasn't sure. It was dark. It had been a very long day. And Gemma was very, very tired.

She undressed, placed her ivory white satin dress on the end of the bed, and entered the bathroom. Gemma was tired, but she needed a long hot bath to relax her. She turned on the hot water. The steam rose from the modern white porcelain bathtub and soon the large mirrors were fogged up and the room filled with steam.

Gemma wiped away the condensation from the mirror and gazed at her reflection. She stood naked in front of the bathtub. Yes, still shapely. Gemma was youthful. She had taken good care of herself. Gemma had been through so much, and her psyche had been badly damaged. The events of the last few months had gone a long way towards healing her damaged emotions. But, was it enough?

Gemma knew what Enoch was hoping for. What Gemma had always hoped for. What she thought she had found with George only to have everything cruelly ripped away from her. Gemma wanted desperately to find love. But would Gemma be able to enter a relationship so soon again? Here was the question that really haunted Gemma: Would she be able to be intimate with Enoch after what she had been through with Grey? Was she truly healed? Could she ever be? Could Gemma really come back from that? Gemma was determined to find love again. To love and be loved. She wanted to be a wife. Could she? Yes. She could. She would. Yes, Gemma would be alright. If Enoch was the one, then she would be alright. She wouldn't allow anyone or anything destroy her chance at happiness. She wouldn't.

Gemma wiped away the condensation from the mirror once more and looked at her reflection in the large bathroom mirror. Yes. Gemma would be happy again.

And Gemma smiled.

Gemma—England—Ptolemy returns to Oxford

THE HOTEL

Gemma stirred in bed. Sunlight filled the white walled hotel room on the corner of Magdalen Street. Gemma had arrived without any luggage, and so she had showered and gone to sleep without a stitch of clothing. Gemma had slept soundly. Under the soft white sheets of the bed in her hotel room, Gemma felt at peace. She was happy and rested. She opened her eyes to the glorious sunshine of a summer day in England.

She lay flat on her back and stared at the white ceiling above her. Only natural light filled the room. At that moment, Gemma felt that that was the way it should always be. Natural light. Sunlight. Ultra-Violet light. The rays of the sun warming and illuminating the Earth. The ancient Egyptians had worshipped the Sun. Gemma felt that that was entirely understandable and appropriate. The blazing Sun swirling in heat and unmatched blinding radiance had given the Earth life. The pulsating and swirling fiery star that mortals referred to simply as the Sun was at the center of it all.

Gemma stretched and then held her soft, pale, and manicured hands in the air. She looked at them. They were small and soft. She gently moved her long, delicate, and tapered fingers. She lowered them back down to the bed and let them rest at her sides above the bed covers.

Gemma inhaled and then exhaled slowly. She wondered if Enoch was still asleep.

She sat up in bed and looked out the window. The heavy dark blue drapes were open, only a gauzy sheer white curtain, which allowed in only natural sunlight, shielded her.

The paned glass windows were closed tight. An unseen air-conditioner cooled the room. Gemma had turned it down a little before going to bed. Gemma preferred a cool or even a cold room in summer.

Gemma's smartphone started to ring softly. Gemma looked around the room for the phone. Ah, there it is, on the desk. She pulled back the white bed covers and walked across the room naked. She picked up her phone and answered it.

'Hello.'

'Good morning, Gem. Sleep well?' asked Enoch cheerfully.

'Heavenly,' replied Gemma.

'How about we meet downstairs for breakfast?'

'Sounds *splendid*, Enoch. I'll be down in forty-five minutes.'

'Alright. I'll wait for you in the lobby.'

GETTING READY

Gemma had enjoyed the hot bath that morning. Not a care in the world. Now only Gemma and Gula remained the unmarried Inseparables. Gemma hoped that that situation would change for both of them. She climbed out of the modern white ceramic bathtub and stood in front of the steamed up mirror. She grabbed one of the large soft white bath towels from the aluminium rack and gently dried herself off. She put her hair up in a white towel, and then after wrapping herself in a large fresh white towel, she walked out of the bathroom.

She looked at herself in the mirror. Yes, Gemma was still beautiful and much of the damage to her psyche had been healed. Yes, Gemma, it's alright now. You can allow yourself to be happy again. You have suffered so much and come through the storm with the aid of true friends. Find happiness, Gemma. Be happy.

Gemma wore the only thing she could wear: the ivory white satin dress she had worn to the wedding the day before. It fit her perfectly and was still immaculate, even after a night at the end of Gemma's full size bed in the hotel room. After putting the dress back on, Gemma stopped and looked at herself in the mirror. Her silky brown hair rested on her shoulders. Gemma gently moved her hand across her bangs. There. All better.

BREAKFAST WITH PTOLEMY

Enoch was sitting in a high back chair downstairs dressed in his black morning coat, white waistcoat, and black striped trousers and reading the Daily Telegraph when Gemma appeared at the bottom of the stairs. She had descended them—panther like—and so quietly that Enoch hadn't noticed. It was only by chance, when turning to the financial columns, that he happened to see her take her final step off the carpeted marble stairs.

Gemma looked at him, and she flashed her beautiful and dazzling white smile. Enoch was entranced. He wished that he could freeze this moment in time and save it. He could then return to it whenever he felt overwhelmed by the day's events. Gemma was truly beautiful. Enoch loved Gemma as much as he ever had. His love for her had not faded in the two decades since they had appeared on stage together. Enoch loved Gemma more than anyone in the world. He needed her. But Gemma was fragile. He knew that. Gemma's heart would have to be won.

Enoch folded the newspaper and stood up. He smiled at Gemma. He walked towards her until he stood in front of her. Gemma, in her white satin dress, looked like a bride.

'Good morning, Gemma.'

'Good morning, Enoch.'

Gemma and Enoch breakfasted in the hotel's dining room. The other guests would occasionally glance in their direction, but most could only assume they were in Oxford for a wedding that day.

The happy and formally attired pair (yes, pair, not couple) breakfasted on golden brown toast and raspberry jam—Gemma's favorite—and freshly squeezed orange juice. Gemma enjoyed listening to Enoch talk about his theatre days and his love of acting; a love he had rediscovered with Gemma's help.

Sitting there with Enoch made Gemma feel nineteen again. Gemma wished that she could go back in time and fall in love with Enoch that night on stage. Then so many terrible events could have been avoided. However,

Gemma knew that was impossible. Life was what it was, and if she were really lucky, she would have a chance to reclaim her happiness.

THE OXFORD PLAYHOUSE

The theatre where Gemma and Enoch had performed that autumn had remained largely unchanged. As they approached the building, memories flooded back to both them.

The sun shone brightly and the warmth of that summer day in Oxford enveloped them. They reached the pavement and stopped. They would have to cross the street. Gemma took Enoch's hand in hers, and said, 'Come on, let's cross here.'

For the first time since they had known each other, Gemma had taken Enoch's hand. Her small hand was soft and warm. Enoch felt that warmth spread through him. It was love. Enoch loved Gemma. And now, on a quiet street in Oxford, on a sunny morning in June, Gemma had grasped his hand. Enoch smiled.

The theatre was closed that morning. No worries. It wasn't necessary to enter. It was enough just to be there standing in front of it. They had returned. And this time as a couple. Well, not a couple, really. More like a pair. Yes, but a happy pair. And there was the possibility that they could become a couple, and if they became a couple, they could become a married one.

They both stood under the Bauhaus style theatre awning and looked through the doors. The large lobby was unlit. The building had been refurbished. It looked quite nice.

'Gemma. How about we go punting down the Cherwell today? It's a perfect day for it. Don't you think?'

'Yes. That does sound nice. It's been *yonks* since I've been out on a punt.'

'But first, well have to buy some new clothes. I don't think we can go boating like this,' said Enoch.

'Oh, I don't know. Drifting down the Cherwell in a black morning coat and a satin dress would make for a much better story, don't you think?' replied Gemma.

And Gemma smiled.

Gemma—England—Always Summer

OXFORD

The punt floated down the Cherwell until upon reaching a bend, Gemma spotted a large stone building: St Hilda's. There were several other buildings along the Cherwell. Some over a hundred years old; some were relatively new. The buildings were partially shrouded in the lush greenery which grew along the riverbank. Green lawns along some parts of the riverbank hosted small wooden docks for the college's own punts.

Külli had taken Gemma out on punts several times during their first term at Oxford. Gemma would occasionally make her way from Somerville to St Hilda's to see her dearest friend in the world. It was at St Hilda's that Gemma would travel to at night to look at the stars hovering above the university from Gula's room on the top floor of the South Building.

Gemma had been fully aware of Gula's true feelings for her by that point. Gemma had not taken Gula's letter declaring her love in their final year at All Saints all that seriously. To Gemma, she was just another one of Gula's school girl crushes. It was only when Gemma explained that any romantic relationship between them was impossible, that Gemma had realized the depth of Gula's love. Gula's reaction had been not only startling, but a revelation. Gula was *truly in love with her*. Gemma had been left in the state of shock. Külli had started to shake, and then tears filled her eyes. She started to cry, and then Gemma knew. She knew at 18 that their friendship would not survive much longer. Eventually, perhaps soon, Gemma would meet someone, and Külli would not be able to handle it.

Külli was Gemma's closest friend. Gemma didn't want to lose her. It was with Gula, the English born Estonian from Surrey, that Gemma had connected with most deeply and almost immediately upon meeting her for the first time on that first day of school in Sussex.

ALL SAINTS BOARDING SCHOOL
August 1991

The alcove room was on the second floor of the dormitory that faced the woods behind the school. The room's hardwood floors, installed in the 1920s, reminded Külli of the deck of a wooden ship. There were four wooden framed beds, white walls, and leaded glass windows. The room looked like an army barracks.

Külli's parents had seen her off at the train station in London that morning. Their only child, a thirteen year old daughter, was going to attend one of England's most prestigious boarding schools. Her parents could not have been prouder. Külli was scared. She had never been away from her parents. She actually liked her school in London and wondered why she had to attend a boarding school in Sussex.

'It's for your future, Gula,' said her father. 'You will meet true English girls there. They are from the best families in England. Do try to make friends. I want you to receive a good education. Don't cry, Gula. This will be a good experience. I just know it.'

Külli placed her tan leather box suitcase on one of the beds and looked around.

Next to the door were four leather and wood travel trunks. The school had requested that the students send most of the required school supplies ahead. Inside the first trunk were Kulli's bedding, a reading lamp, extra shoes and a pair of leather riding boots her father had made for her himself. There was also a large dictionary her father had purchased for her. Oh, and some regular clothes that she could wear on trips away from school like faded blue jeans and a couple of jumpers. And a few other things which Külli couldn't be bothered to remember at that moment, she was nervous about who her roomates would be. She had never had a roommate before, let alone three.

GEMMA
The diminutive and slender Gemma made her way down the wood paneled

hallway towards her room. At 13, Gemma was expected to board at a school in Sussex, far away from her grandparents in London. The previous year, Gemma's mother had passed away and her older brother had departed for Hong Kong. Her father hadn't so much as said a word to her since she was eight years-old. Now, the tiny and gentle Gemma would attend All Saints. Yes, for the next five years, this all-girl boarding school in the wilds of Sussex would be Gemma's home.

Külli worried about many things. The most important was that fact that while she was British—at least she felt she was—she was not English. Nor was her family listed in Burke's Peerage. She was a commoner. She had entered All Saints, the domain of the English nobility, through academic merit. That her father could easily afford the tuition had no doubt also played a role in her admittance. Külli wondered how the other girls would view her, and if they would accept her or shut her out completely. For the first time in Külli's life, she was really scared.

Külli sat down on a single blue and white striped mattress. The afternoon sunshine filled the room. The air conditioning worked well. The alcove was rather cool, almost cold. Külli looked out of the windows at the green leafy trees outside.

'Hello. You must be one of my roommates,' said a gentle voice from behind Külli.

Külli looked in the direction of the voice and then her heart skipped a beat. Standing in the doorway was the most beautiful being she had ever seen. Külli could only stare. The tiny, slender, and fresh faced girl that stood before her in a white cotton blouse, pleated blue skirt, and black patent leather shoes was angelic. Her long brown hair and bangs framed her tiny pale face. The young girl's blue eyes were gentle. This girl seemed to radiate gentleness. The slender English girl smiled.

Külli stood up. And when Külli stood up, people noticed. At 13, Külli was already 5' 9". How much taller would she grow? She could only wonder. She slowly approached the young girl standing in the doorway. She stopped and then glanced down at her.

'My name is Külli,' said the young Estonian. She then continued to stare

108

unsmilingly at Gemma.

Gemma didn't know what to make of the giant that towered before her. She didn't seem to be friendly. She didn't seem hostile either. Gemma, being Gemma, decided to do what she liked to do the most: she smiled.

'Hello, Külli. My name is Gemma. It's nice to meet you.' And Gemma smiled.

So, that was her name: Gemma.

Külli suddenly felt a warmth start in her center and move outwards from there to every extremity. She had never experienced anything like it.

Külli had always known she would never have any interest in boys, only girls. She had never questioned why or felt there was anything strange about herself. She simply was what she was. There had been no soul searching. No dilemmas had ever had to be navigated; no doubts had ever filled her. She was sure. She was guiltless. This is what she was. Külli's heart was reserved for girls and only girls. Well, to be more accurate, one girl. The girl that Külli knew, even at that tender young age, she would find one day.

That day had arrived. For sure. For sure.

Gemma—England—The Maze

OXFORD

Nightfall in Oxford is beautiful; perhaps more beautiful than any other place in the world. The domes and spires of Oxford University catch the red, blue, yellow, orange, magenta, and purple hues of twilight like no place else.

Gemma and Enoch were sitting on a low grey stone garden wall in the twilight. Neither spoke. They simply watched as the twilight slowly faded to night. The air was still a little warm and a gentle breeze cooled them.

Gemma's tortoiseshell sunglasses rested on her head and she was holding her straw hat in her left hand. Her silky brown hair was intertwined with the white collar of her open neck cotton blouse.

'Thank you for today, Enoch. I had an absolutely *splendid* time. I haven't been here in *yonks*,' said Gemma in her natural Sloane way.

Enoch, sitting next her, turned his head slightly and replied. 'Thank you, Gem. I was happy to spend the day with you—here.'

Gemma slowly turned her head to look at Enoch, the final twilight rays of blue illuminating her smooth pale face. Her eyes slowly examined the rather youthful man that sat next to her on the wall. His white button down Oxford dress shirt illuminated in the bluish twilight.

Enoch's blue eyes then met hers. He did not break his gaze but instead continued to look directly at her. Enoch's gaze was gentle, soft. Yes, Enoch was handsome.

'I think I left my *gigs* back at the hotel. At least I hope I did; otherwise, I'm going to have a *terribly* difficult time trying to use my phone,' said Gemma quietly.

'I'm sure we will find them, Gem.'

Gemma then sat up and took a few steps into the garden. It was now dark outside, save for the light given off by some tall cast iron lamps in the lush, green, tree filled garden. She dusted off her blue cotton trousers and then spun around to face Enoch.

'What would you like to do now?' asked Gemma, and she smiled.

Enoch exhaled.

'Gemma, what are you doing tomorrow?'

'I have tomorrow off. I'm now on summer holiday until the end of the week,' replied Gemma.

Enoch seemed to reflect for a moment in the light of the iron lamp and then got up from the low garden wall and walked over to Gemma. 'Gem, how about we visit my country house tomorrow? It's close by in the Cotswolds. I'd like you to see it.'

Gemma smiled. 'I'd love to. Tomorrow then?'

Enoch smiled. 'Yes. Tomorrow. But, now, we still have the entire evening ahead of us. What would you like to do?'

'Go back to the hotel and take a long bath,' replied Gemma.

'And then?'

'Have a quiet dinner with you somewhere. Anywhere.'

THE HOTEL
Gemma had a long hot bath followed by dinner with Enoch downstairs in the hotel's restaurant.

They had both purchased two pairs of cotton trousers that morning at a local Oxford outfitters along with two white cotton shirts. Gemma had bought two identical pairs of blue cotton narrow legged trousers. Enoch's cotton trousers were both dark brown. After bathing, they had changed into the unworn clothes purchased that day. They sat at a small table near the window that looked out on the cobblestone street in front of the hotel.

Both of them were tired after a long day of punting and exploring the nooks and crannies of Oxford. Memories flooded over them at every turn. And today, together, new memories were being created. There had been very little discussion during dinner. They were both hungry and were happy to relax and enjoy their meals.

'Would you like anything for dessert?' asked the young blonde waitress.

'No, thank you,' answered Enoch. 'Just coffee, please.'

COFFEE

Gemma poured a small amount of cream into her coffee and then stirred it with a small silver spoon.

'Enoch, may I ask how you got into finance? I mean, of all the things in the world, why finance?'

Enoch smiled. He then slowly lowered his white coffee cup and placed it on the white bone china saucer on the white table cloth of the table. 'I never dreamed I would. I mean, my mother convinced a former classmate of hers to give me a chance at his hedge fund, and, the rest, as they say, is history.'

Gemma looked pensive for a moment and then looked at Enoch. 'You're a mystery to me, Enoch. I can still only see the young enthusiastic actor, not the mysterious Mr Enoch Tara.'

'Had you known of my life in finance before I sent you your crown?'

'No. To be honest, I'd not given you that much thought. I mean, after everything that had happened to me, you were just a distant but happy memory. That night on stage meant something to me. It really did. It does now, but I had no idea what had ever happened to you. I only wondered why I had never seen or heard anything about you in the theatre.'

Gemma sighed. 'My life has been rather tumultuous. So many people have disappeared from my life.'

Enoch tilted his head to one side slightly and sighed. 'I'm sorry I didn't help you during the trial, Gemma. I wanted to, but I didn't, and I don't understand why I didn't.'

Gemma looked around the hotel dining room. She looked at Enoch and shook her head. 'Please don't feel guilty about that. There was nothing you could have done.'

'I could have paid your legal fees; given you a job at my firm; taken you away from London.'

Gemma shook her head again. 'I wouldn't have accepted. I had Poppy. She has always been there for me. It was a very difficult time. I wouldn't have wanted to see you back then. I was a wreck. It's better you didn't see me. You wouldn't want to have seen me back then.'

'Not true, Gemma. I have a lot of regrets. Not helping you will always be the biggest.'

'Enoch. That's in the past. I have moved forward. Let's not dwell on this anymore,' said Gemma. She smiled and said, 'I'm happy you saved my crown and returned it to me. Thank you.'

Enoch smiled. 'I'm glad I got that part right.'

'Yes, you did,' she replied. And Gemma smiled.

THE COTSWOLDS
The next morning, wearing their cotton trousers and white cotton collared shirts, Gemma and Enoch left Oxford and drove to the Cotswolds. The morning drive had been a quiet and uneventful one. The countryside was an endless sea of vibrant greens and fields of Cotswolds lavender. The blue sky was partially filled with giant white clouds that moved slowly along in the summer breeze.

THE HOUSE
The Edwardian house lay at the end of a long winding road shaded by large leafy trees. The relatively modest two storey structure was constructed of red brick and had large sash windows, the frames of which had been painted white. The large glossy white front door was set back in the center of the house and had a large white arched entry. Above the front door, and suspended from the ceiling of the archway, was a silver lamp.

The house was surrounded by well managed box cut grass lawns and heavily shaded by dozens of large smooth and grey beech woods, willows, maples, ash, and a few gigantic towering oaks. There were also white, purple, red, lavender, and yellow wild flowers interspersed within the untamed wilderness which grew further out from the main house.

What truly made the house impressive were the woodlands which surrounded and shaded it, not the structure itself. Yes, this house was unusual. The previous owners had wanted shade and privacy rather than smooth green lawns.

Gemma's white hatchback slowed to a crawl as they pulled up to the house.

'The house was in a rather terrible state when I bought it. It had been badly neglected. No one had lived in it since the late 1970s. The previous owner had used it as a storage shed for decades. When I was shown the house, the estate agent suggested I could do the same, such was the condition of the house,' said Enoch.

Gemma parked the small white car in front of the house and turned off the engine. Beams of sunlight broke through the leafy branches; creating an undulating patchwork of light and shadows around the house.

'I had the house restored to its Edwardian splendour,' said Enoch somewhat melodramatically. And Enoch smiled innocently. Yes, innocently.

The longer Enoch spent with Gemma, the more he seemed to be reverting to his previous self—the stage actor and thespian spirit he was meant to be. Enoch could relax completely around Gemma. He felt safe. He knew Gemma would never harm him. Gemma was gentle, kind, good, and true.

Gemma and Enoch exited the white Peugeot and stood staring at the house. They stood under a canopy of thick branches and large green leaves. The air was much, much cooler in the shade.

'Originally the house had only a few small trees and wide lawns. The previous owners purchased the house in the 1960s and did nothing with it. The trees were allowed to grow and grow. And grow. I'm glad. I like the sense of seclusion it gives the place. It's more Jungle Book than Cotswolds,' said Enoch happily.

'I *rather* like it, Enoch. *Terribly* lush,' replied Gemma in her Sloaney intonation.

'Please allow me to show you around the house, Gemmy.'

Gemma raised her sunglasses and placed them back on her head of glossy brown hair as she walked towards the house.

The house itself was almost a disappointment. It was practically empty. The glossy hardwood floors had been restored and the white panelled walls almost seemed to glow. The tiled bathrooms had clawed iron white bathtubs, which Gemma quite liked. The Edwardian tile work had also been faithfully restored. The kitchen had modern appliances, but they fit in surprisingly well with the original and carefully restored interior.

The only semi-furnished rooms were the bedrooms and the drawing room. The white walled bedrooms had simple modern wood frame beds and new mattresses, but were unmade. In the center of each of the beds (in each of the four bedrooms) was a cardboard box filled with white Egyptian cotton sheets and pillow cases. There was also a beige wool blanket with red edging neatly folded up on each bed and two pillows, which were still wrapped in plastic.

'I still have some work to do in the bedrooms,' said Enoch cheerfully.

The drawing room was truly beautiful. The white panelled walls were left bare and stood in stark contrast to the polished hardwood floors. The high ceiling and large sash windows allowed natural light to fill the entire room. The drawing room was at one end of the house and had windows on both sides. This part of the house was also unusual in that it was not as heavily shaded by trees as the rest.

The furniture was mid-century modern. Sleek and retro, the furniture was brand new. The sofa and chairs had all been upholstered in snow white fabric. There was also a mid-century modern wooden coffee table. There were modern end tables with white Art Deco ceramic lamps (with white lamp shades) that had quickly caught Gemma's eye as she entered the room. There were also three standing mid-century modern lamps.

There were large white drapes framing the large sash windows, and they been left open to allow in natural light. Other than that, there was nothing else in the drawing room. The overall effect was, however, quite nice.

'I know the room is far from Edwardian,' said Enoch. 'I believe a house should be a home. A place of comfort. And I don't want to worry about breaking anything expensive.' Enoch then smiled innocently. Yes, the young actor had returned. 'Please have a seat, Gemma.'

Gemma adjusted the sunglasses on her head of glossy brown hair and sat down on the white sofa at an angle and looked out of the large windows on one side of the drawing room. Her blue cotton trousers contrasted vividly against the white fabric of the sofa. She placed one arm on the armrest and leaned back against the soft white cushions.

Outside was a wide, shaded, green lawn. Gemma suddenly felt a cosmic tug, and she turned her head to look out the windows on the other side of the room. And there it was: the maze.

THE MAZE
On the other side of the house, there was a large, green hedge maze. A series of vertical hedges all carefully cut and maintained. Gemma recognized what it was immediately, almost instinctively. The maze was partially shaded by maple and willow trees. It stood a very short distance from the house.

'A hedge maze,' said Gemma excitedly as she looked out of the window.

'Yes. It was an overgrown mess when I purchased the house. It's what most attracted me to the house.'

'I haven't been in a hedge maze in *yonks*,' said Gemma.

'Would you like to explore it?'

'*Rather*,' replied Gemma, and she smiled.

The pair made their way outside, through a large glossy white door and stepped onto the lush box cut lawn. It was smooth and soft under foot. Gemma let her tortoiseshell sunglasses rest on her bangs as she leisurely made her way with Enoch to the vertical hedge wall. Enoch, crisply attired in a white button down Oxford dress shirt, dark khaki trousers, and rubber soled leather shoes walked along side her.

The warm rays of the sun caressed Gemma as she walked across the green lawn. The hedge maze was surrounded by tall leafy green trees that swayed in the summer breeze. Gemma stopped at the entrance of the green hedge maze and folded her arms. She gazed at Enoch and said, 'Is there a Minotaur waiting for us inside?'

'Perhaps,' smiled Enoch. 'But I shall protect you. Always,' replied Enoch with a bat squeak of emotion.

'Then guide me, youthful Ptolemy,' said Gemma gently, softly, and quietly. Gemma smiled, and at that moment Enoch realized that Gemma, the one being he loved most in the world, was developing feelings for him. Enoch felt as if he was floating. He smiled. Enoch took Gemma's small soft hand in his and smiled.

'I'll lead you to the center, Gem. To the Minotaur's lair. Let's see if he's there. Or, perhaps we'll encounter him wandering about the maze. Either way, it's a beautiful day to explore it.'

THE LABYRINTH
The vertical thick green hedge rows which made up the maze were meticulously maintained. The maze was made of yew trees and a team of landscapers would appear on weekdays to carefully manage it. Enoch employed some of the best landscape architects in England. This maze was more than ample proof of it.

Enoch led Gemma into the maze, the thick green hedges towering high above them both. The sunny summer warmth was quite pleasant and occasionally a cool light breeze would make its way through the hedge rows as they walked together down the earthen paths.

'How long have you owned this house, Enoch?' asked Gemma.

'I bought it four years ago. I haven't lived in it; the renovations have taken much longer than I expected. I left the trees alone, but I have restored the lawns, even if they remain obscured by the trees and shade. The maze was so overgrown that it was impossible to navigate. It took months of work by a team of landscapers to tame it.'

'I think we're lost,' said Gemma in a slow quiet voice, and she smiled.

Enoch, as if acting on cue, stopped and looked around, his light brown hair blowing slightly in the breeze. He arched an eyebrow. 'Did you hear something,' he said in barely a whisper.

'No. Should I have?' whispered Gemma.

'I think it's close, Gemmy.'

Gemma froze somewhat melodramatically and slowly turned to look towards the center of the labyrinth. 'I think I can hear it too.'

Enoch smiled and held Gemma's hand a little tighter. 'Come on, Gem. Let's see if the Minotaur knows how to make a proper cup of tea.'

The pair made their way through the maze, first down one path, then a sharp turn right, followed by another turn to the left, until finally the entered the center of the maze.

THE CENTER
The center was fairly small, but then again, the maze really wasn't that large. What made the center so interesting was that it consisted of a stone square set in the middle of a small green lawn. The cream colored stone had been quarried on Crete. In the center of the stone square was an elaborate tile work which depicted the ancient Minotaur. It looked as if it had been made thousands of years ago in Minoan Greece. It had.

Enoch, still holding Gemma's hand, led her onto the stone square that was level with the lush green lawn. 'This was installed by the original owner in 1902; the year the house was completed. It had been buried under soil and hedge for decades until two years ago. And now, the Minotaur has been restored to its rightful place as guardian of the maze.' Enoch, his explanation now complete, bowed slightly. He smiled.

At that moment a cool breeze made its way through the labyrinth and blew Gemma's hair up into her face. She brushed it away with her free hand, and then pulled Enoch towards her with her other. She hesitated for a brief moment, and then she leaned forward and gently, very gently kissed Enoch. She then pulled her head back and looked at him. Her clear blue eyes radiated gentleness and *strength*. Gemma smiled.

Enoch was elated. He said nothing, but his heart raced. Finally, the moment that he had hoped against hope for, waited an eternity for, had arrived. He smiled slightly. His breathing seemed to pick up, and then slow down. Enoch, attempting to gather his thoughts, continued to hold Gemma's hand, but said nothing.

Gemma smiled shyly and then released Enoch's hand. She used both of her hands to pull her slightly longer than shoulder length glossy brown hair away from her face and behind her shoulders.

She gazed at Enoch once more. Gemma smiled and then said, '*Terribly thrilling* maze. *Rather.*'

Gemma—England—Tea with the Minotaur

THE COTSWOLDS
Enoch stood in the kitchen. He looked around. He opened the door to the stainless steel refrigerator and looked inside: nothing. The ice cold refrigerator was quite large, quite nice, and quite new. It was also quite empty. It had never occurred to Enoch that he had never had the kitchen stocked by the staff. The cupboards, designed and installed by one of London's best kitchen designers, were also barren.

Enoch had spent most of the last two decades absorbed in finance. Such mundane things like groceries, tea pots, spoons, scones, and sugar had rarely entered his mind. He employed people to take care of the details of daily life. Enoch's domestic staff was good at anticipating his needs, but even they couldn't have anticipated that he would need refreshments in a house he had never spent a single night in.

What to do?

THE DRAWING ROOM

Gemma was sitting comfortably in one of the large high back white armchairs in the drawing room. She felt good. She was happy. She stretched a little and then adjusted the collar on her open neck white cotton blouse. She could feel the small silver cross of St Albans against her skin. The slim sterling silver chain was hidden under her white blouse. Gemma pulled the silver chain up and the ankh like Christian cross appeared before her. It was engraved with the words: **Worship and adore God.** Gemma's mother had given her the cross before she had passed away. It was Gemma's most precious possession.

Gemma's mother had usually referred to her as Ophelia. Ophelia was Gemma's middle name. Today Gemma Ophelia Ripley was feeling introspective. She looked out the large window at the maple tree that swayed in the breeze outside. It had a calming effect on her.

Gemma had finally revealed to Enoch how she felt about him. And, at the same time, Gemma had revealed to herself how she felt about him too. It wasn't until that moment, until that gust of cool air had tousled her hair, that Gemma realized that she really loved him.

It had all happened so fast. One moment she was looking at an ancient piece of stone from Crete, and next she was gently kissing Enoch. Yes. It had all happened so quickly. She hadn't had much time to think. She had hesitated momentarily before she had kissed him; was this how she really felt? Yes. She was sure. Be brave, Gemma.

'Gem. I'm afraid I haven't anything to serve you. I forgot to inform the staff. There isn't so much as a blueberry scone to be had,' said Enoch, and he sighed. 'How about we drive into the village and have tea there?' asked Enoch.

'You're *rather* fortunate, Enoch, that I have everything needed for tea with me. In the hatchback. I picked up a few boxes of tea and a set of cups and saucers from a mostly forgotten tea shop in the village near Poppy's castle in the Lake District last weekend. And since I had forgotten the tea in the boot, we can have tea with the Minotaur after all,' replied Gemma, and she smiled impishly. Yes, impishly.

THE LABYRINTH
Enoch accompanied Gemma out to the white hatchback parked in the shade of a large oak in front of the house. Gemma raised the hatchback and looked inside the boot.

Ah, there it is. Just where she left it. Gemma picked up the cardboard box—'No, that's alright, Enoch. I can carry it'—and made her way to the white walled kitchen.

She placed the cardboard box on the counter, opened it, and removed the polished silver tea pot, white ceramic sugar bowl, four cardboard boxed white tea cups and saucers, a set of silver spoons, a box of sugar, a small glass jar of locally produced honey, and two white and red boxes of tea.

'Please allow me to show the Minotaur how to make a proper cup of tea, Enoch,' said Gemma as she moved about the kitchen.

Enoch smiled and decided to stand near the window and watch. The window was open just enough to allow fresh air, cool breezes and the vanilla scent of the Cotswolds lavenders fill the room. Besides, Enoch had a lot to think about.

Gemma's kiss had blindsided him. He hadn't expected it. Not then, nor perhaps ever. The softness of it. Yes, that moment. He hadn't really reacted at all. Gemma had simply smiled and taking him by the hand, led him back through the green hedge maze to the house. It was more like a dream than anything else.

'I'm so glad I forgot to take this out of the car. You'll love the honey. A local beekeeper sells it to the shop. Oh, and the tea cups were made locally too. Aren't they nice?' said Gemma happily.

'I'll get one of the blankets from upstairs. They are perfect for impromptu picnics,' said Enoch happily.

I didn't take much to make Gemma happy, thought Enoch. Gemma was not such a complex person. She was good-hearted and kind. And she wanted to love and be loved. Gemma had never really asked that much of the world, and what little she had asked for had not been given. Enoch was determined to change that. Enoch had dreamed of this moment and it had finally arrived. Enoch closed his eyes momentarily in silent prayer. He prayed that he be allowed to bring Gemma happiness and protect her the way she should have been protected all along.

Gemma placed the polished silver tea pot in the cardboard box along with a box of tea, the bowl of sugar, two spoons, and the glass jar of honey. She smiled and looked at Enoch. 'Would you mind *terribly* carrying the tea cups for me?'

'Gem, please let me carry the box.'

'Oh, okay. That would be better. For sure,' said Gemma.

The ~~pair~~ couple exited the house and made their way back through the green vertical hedge maze to the Minotaur's lair at the center of it. Once they arrived, Enoch placed the blanket on the grass lawn next to the ancient stone square. Gemma carefully unpacked the contents of the makeshift tea basket onto the Minotaur's stone. When she was done she stood back up and faced Enoch.

'Tea is served, shy one.'

Gemma then sat down on the blanket; Enoch joined her. She carefully poured the hot tea into his white cup.

'Sugar?' she asked happily.

'Yes, please.'

They happy couple then had tea with the silent Minotaur in the center of a deep green hedge maze of yew on a breezy, sunny, summer day in the Cotswolds.

Anything was now possible.

Even happiness.

Gemma—England—The Lagonda

THE COTSWOLDS
A short distance from the hedge maze was a large red brick structure. It had two large gate like wooden doors, both painted bright white. The structure was heavily shaded by large oak and maple trees.

'I have one more surprise for you today, Gem,' said Enoch as they walked towards the red brick building.

Enoch approached the first wooden door, grabbed the metal handle, and pulled the gate open. The white walled interior was windowless and had a concrete floor. Inside was, apparently, an automobile covered with a beige car cover. Enoch walked to the front of the vehicle and very carefully pulled at the cover and revealed the car hidden underneath.

THE LAGONDA
The navy blue 1927 Lagonda looked brand new. It was a convertible; it's black canopy was up. Enoch opened the driver's side door, looked around inside, and then he turned the latch. He pulled the canopy back and locked it in place.

Gemma was impressed. She loved classic cars. This particular vehicle was truly beautiful to behold.

'I had it restored last year. I rarely have time to drive it. It's a bit of a beast to drive actually,' said Enoch.

Gemma smiled.

'How about we take it for a spin?' suggested Enoch.

'*Yah!*' said Gemma in her posh Sloane accent.

She walked over to the car and Enoch opened the automobile's glossy metallic blue door. Gemma carefully climbed into the rather uncomfortable 1920s automobile. It was built like a truck.

After closing the passenger side door, Enoch walked around to the front of the car and gave it a few cranks with an iron hand crank that seemed to appear from nowhere. He then walked to the otherside of the car and got in. He looked at Gemma and smiled. Suddenly Gemma pointed forward dramatically and in a near shout said, 'Launch the Lagonda!'

Enoch smiled and started the Lagonda, which started up easily. The car moved forward slowly and out of the garage and then moved down the shaded road past the house and Gemma's small white hatchback.

The Lagonda started to pick up pace as it moved down the heavily shaded road leading away from the house. Enoch and Gemma both put on their dark sunglasses and enjoyed the feeling of the wind blowing through their hair. Gemma leaned back in the large black leather seat. The warmth of the Sun caressed her and the winds cooled her at the same moment. Gemma looked around in all directions as they drove down the road. Riding in a car with the top down was enjoyable for Gemma, especially on a beautiful summer day such as this.

'A day in the winds is a day well spent,' said Enoch as he shifted gears. Enoch smiled and continued to pilot the large car down the road.

Enoch reached the end of the road leading out of the of his estate and stopped. He looked both ways, and then signaling with his hand, he turned onto the country road that led to a village. The car sped up. There were very few cars on the road that afternoon.

Gemma would occasionally glance at Enoch as he piloted the car carefully down the road. Would this work out? Was Enoch really the person she had been searching for? Gemma hoped so. Enoch was so different from most men. But he remained an enigma to her and everyone else.

THE DINNER PARTY
June, 2019
At the dinner party at Gemma's flat a few weeks ago, Enoch had said very little. He mostly listened to what others had to say. Brian was in awe of him, so he said little to him. The only one who seemed completely at ease with him had been Violet. She was from a family of vast wealth that had married into a vastly wealthy family. Enoch was a parvenu to Vava, albeit an interesting one. Violet never asked Enoch about his career in finance; she really wasn't interested in it. Violet happily quizzed Enoch on a topic dear to his heart: his acting.

Violet had played Cleopatra in a school play at All Saints. She had starred in the Shakespearean version , it was the modern American one, written by Jubal Wyatt, that Gemma and Enoch had performed in. Violet had been a very good actress in school, so she could more fully appreciate Enoch's acting abilities.

Poppy also asked Enoch about his performance. She told him how emotional it had been for her.

It was at this moment, seated next to the beautiful twenty something Octavia, that Külli spoke. 'I thought your performance was amazing, Enoch. It was deeply moving.'

The other girls all turned and looked at Külli in amazement.

'You attended the performance?' asked a stunned Gemma.

'Yes.'

'I didn't know that, G,' said Gemma.

This had been a revelation to The Inseparables. There was an awkward silence. Octavia, completely unaware what had transpired between the girls all those years ago, could only arch an eyebrow.

Gemma smiled. 'I am so happy that you attended, G. Truly,' said Gemma.

Yes, all The Inseparables knew that Gula had been the catalyst for Gemma's performance that night. What had been a strange experience for Gemma suddenly meant even more to her. Gula had witnessed it. That performance had been a testimony of her love for Gula. There was no need to explain it. All the Inseparables knew what it meant. Gemma looked directly at Külli and smiled. No further words were necessary.

Octavia, the youngest by at least a decade, had been slightly uncomfortable, but was well recieved. The others went out of their way to be kind to her. Külli was supremely grateful and happy. Several times during dinner, Külli would discretely grasp Octavia's soft hand and caress it. Octavia would always look at Külli and smile; sometimes she would blush. The evening had gone extremely well for Octavia. She felt accepted; exactly what she had hoped for.

Enoch, sensing Brian's unease, sometimes looked in his direction and smiled. Brian always nodded slightly and returned it.

The potluck dinner had not only been a social success, the food had been delicious and the conversation enjoyable.

4 THE FAMILY PILE

Gemma—England—The Family Pile

THE CASTLE

The castle ruins in summer rested on a beautiful and well maintained green lawn. The grey stone of the remaining walls and towers stood in stark contrast to the lush green surroundings.

Just beyond the green lawn were a variety of trees, some of them ancient. The most common among them were English oaks, many of them stood almost forty meters in height; their branches weighed down with large green leaves and brown acorns. The ancient trees, some of them over 500 years old, had become fissured with age. The English oaks provided ample shade for those seeking respite from rare sunny summer days. The sunlight that managed to penetrate the thick shield of green leaves appeared as undulating translucent waves of gold.

Poppy's family had used the wood from these trees to build numerous structures on their land for hundreds of years. The wood had always been used sparingly so as to preserve the forest and supply future generations with wood when needed. None of the trees in the forest which surrounded the castle and the main house had been cut down in Poppy's lifetime. Staff would gather fallen branches for firewood when needed.

There were also Field maples, whose leaves turned golden-yellow and blanketed the forest floor in autumn. Its winged fruit was dispersed in the summer breeze. The trees had been planted by Poppy's great-great-grandfather after he returned from suppressing the Sepoy Mutiny in India in the 1850s.

Mixed in with trees was purple Buddleia which gave off a honey like fragrance in summer and attracted butterflies which fluttered around them. Poppy liked these purple flowers so much that she planted some under the windows of the drawing and dining room, so that when the windows were opened on mild spring and summer days, honey scented breezes would fill the rooms.

There was also wild privet, which in summer had white flowers and in winter matt-black berries which were poisonous to people but happily consumed by birds. The poisonous black berries of the purging buckthorn also grew intertwined with the flora and fauna of the forest.

Spindle trees dotted areas of the forest closest to the castle ruins; their bright pink-and-orange berries appeared in the autumn. Poppy was usually the first member of the family to notice them on her chilly morning walks through the castle grounds.

Külli had always loved trees more than flowers. Gula especially liked the colourful berries of the Spindle trees. She also loved maple trees.

The girls would enjoy leisurely walks on foggy mornings on weekends away from school. Clad in faded blue jeans and bundled up in their navy blue duffle coats and the purple, red, and blue scarves of All Saints, the girls would make their way to the castle and explore the ruins. Gula would take Gemma by the hand and lead her up the stairs to the top of the tower. From there the girls could enjoy breathtaking views of Poppy's ancestral lands.

Poppy loved nature, as did her entire family. Poppy had enjoyed listening to the stories her grandmother would tell her of the fairies that supposedly lived in the forest just beyond the castle when Poppy was a little girl. The stories of woodland sprites and fairies made the forest seem magical to her. Poppy spent many an afternoon looking for woodland creatures to no avail. Poppy used to leave biscuits out for the fairies, but only birds would eat them.

Poppy, at 41, still wondered the woods in search of woodland pixies, sprites, and fairies. She felt at peace here. Happy memories appeared like phantoms as she moved about the woods and castle ruins.

Brian would always accompany her on these walks when he stayed with the family on weekends. Brian was now serenely happy. He wanted to spend every minute he could with Poppy. He regretted that he had been unable to take time off from work that summer, but the financial world was in an uproar and the bank director needed him more than ever.

Poppy's pregnancy had made Brian re-evaluate his life. Brian had married late. Most of his classmates from Harrow and Oxford already had children, many of them preparing to attend university. Brian had no regrets in that regard. Poppy had been worth the wait. And Brian was lucky in another regard: Poppy's family was as loving and caring as she was. Brian could now only think of his life with Poppy. Brian would always smile when he imagined what Christmas holidays would be like at either his parents' modest country house in Surrey or Poppy's baronial home in the Lake District. With James' twins, the house would be bursting with children and happiness.

Poppy would often return from her autumn and winter walks frozen to the bone. A hot breakfast was in order and the staff always served an excellent one. Sitting alone at the long dining room table, which was draped with a white table cloth, Poppy would sip hot tea from an ivory white porcelain cup edged in gold. She would spread fresh butter on golden brown toast with a sterling silver butter knife. Sometimes she would breakfast alone on fried sausage, bacon, baked beans, portobello mushrooms, scrambled eggs, and toast while reading the local newspaper. Poppy enjoyed the occasional spell of solitude. She could have breakfast at a leisurely pace and relax.

Inhale. Exhale. Inhale. Exhale.

Yes. It was at the family pile in the Lake District that Poppy truly felt at peace.

ALWAYS SUMMER

That year, Poppy, now pregnant, had decided to spend the entire summer in the Lake District with her parents, Helen, the twins, and occasionally Brian and James, on the weekends that they were able to get away from the tumult that was now London.

Life at the family pile that June and July was a summery blur of glorious sunshine, warmth, and cool, even cold days. The trees, shrubs, and flowers around the house produced a vibrant mix of greens, whites, and purples with splashes of orange, blue, and red berries.

Poppy had always loved purple. Purple, and the varying shades of it, were beautiful and majestic. Purple was born in antiquity and use to only adorn royalty. Purple meant Roman emperors in the West and Byzantine emperors in the East. Purple meant ancient Rome. Purple meant Byzantium. Purple fluttered from Carthaginian military standards. Purple represented mystery and magic. Purple was even Asprey's chosen color. A purple box from Asprey invoked memories. Purple calmed her and more than that, it made her feel happy.

The grassy fields beyond the carefully maintained lawns were ablaze with lilacs, Buddleia, and lavenders. Poppy had planted them herself while on holidays during her time at All Saints. The honey scented purple petals of the Buddleia which grew under the windows of the drawing and dining rooms and the lilacs and lavenders that filled the fields around the house gave the house a pleasant air that hadn't had before. It softened the harshness of the medieval grey stone the house had been constructed from. The purple did not so much contrast with as augment the vibrant shades of green which pulsated and swirled around the house in spring and summer.

The surrounding forest and the land further on from the house were also populated with Grey willows, Wayfaring trees, and Midland hawthorn shrubs which bore white blossoms in summer and haws in winter, the red fruit quite noticeable in white winter landscapes. It was considered bad luck to cut one except when they were in flower, but even then, people had been warned never to bring the sprigs into the house. Such was the local folklore...

THE DRAWING ROOM

That summer found Poppy spending most of her time in the drawing room. The three polished burl wood panelled walls and hardwood floor, which had been installed in the 1920s, were modern when compared to the light grey medieval stone that remaining walls and fireplace had been constructed from.

The surprisingly comfortable wooden Art Deco furniture, upholstered in purple with lavender piping the same color as the lavenders which grew all over the estate, were arranged around a low wooden and highly polished Art Deco coffee table. Poppy enjoyed sitting on the large purple velvet sofa and reading the daily newspapers that were brought to her each morning by a member of the uniformed staff. She also read (or rather re-read) her favorite books.

Usually the only sound that could be heard in the room was the gentle ticking of the silver Apsrey clock on the mantle of the stone fireplace, unless, of course, it was winter. In winter, the crackling of the fire was augmented by or perhaps competed with, the sound of the silver clock.

In the spring and on mild summer days, the leaded glass windows would be opened and the honeyed scent of the Buddleias would carry into the room, often along with its telltale purple petals. The soft sounds of gentle breezes would fill the room, but beyond that, very little else.

The family pile was Poppy's refuge from an outside world that was growing more and more chaotic with each passing day.

Gemma—England—Egyptian Art Deco

THE LAKE DISTRICT

July 2019
THE HOUSE
The summer heat kept Poppy indoors most of the time. She was three months pregnant and already starting to show. Poppy was a bit perplexed. I mean, she had never been pregnant before, but many of her friends and co-workers had, and none of them had put on weight this rapidly. Well, that is except for Helen, her sister-in-law, and she had given birth to twins. Twins. Twins? Twins! No. It can't be twins. Oh, no. Twins?

Poppy was reclining on the Art Deco sofa in the drawing room of the family's country house. The Bauhaus style wooden sofa had just been re-upholstered in purple velvet with lavender piping, a wedding gift from James and Helen.

'I have always *rather* liked the purple,' said James as he and Helen escorted Poppy into the drawing room when she had arrived at the house a few days before. They had wanted to surprise her with something really special. 'We figured that since you would be spending the next few months at the house, you would like a new splash of purple,' said Helen cheerfully.

Helen was beautiful. Helen had always been beautiful, and quite posh. She was always smartly dressed, and even in her mid-forties still radiated youthfulness. Helen's long silky blonde hair was kept loose and was often complemented with a pair of dark sunglasses which usually rested on her head when she wasn't wearing them. She was still slim and at 5'8", relatively tall.

Helen had studied Ancient History while at Oxford University. She had attended Somerville, the college that Gemma, Poppy, and Violet would attend a few years after she had graduated. Helen, like Gemma and Külli, had been a first rate student.

After graduation she got a position at a Japanese bank in the City. Helen excelled at banking. She had a keen understanding of finance and soon gained the trust and support of the Japanese bank directors who assigned her to the group's most important projects. She advanced rapidly up the ranks. The sky was the limit. However, this all meant delaying something that had been extremely important to her: children.

Helen and James had both wanted children and had planned to have them soon after they married, but Helen's career, so brilliant and exciting, kept intervening. 'Just one more year, and I'll be ready for children,' she would tell James year after year. The years past, and one day Helen woke up in the white walled bedroom of her London semi-detached and realised that she was 38 years-old and childless. She started to cry.

James, for his part, had never pressured Helen about having children. He had promised to support her career in banking, and James always kept his promises. At that moment, Helen wished he hadn't.

Helen had lived in Tokyo—away from James—for two years and become fluent in Japanese. She had become a millionaire in her own right, and the bank was expecting even greater things of her, and yet, Helen, on that warm and sunny spring morning, felt as if she was an utter failure.

The devoted James truly loved her. He had always supported her ambitions, and he had never complained whenever assignments had taken her from him. He had never complained that 19 years had gone by since they first met as undergraduates at Oxford and had remained childless. Helen had promised him before they married that she would be a devoted wife and mother. She had let James down, and on this sunny morning, she realized how self-centered she had been.

That was the morning that she told James over breakfast how sorry she was that they had not had children. James became emotional as he listened to her, and then started to cry. Helen gently took one of James' hands in hers and told him that they would have children within a year, if it were still possible for her to have any.

After extensive medical treatments, Helen became pregnant and gave birth to a set of healthy flaxen haired twins, a boy and a girl.

Helen quit her position at the bank and in order to become a full-time mother. The Japanese bank director, upon hearing the news, started to become emotional. Helen had never seen him show much in the way of emotion, and she found it to be quite moving.

Helen was a fantastic mother, and the twins had turned out to be polite, thoughtful, and kind. The twins were also adorable. Their daughter, Lucy, was very sweet and wanted to be a ballerina. She really liked cherries, which was also Gemma's favorite fruit, and so she would spend the mornings at the family pile at the cherry trees behind the castle with her father picking them. Her son, Henry, was just as sweet as his twin. Henry wanted to be a soldier, like most of his ancestors had been.

Helen had watched Poppy work long hours in the City, toiling away in the offices of a British bank. She worried that Poppy would never have any children. Helen knew how much Poppy had always wanted to children. When Poppy announced that she was pregnant the day she had married, and just before Brian and Poppy departed for their honeymoon, no one had been happier for her than Helen.

A CLOCK, A BRACELET, AND A TIARA

Shortly after Poppy arrived at the house, Poppy's father, the 12th Baron, found her alone in the drawing room. Brian was in London working on an important banking project, and Poppy was spending the summer at the house with her parents.

The baron had retired that spring after a long and moderately successful banking career in the City. Poppy's parents had decided to keep their modest house in London (a semi-detached), but live full-time at the family pile in the Lake District. Both were happy to leave London. The city was becoming more and more chaotic with each passing day. They were also happy to have Poppy staying with them.

It was on a summer afternoon in July that the white haired and clean shaven 12th Baron entered the burl wood walled drawing room holding a large blue leather box. He was wearing a white cotton button down Oxford dress shirt and a pair of grey trousers. He smiled as he greeted Poppy, who was seated at one end of the sofa. She had been reading the morning edition of the Daily Telegraph.

Poppy, already showing and now being too big to fit into most of her wardrobe, was wearing loose fitting navy blue (with white piping and a white draw string waist) cotton pyjamas and a white waffle weave bathrobe that she had brought with her from London. Her mother had ordered some maternity clothes from a London dressmaker, but they had yet to arrive. Poppy looked up from her newspaper and smiled.

'I have wanted to do this for a long time. I think now would be the right time to do it,' said the baron. He sat down and placed the medium sized blue leather box on the purple upholstered sofa between them.

'Jane, as you know, returned from Germany with a lot of beautiful objects and jewellery. I inherited all of them upon the death of my father. I would like to give you a few pieces of jewellery, Poppy. Jane would not want them to sit unused forever.'

Poppy's adjusted herself on the sofa and looked carefully at her father. What did this really mean? Was something wrong? Was her father unhealthy?

'Poppy. Jane's life was tragic. She died alone of a broken heart. There has been so much sadness in this family. That you have married and are expecting means the world to me and your mother. Jane left instructions in her will that her jewellery should be given to the daughters in the family line. She wanted that. Well, you were the first daughter born since Jane. She had instructed that as each girl married, she would be given certain things. Now that you are married, I am here to fulfill Jane's final request.'

Poppy felt a wave of emotion sweep through her. Sadness gripped her, and tears started to fill her eyes. She knew Jane's story well, and had shared it with those closest to her.

Her father opened the faded blue leather box. The box's white silk lining also showed signs of age.

The blue leather box had been made in Berlin at the request of the young Prussian Junker Eugen. Eugen had loved Jane, but Jane's English family had refused them permission to marry. Jane had wanted to defy her family and marry him anyway, but Eugen refused. He didn't want Jane to become estranged from her family. Eugen had loved her that much.

Poppy leaned forward. There were several small leather boxes inside along with one that was relatively large. The baron took out a long blue leather case and held it out to Poppy. Poppy grasped it carefully with both hands. She looked up to her father.

'Go on, Poppy. Open it. I believe Jane has been waiting for this moment for a long time.'

Poppy opened the narrow case to reveal an Art Deco bracelet of linked sterling silver panels. Each panel was decorated with Egyptian hieroglyphics. The bracelet, though heavily tarnished, was beautiful in its simplicity. It had been made by one of Berlin's best known jewelers. Neither the family that produced the bracelet, nor the jewelry store it had been created in, would survive the Second World War.

'Try it on, Poppy,' urged the baron.

Poppy put the slender blue box on the sofa and then unlocked the silver clasp on the bracelet. The bracelet was now open. Poppy placed the metal bracelet on her slender wrists and closed it. She locked the clasp in place and then held up her hand. The metal was cold against her wrist.

'It fits perfectly, father. Thank you. Thank you so much. It's beautiful.'

The baron smiled. 'There is some metal polish in the kitchen that will remove that tarnish easily.'

'I'll polish it immediately. I'll be heading to the kitchen for a slice of cold pizza in a moment, and I'll ask the staff where the metal polish is.'

'We have cold pizza? And you didn't tell me?' smiled the 12th Baron.

Poppy smiled. 'I had Edward make me a large thin crust Hawaiian pizza last night. It was delicious. However, it was so large that even the baby and I couldn't eat it all. So, it's been sitting in the refrigerator all night.'

The baron smiled. 'I'll have to remember that.' The baron then took out the medium sized black leather case and placed it on the sofa between them. 'One more thing.'

Poppy opened the black leather case to reveal a small sterling silver box. It was slender and there was a seam down its middle.

'What is it?'

'A travel clock. Eugen had it made for Jane. She was a frequent traveller. It's unusual. Well, see for yourself.'

Poppy held the small sterling silver travel clock in her hands and carefully and slowly opened it. There was a white clock dial adorned with Arabic numerals in blue. Blue had been Jane's favorite color. The front of the clock around the clock dial had been enamelled in blue. It was strikingly beautiful.

'There is a silver key in the box. You have to wind it with the key. The clock works quite well,' said the baron.

'It's beautiful, father. Thank you,' said Poppy. I think I'll keep this bracelet on from now on,' said Poppy. And Poppy smiled.

The baron then removed three more small leather cases and placed them on the highly polished coffee table. At the bottom of the large blue leather box was a large purple leather case. It was saucer shaped and tall. There was an ornate highly stylized cursive signature stamped on the top of the box in gold. Poppy's father placed it on the sofa. The leather box was large enough to hold a pitcher. Poppy wondered if some kind of vase or decanter was inside.

The baron, in a moment of reflection, looked off to one side. He then gathered his thoughts and looked back at Poppy.

'There are a few smaller pieces of jewellery that I am saving for Lucy. This final piece was Jane's most prized possession. Eugen had it made for Jane as a graduation gift. He gave it to her the day she graduated from art school in Berlin. Jane loved it. She loved everything that Eugen gave her. She had worn the bracelet every day. This, however, is very special. Jane wore it numerous times while living in Weimar, Germany. I have never shown you the photos of her wearing it. She kept them in a small envelope in the case. I would like you to have it, Poppy.'

Poppy unlocked the small silver clasp on the purple leather box and carefully opened it. Inside was a strikingly beautiful and highly unusual tiara. It was made of silver and now heavily tarnished. It was unusual in that it was an Art Deco version the Egyptian vulture crown in sterling silver.

THE TIARA

The tiara—if one chose to call it that—was fantastic. Poppy slowly lifted it from the leather case and looked at it carefully. It was surprisingly lighter than one would expect. Yes, gold would have been not only exponentially more expensive, but substantially heavier. On the underside of one of the wings were the stamped hallmarks denoting the purity of silver and the manufacturer. The vulture wings were hinged together and when wore would frame the wearers face. The Art Deco vulture head seemed to almost hover at the top of the crown. The features of the vulture were done in simplistic Art Deco designs and patterns. It was amazing. Poppy had never seen anything like it.

'Father, it's beautiful. Like nothing I have ever seen,' gasped Poppy. 'I wonder if it will fit me?' Poppy placed the tiara back in its case and then using both of her hands, she pulled her shoulder length blonde hair back behind her ears. She picked up the Ptolemaic tiara and carefully lowered it onto her head. She had to adjust it a few times until it fit her comfortably. She stood and then looked at her father. 'Well, how do I look?' asked Poppy.

The baron stood up and looked at Poppy for a moment. 'Amazing, my dear Poppy. Amazing.'

'Let me see for myself,' said Poppy.

Poppy stood up and walked over to the fireplace. She looked into the gilt framed mirror which rested on the stone mantle. The diminutive Poppy, wearing dark blue pyjamas with white piping and a white waffle weave bathrobe examined her reflection carefully in the mirror.

The sterling silver vulture crown appeared to fit her perfectly. Her silky blonde hair poked out from around the edges of the tarnished silver metal plates that made up the Ptolemaic tiara. Or was it a crown? Or perhaps a silver helmet? Hmmm. Well, what did it matter? It was fantastic. It looked fantastic on Poppy, and Poppy looked fantastic wearing it.

Poppy glanced over at her father. He was standing ramrod straight. The 12th Baron was still every inch the soldier he had been since serving as an officer in the Life Guards. His white hair cut was like a British officer and he walked and spoke like one. At that moment, Poppy could only see her father standing before her. He was kind, gentle, brave, honourable, and intelligent. He had instilled all of those virtues in his children. Poppy, the bantam daughter of the 12th Baron, loved him with all her heart. He had never been cruel to her. He had always protected and supported her. Poppy was proud of her family and her father. She had always known she was blessed to be born into a family like this, but at that moment, she realized how truly blessed she was.

Poppy, her voice breaking with emotion looked at her father and said, 'I love it. And I love you,' said Poppy. 'I don't have the words to describe how much I love you, father.' Poppy then started to cry.

The baron walked over to Poppy and gently hugged her. 'Now, now, my little Poppy. Let's not cry. Jane is watching, and she wants you to be happy.'

Poppy, still in her father's embrace, looked around the drawing room. It was quiet—save for the gentle ticking of the silver Edwardian Asprey clock on the mantle. The drawing room's polished Circassian walnut walls gleamed in the summer sunshine. The room was cool, the newly installed air conditioning system worked marvellously, and Poppy suddenly felt at peace. Was Jane really there? Poppy wasn't really sure. But, she felt something or someone was. For sure. For sure.

Gemma—England—Freya and Louise

THE LAKE DISTRICT
Freya and Louise stood on the side of the road next to the white Volkswagen Polo. The hatchback was parked on the shoulder of the country road. The English countryside in July was a sea of green variables. The long branches of leafy green trees swayed in the summer breeze. The sky was blue and filled with large bilious white clouds.

Freya looked at her smart phone. They had taken a wrong turn, and now they were lost. And to make matters worse, there was no cell phone signal. Freya sighed.

A sudden breeze came up and Freya's long glossy blonde hair blew in the wind. Freya felt better. She put her mirrored Gentle Monster sunglasses back on and walked back to the small white car.

Summer in England is a curious thing. Warm, then hot, then suddenly cool, then cold, then warm again—all in one hour. It was best to keep a quilted jacket or a jumper in the car—or tied around your waist. Louise kept one of her cream colored cable knit All Saints cricket sweaters in the backseat of the VW. The cuffs and v-neck collar of the sweater ringed in the school's red, blue, and purple. It was not only warm, but quite fashionable.

Louise, wearing a white blouse with a large collar, khaki cotton trousers, and brown leather shoes, opened the glove compartment and took out a paper map. She unfolded it and looked at it carefully.

'Freya. If we take the next turn off, we will be back on the main road. Gemma's house is near a small village. If we can find it, then it will be easy to find Gemma's house.'

Louise's strawberry blonde hair, once again in the chin length bob that Freya had given her three years earlier, framed her face. Louise showed Freya the paper road map.

Freya tilted her sunglasses back on her head and looked carefully at the road map.

'Yes. It's a good thing Mummy insisted I have a paper road map in the glove compartment. Otherwise, we would be hopelessly lost out here. I can't believe there isn't a signal. At this rate, the next village won't even have electricity,' said Freya and she laughed.

The girls both put on their sunglasses, got back into the white compact car, and drove off down the road.

THE HOUSE
The drive out to the Lake District had been a pleasant one. The sky was blue and the clouds were white and majestic. The country roads were lined with lush green scenery and surprisingly little else.

Freya had decided to purchase the White VW hatchback because it was easier to get around in and could also hold four passengers. The much beloved Bristol Fighter had been left at her grandparent's house in Mayfair.

The small white car cleared the hill and the former Royal Air Force training centre appeared in the distance. Yes, just as Gemma had described it: a collection of brick buildings hidden amongst lush green trees.

The large red brick building off to the side had a white hatchback parked in front of it. That must be Gemma's house.

Freya decelerated and signalled. The VW turned off the main road and headed down the road that cut through the forest. After a few minutes, the car came to a stop in front of a red brick building. Freya and Louise got out of the car and walked to the front door. Well, the front door was actually a set of wooden double doors. Freya knocked and one door opened.

'Freya! Louise! You made it! It's so good to see you. Welcome to my home,' beamed Gemma.

The girls took turns hugging Gemma and then they entered.

The large room that awaited the girls had been recently painted white. The walls had been sheet rocked and new wooden sash windows installed. The hardwood floor had been sanded and polished. It looked quite nice. The room had a high ceiling and the standard sized windows allowed natural sunlight to fill them room.

Gemma had installed simple white wooden book cases in between the windows along all four walls. The book cases all stood empty.

In the center of the room were a dozen cardboard boxes of various sizes, several folding metal chairs, and a wooden coffee table. There were two small wooden night stands in the room, each with a shaded white lamp on them.

There were also several yellow work lamps in one corner. Their power cords had been coiled up and hung from hooks on the lamps.

There was little evidence of the former Royal Air Force training centre facility left. Most of the large building consisted of Gemma's drawing room—well, such as it was. There was a bathroom, two bedrooms, and a kitchen at the very end of the building. The other rooms were all relatively small. The walls had all been painted white, with the exception of the bathroom, which was entirely in glossy white tile.

'I have a cot in the back room. I haven't spent the night here yet. I stay with Poppy at the house. Poppy is almost four months pregnant. She is really showing now. She is spending her summer holiday with her family in the Lake District. Brian visits on the weekends. He's working on a huge banking project now. Please, have a seat.'

The girls arranged three of the folding metal chairs around the wooden coffee table.

'I'll make some tea. I picked up a box of scones this morning at the bakery and I have raspberry and strawberry jam too. And fresh clotted cream. Oh, and I made some raspberry and chocolate biscuits for you,' smiled Gemma.

'Thank you, Gemmy,' said Freya and Louise at the same time, and they smiled.

The girls looked around the drawing room—that's what Gemma called it— and marvelled at the transformation. The room looked nothing like the photos they had seen of it a month earlier. The room looked quite nice. Louise then noticed the rather unusual clock on the wall. She stared at it for a moment and then spoke.

'It's an old RAF Sector clock from World War Two, Freya. The red, yellow, and blue triangles denote five minute intervals. It was used for Ground Controlled Interception.'

'Exactly right, Louise,' said Gemma as she entered the room carrying a silver tray. She placed the tray on the coffee table.

The girls took their respective places around the table and Gemma served them tea from a white ceramic tea kettle. Gemma expertly poured tea into white bone china tea cups that were edged in gold; the bone china saucers were white. She then offered the girls lumps of sugar from a glass sugar bowl with a silver lid. The girls stirred their tea with sterling silver spoons.

'The clock came with the building. I really liked it, so I cleaned it and installed it on the wall of the drawing room.'

Gemma was happy to be back in a space she owned. She owned this building. Mars had asked that the price be lowered so that Gemma could afford it more easily, and the developer (who was also Mars' Oxford classmate) had agreed. Gemma had been able to pay cash.

The building was in good condition, but the former workshop needed a lot of work if she were going to live in it on weekends and the occasional holiday.

'Who owns the other buildings?' asked Freya.

'They are still for sale. Mars said the developer is considering tearing down the other structures and just selling the land. I hope that doesn't happen. The buildings are all in excellent condition.'

'I'm going to renovate this building room by room. It will take a while, but when it is done, it will be my secret lair. Of course, you two are always welcome here.'

Freya and Louise both smiled.

Freya, clad in faded blue jeans, and a white cotton open collared top, leaned back in the chair and looked up at the ceiling. Her eyes scanned it for details. The thick wooden beams hovered above them. She lowered her gaze and looked at Gemma.

'God mother. Enoch is *rather* attractive,' said Freya in her posh accent. Yes,

Freya's accent was quite posh. Freya was now spending a lot of time with her mother and slowly picking up more and more of her mannerisms and acquiring a *terribly* Sloaney accent along the way. Gemma was happy at this turn of events. Vava had changed completely and her life had opened up completely and Violet had found joy, happiness, and love awaiting her. Freya was happy too. But back to the conversation…

'Oh, you like him, Freya?'

'Yes. He's quite sweet and interesting. I talked with him at the wedding reception. He really loves you. We didn't talk about you, but I saw how he looked at you. Mummy says he is *terribly* important in the world of finance. Enoch Tara is quite the mystery. That's what everyone says.'

Gemma arched an eyebrow. 'Freya. What do you want to know?'

'Nothing. If he makes you happy, that's all that matters to me,' replied Freya happily.

Louise had been sitting quietly drinking her tea and slowly consuming a chocolate raspberry biscuit when her smart phone pinged. She looked at it and then put the phone back down on the coffee table. 'Poppy just text me. She wants to know if we would like to stay at the house with her tonight.'

'That's sounds *splendid,* Louise. Please text her back and tell we would love to,' answered Freya.

'Poppy loves spending time at the house. She is enjoying having nothing to do. She is reading books on interior design. She plans to re-decorate the nursery at the family pile. She is also thinking about how to decorate the nursery at Brian's townhouse in London. Oh, and she is looking for a nanny. She wanted to hire Karmen, but Violet's sister-in-law refuses to give her up.'

'I want Karmen for my baby. I want her to grow up speaking Croatian,' said Freya. And Freya smiled.

'I am going to raise my baby in the countryside with fresh air, green grass, ancient trees, and crystal clear lakes,' said Louise. 'I want my children to grow up happy and safe. I want them to know they are loved.' Louise sighed and her gaze turned inward for a moment. 'To love and be loved is what really matters,' said Louise quietly.

Gemma smiled. 'You will find love one day, Louise. You will. For sure. And you will be happy.'

'Yes. You are right, Louise,' said Freya. 'Mummy said the same just before she departed for the country. She's spending it with grandfather and grandmother. Father has been called away on business to Borneo. Somewhere around there.' Freya smiled and said, 'Yes. Mummy really said that.'

Louise smiled. Your mother has invited me to a fox hunt in October. I told her I would attend. She said they no longer really hunt foxes anymore because of an Act of Parliament , but that it is still *terribly thrilling* . And it would be a chance for me to wear jodhpurs and spurs,' said Louise happily.

And all the girls laughed.

'Yes, I'll be there too. It will be good to see you again, Louise. We will have been apart for months at that point,' said Freya quietly.

Louise, easily sensing Freya's distress smiled and said, 'Don't worry. I will be the same as always. And I will always be your friend.'

Freya smiled and reached over and held Louise's soft tiny hand. 'You always know what to say, Louise. Thank you.'

'I'm going too,' said Gemma. 'I haven't been on a fox hunt in *yonks*, but so much has changed since the 1990s.' Gemma reflected for a moment and then said, 'It seems everything has changed.'

'That's what Mummy told me last weekend. Everything has changed. She said she wished she could go back and relive her youth just one more time.

145

If she could do that, then she could face the present more calmly,' said Freya.

Freya then took a sterling silver butter knife and spread strawberry jam on one of the split scones. And then, like one of the denizens of Cornwall (or London), she topped it with a spoonful of clotted cream. There. **Perfect.**

Gemma—England—Languorous Summer

THE LAKE DISTRICT

Gemma, Louise, and Freya drove to Poppy's country house late in the day. Being summer, the sun would not start to set until almost half past ten in the evening.

Twilight in the Lake District is amazing in summer. The setting sun reflected off of the lakes as Gemma, driving in her white Peugeot hatchback, piloted her way along the lake's edge on the way to Poppy's country house. The sunlight painted the fells in shades of orange, red, blue and purple. The panorama which stretched out before the girls was amazing, even phantasmagoric. The shades of light which reflected off the water were constantly moving and changing as the sun disappeared behind the mountains.

Freya drove her white Volkswagen Polo with Louise a short distance behind Gemma's hatchback. Freya paid careful attention; she didn't want to lose sight of Gemma.

Louise rolled down the window and let the cold wind tousle her strawberry blonde hair and cool her. Louise smiled. The vanilla and honey scents of the lilacs and lavenders filled the air. Louise leaned back and enjoyed the scenery which was ablaze in color. As the swirling perfect disc called the Sun slowly drifted downwards, the colors grew darker, from vibrant oranges and reds, to blues, magentas and purples and filled the small white hatchback's interior.

Freya tilted her sunglasses back on her head; she wouldn't be needing them until tomorrow. She accelerated as Gemma turned off the main road and headed up a mountain road. As soon as Freya reached the turn off, she slowed down and used her turn signal as she turned onto the mountain road. She then accelerated and the occupants were pushed back against their car seats by gravity as the car made its way up the steep incline. As the car cleared the top of the mountain road and they were making their way through the mountain crag, a few jets of purple and blue light faded away and the Sun finally disappeared. It was now dark. Freya turned on the headlights and moved steadily through the darkness.

THE GATES

Gemma slowed down as she approached the gates of the baronial lands. It was dark and the headlights of the Peugeot illuminated the country road ahead of her. The stone gates suddenly appeared. The gates consisted of heavily weathered and ancient stone pillars. The ornate iron gates, installed during the Victorian Era, had been taken down and donated in a scrap metal campaign during the First World War and had never been replaced.

On either side of the stone pillars were the remnants of the medieval stone walls that had been built almost nine-hundred years ago. Much of the stone had been carted away for use on other building projects over the centuries. The stone walls had been largely replaced by hundreds of tall and ancient oak and maple trees. Their leafy branches provided a natural barrier that hid much of the lands beyond the stone gate.

Gemma slowed and then pulled off the road and parked in front of the gates. She kept her lights on. She got out of the car, keeping the driver's side door open. The headlights illuminated the stone pillars and the heavily shaded entrance.

The wind would occasionally rise and whip through the trees. The temperature had dropped considerably that evening. It felt good. Gemma put on a blue quilted Burberry jacket and waited next to the car holding her smartphone, just in case Freya or Louise called. She hoped they weren't lost.

After a few minutes, a pair of headlights appeared. They moved swiftly through the darkness. The small white German hatchback then slowed down and came to a stop directly in front of the stone gates adjacent to Gemma.

'Thank you for waiting, Godmother. I was a bit lost coming through pass. I saw the gates in your headlights and just drove in the direction of the lights,' said Freya as she got out of the car.

Louise got out of the passenger side and approached Gemma. The slender and diminutive Louise rubbed her arms to warm herself against the cool night air as she walked through the pale darkness, partially illuminated by two sets of headlights which were set at different angles.

'The sunset was beautiful, Gemma. I love the Lake District. One day, I will build a small cottage here for me and my family. My future husband and children will spend their summers here. Also, their Christmas vacations. We will attend church services at the village church with everyone,' said Louise happily.

Gemma smiled. Louise was so cute and chirpy. She liked having her around. Louise had really come out of her shell in the last few months. It seemed everyone in the group had changed a lot since the winter. Gemma smiled.

'Well, girls. This is it. The northern entrance. It's normally used by the leaseholders to move livestock and trucks through. There are small farms on either side of the road. Be careful you don't hit any lost sheep when driving tonight. I always go slowly through here. The main house is just a few miles away, on the other side of the forest.'

Gemma's smartphone began to ring. It was Poppy. Gemma answered.

'Hello. Sorry, Poppy. We got off to a late start tonight. It's my fault.'

'That's alright, Gemmy. Have you had dinner?'

'No. None of us have.'

'Fantastic!' said Poppy happily. 'I have no less than three cold pizzas waiting for you. I have been having Edward make pizza for me two or three times a week since I arrived. I made extra for you girls. They were hot a few hours ago, but when I suspected you weren't going to arrive in time, I put them in the refrigerator.'

'Poppy. I love cold pizza.'

'I know, Gem.'

Gemma then lowered her cellphone and said, 'Girls. Tonight we are having cold pizza.'

Freya and Louise cheered happily and loudly enough that Poppy could hear them over the phone. Gemma and Poppy smiled.

'Alright, Poppy. We'll be there in about fifteen minutes. We are at the north gate right now.'

'Okay, Gem. Be careful driving through the woods tonight.'

'We will,' replied Gemma.

THE FAMILY PILE
Poppy was waiting in front of the glossy black double doors of the house with Kata, one of the black-uniformed Croatian servants, when Gemma's car pulled into the long driveway. The girls arrived a minute later in Freya's VW. The front of the house was illuminated by exterior house lamps.

Gemma exited her car and approached Poppy, who was now starting to show. Poppy, still waiting for her bespoke maternity clothes to arrive, was wearing a white waffle weave bathrobe, navy blue pyjamas with white piping and a pair of white slippers.

'Poppy! I'm sorry we arrived so late. I lost track of time showing the girls around my new house.'

'It's not Gemma's fault, Aunt Poppy. It's mine. I got lost and spent most of the day touring the Lake District with Louise,' said Freya laughingly as she walked towards the House. Freya was starkly beautiful. Her long, glossy, blonde hair was in a double ponytail, with each braid resting on her shoulders. Freya was radiant. She smiled as she walked towards Poppy and Gemma.

'Freya! I'm so glad you could join us in the Lake District. It's so peaceful and quiet here. It will be hard to return to London next year with the baby. I think the slow pace and quiet of the countryside is agreeing with me way too much,' said Poppy and she smiled.

Freya and Louise stopped in front of Poppy and noticed the baby bump underneath of white bathrobe. 'Poppy, is that the baby or too much pizza?' laughed Freya.

Poppy laughed and then hugged Freya, who stood at least six inches taller than her. 'I'm telling everyone it's the baby,' replied Poppy as she hugged Freya.

Louise smiled and said, 'You're more beautiful than ever, Aunt Poppy.'

Poppy smiled and then opened her arms to embrace Louise. 'Thank you for coming to stay with us, Louise. I'm happy to have you with us. Tomorrow we will search the castle and forest for fairies and sprites.'

Louise smiled as they embraced. Louise tilted her head to one side and said, 'Are there a lot of them in the forest? Gemma told me the fairy queen lives somewhere close to the castle.'

'That's true. I used to leave biscuits out for her and the other fairies when I was young, but I don't know how many they were able to retrieve before the birds got them,' replied Poppy happily.

THE EGYPTIAN ART DECO CHAMBER
The girls decided that a pizza party would be the best way to celebrate their first night together that summer. Poppy led the girls into the cavernous

kitchen and to one of the large stainless steel refrigerators.

Gemma and Freya took out the three pizzas. They had already been cut into slices by Edward. All three pizzas were carefully broken up and stacked into four large clear plastic containers with resealable plastic lids. There was a lot of pizza.

Poppy directed Louise to put sterling silver shakers of salt, black pepper, and red pepper into a wicker picnic basket that Poppy had taken out of a cabinet in the kitchen.

Poppy directed Freya to get four glasses and four white bone china plates (with gold edging) from the cupboard and place them in the wicker basket that Louise had placed the condiments in.

'Okay, I'll carry the basket, and girls, you can carry the pizza. I keep a lot of bottled water in the small refrigerator in my bedroom,' said Poppy happily.

'No,' said the other three girls simultaneously.

Gemma, holding one plastic container of pizza slices, picked up the silver handled wicker picnic basket with her free hand. 'I'll take the basket. Please take it easy, Poppy,' said Gemma.

Poppy smiled and said, 'Thank you, Gem.'

The four Inseparables then made their way out of the kitchen, through the wood panelled dining room, and down the narrow hallway to the landing in front of the stairs. Poppy went up first, followed by the other girls, all laden with the night's supplies.

It was almost midnight and the house was very quiet. Kata had been summoned upstairs shortly after the girls had arrived to assist the baroness with something. Marija, the other Croat servant, was probably asleep in her cottage. The baron had still not returned with Hector from meeting with some of his tenant farmers. The house was still fully lit. The servants usually turned out most of the lights at midnight, keeping on only a few lamps to provide minimal illumination for anyone wishing to navigate their way through the house. Summertime in the Lake District was always a busy time of the year. It was normal for the family to sleep late and awaken late.

The girls entered Poppy's room. The white walled room was dimly lit. Light came through the plaster Egyptian Art Deco hieroglyphic crown molding which lined the upper walls. The effect was beautiful, it bordered on the mystical. There were shaded lamps on the nightstands on either side of Poppy's bed. The lamps both cast bursts of light from them. The ceiling lights remained off. Outside the large bedroom windows, the illumination of the exterior lamps cast additional light into the room.

The girls put the plastic containers of pizza and the wicker picnic basket on the polished wooden table next to the large sash window.

'Oh, no, we forgot the utensils. I guess we will just have the pizza without them,' smiled Poppy impishly.

The girls stood around the small wooden table and started to unpack their midnight dinner.

'Edward made one cheese pizza, one pepperoni, and one Hawaiian pizza. There is enough to feed an army here. Or, perhaps, just four hungry girls and a baby,' said Poppy and she smiled.

Freya laughed and said, 'It is so good to be back here with everyone. I missed you so much. What is life without pizza and good friends?'

'You are all always welcome here. I love you,' Poppy said to the girls standing opposite of her. 'I always will.' Poppy then arched an eyebrow, smiled mischievously and said, 'Now let's have some pizza; the baby is famished.'

The girls each selected two or three slices of pizza each and then placed the remaining pizza into the small refrigerator Poppy had had installed in her room next to the table. She wanted a ready supply of cold drinks nearby so that she would not have to tread up and down the stairs so much that summer.

Poppy made her way to the large bed. The bed was unmade. Poppy had been resting much of the evening in it, reading different books and napping. The bed's soft white sheets and white Egyptian cotton duvet reminded Gemma of a snow drift or a snow capped mountain chain. There were also several large white pillows scattered across it.

Poppy got into bed carefully and sat down in the ocean of white cotton. She smiled happily. 'This pizza is really good. I love thin crust pizza, and Edward makes the best pizza in England. Come join me, Gemmy.'

Gemma, carrying a plate of pizza slices and a glass of cold water, walked over and sat down on the edge of the bed. She placed the glass of water on the night stand next to Poppy's glass, and then laid back against a large pillow. Gemma gazed upwards at the ceiling. The plaster hieroglyphic crown molding cast unusual patterns across the ceiling and onto the walls. Gemma then lowered her gaze and picked up a thin slice of cold pepperoni pizza. She bit into it and smiled. It was delicious. And now, here, in the warm and inviting soft bed of her dearest friend in the world, Gemma felt a wave of happiness sweep over her.

Gemma was truly happy. She had found love again. Well, this time, she felt it was mutual. Gemma now doubted that George had ever loved her at all. It used to bother Gemma terribly when she had thought about her youth being wasted on such a vile and useless human being. Why had God allowed that to happen? Why couldn't Gemma have met someone else at Oxford? Why couldn't she have fallen in love with Enoch during rehearsals? Gemma's life would have turned out so differently. She would not have had to endure so much suffering.

Gemma's life had been brutal. Her harsh childhood, scandalous divorce, and swift downfall had been horribly traumatizing. Her experience with Grey had left even deeper scars. Why had God allowed all of this to happen? This question still haunted Gemma. Her faith in God was surprisingly unshaken, but still, she wondered: what purpose had all of her suffering served?

Gemma closed her eyes for a moment and thanked God in silent prayer for bringing her through the storm with the aid of loyal friends. She opened her eyes and saw Poppy slowly chewing on pizza and staring at her. The look in Poppy's eyes seem to ask: Are you alright, Gemmy? Gemma smiled. She was. Gemma was alright. Now she was.

Freya and Louise sat at the edge of the large bed and chatted happily while they ate slices of cold pizza.

Gemma crawled over and sat up next to Poppy. Gemma, still in faded blue jeans and a white cotton top, slowly rested her head on Poppy's shoulder.

'I love you, Poppy.'

'I love you, Gemmy.'

Gemma, took another bite of cold pepperoni pizza and closed her eyes. She thought about Enoch. What should she think of him? Could she trust him? Enoch seemed so pure, just as she remembered him. Enoch Tara. The mysterious Enoch Tara. Enoch was a venture capitalist of awe inspiring abilities and untold wealth—not that that mattered to Gemma, it didn't at all.

Gemma worried that someone with that kind of reputation and wealth might have a dark side to them that she was unable to recognize. George and Grey had both been able to deceive her easily, too easily. Was Enoch like them? No. Gemma. Don't be stupid. Of course not. Enoch was different. Gemma could sense that. Gemma had to trust Enoch. Most importantly, **Gemma had to learn to trust herself again.**

'This pizza is *marvellous*, Poppy,' said Louise in her Sloaney accent. 'It's better cold. Yes, it is much better cold,' said Louise happily. Louise then sprinkled more black pepper on her pizza.

'Louise, would you like some pizza with that?' asked Freya laughingly.

'I like pepper, Freya,' chirped Louise happily.

The girls both laughed.

Gemma opened her eyes and sat up. 'Poppy, what would you like to do tomorrow?'

'I thought we could take a walk after breakfast and explore the castle. I'm going to look for fairies and sprites tomorrow.'

'I remember doing that when we visited while still attending All Saints. We had such a good time. You used to tell us so many interesting stories about the woodland creatures that live in the forest,' said Gemma.

'Yes, my grandmother told me all about them when I was growing up.'

'Are they real, Aunt Poppy?' asked Freya while arching an eyebrow.

'They are. If you want them to be,' replied Poppy.

'I want them to be,' said Louise.

'Then they are, Louise. You have to believe in something. Why not believe in fairies and sprites?'

'Yes. That sounds about right, Aunt Poppy,' said Freya thoughtfully.

'Then it's settled. Tomorrow we search the forest and castle for sprites and fairies,' said Poppy happily.

'Don't forget to bring along some biscuits, girls,' said Gemma. 'Fairies love biscuits. So do sprites. And birds,' said Gemma, and Gemma smiled.

'Freya looked at her silver Cartier watch and said, 'It's past midnight. Are you alright to stay up this late?'

'I've been asleep half the day, Freya. I'm wide awake. The question is: How are you? You have been driving all day. How about we go to bed in half an hour? Then tomorrow morning we can have the last of the cold pizza for breakfast and explore the castle?'

'That sounds good,' replied Louise sleepily. She then took another bite of Hawaiian pizza and smiled.

Gemma—England—Lucy

THE LAKE DISTRICT

Lucy looked out the window of the large dark blue Range Rover as it approached the 12th Baron's country house. It was July and the mid-summer heat was kept at bay by the droning air conditioning system.

The 1984 five-door Range Rover had been restored by the baron the previous year. The baron liked classic British vehicles, but these days, with the country's automotive industry owned and operated by foreign conglomerates, 'British' cars looked anything but British. The cars produced globally today all looked the same. The baron would have to put on his black-framed reading glasses and look carefully at the car badge to tell a British car from a Japanese or German one. But a lumbering 1980s Range Rover was unmistakably British. Therefore, it was only natural that the baron had had it restored. On top of that, the car was easy to maintain because it lacked the electronics and computers of modern vehicles.

Today, James' mother, the baroness, was behind the wheel of the blue behemoth as it made its way towards the family pile.

James, Helen, and the twins had finally gotten away from London for a summer holiday in the Lake District. For the twins, Lucy and Henry, the Lake District meant visiting their kind grandparents and having the opportunity to play in lush green fields and in the trees that surrounded the baronial manor house. For the twins it also meant spending time with their father, who was rarely seen when they were in London. And for Lucy and Henry, it also meant a chance to search for the sprites and fairies which hid in the castle grounds.

WOODLAND CREATURES

For centuries, local folklore had it that fairies could be seen flitting about the forest on gossamer wings, and that brownies, sprites, even the occasional hobgoblin, could be found wandering the woods and fields around the baronial castle. Local children had always been allowed to wander the woodlands that surrounded the local villages in search of them, the 'Hidden People' as they were also known, and enjoy foraging for wild berries by all twelve barons that had protected these lands.

Poppy's grandmother had truly believed in them. And she enjoyed telling the young Poppy stories about them on their daily walks through the woods and castle ruins.

Poppy, when young, had spent a lot of her free time earnestly looking for them and using biscuits to lure them out of their hiding places.

The young, flaxen-haired Poppy would consult with her beloved grandmother about which biscuits fairies and elves liked the most. After making a list, Poppy would travel with her mother to the bakery in the local village (which was still open) and buy an assortment of biscuits suited to the task. Sometimes, Poppy and her grandmother would bake the biscuits themselves. It was her grandmother that had told Poppy that fairies favoured raspberry chocolate biscuits; which also happened to be Poppy's favourites too. Alas, it seemed that it was the local birds that benefited the most.

Poppy would leave a few biscuits in a wide variety of places throughout the woods and castle grounds. Poppy would then lay in wait. Usually local birds like wrens, ravens, and magpies would land and take them before the hobgoblins or brownies could find them.

It was all so sad, Poppy would sigh. The fairies and brownies must be so hungry. Poppy's grandmother would always assure her that not all of the biscuits had been taken by the birds. The fairies were adept at grabbing them when no one was looking. Poppy would then smile

THE FAMILY PILE

1986

The flaxen haired Poppy sat on the pale blue sofa in the family drawing room. Sunlight filled the drawing room and a gentle breeze entered the room through one of the large open windows of the house. Poppy, at seven, was perplexed. How would she ever be able to spot a fairy or a brownie, or even a hobgoblin, if the birds kept snatching away the biscuits she laid out in the forest for them?

It was spring. The fairies would now be at their most active, for sure. Poppy looked forlornly at the swaying leafy trees which surrounded the house. She sighed heavily. What to do?

'What's wrong, my little Poppy?' asked Poppy's white-haired grandmother, the baroness.

The slender baroness was wearing a pair of khaki jodhpurs, leather riding boots, and a white cotton blouse with a large white collar. She was preparing to walk to the stables for her daily ride.

'Grandmother,' said Poppy, 'The birds keep taking all the biscuits that I leave in the forest for the fairies. They must be cold and hungry.' Poppy sighed and leaned back against the soft cushions of the Art Deco sofa, her long, blonde hair laying about her in stark contrast to the pale blue upholstery which surrounded her.

Poppy was worried; her grandmother could tell that easily. Poppy had always been easy to read. Her grandmother knew just what to say.

'Poppy, please don't worry. The fairies are very adept and taking biscuits when people aren't looking. It's a game for them. It's how they play with good-hearted children. The fairies only play with the good-hearted. You see, the missing biscuits prove that. Do you think the birds can take all of them? Of course not. The fairies get more than their fair share. I'm sure they feasting on some of the chocolate and raspberry biscuits that we made this morning right now.'

Poppy's grandmother sat down next to her and held Poppy's tiny, soft hand. The baroness smiled. 'Poppy. I'm sure they are alright.'

'How do you know?' asked the tiny young girl seated next to her grandmother.

'Because if the fairies are hungry. They will knock on the front door of the house and leave a pile of stones in front of the door to let you know. That's how fairies ask for things. And if the fairies like the biscuits you leave outside for them, they will send butterflies to hover around the house on sunny days. That's how you know they like your gifts. It's also a way of telling you that the fairies are happy.'

'Really?' asked Poppy quietly as she looked at her grandmother.

'Yes. Really. Let's go look outside. Shall we?' asked the baroness.

The two of them walked down the hallway until they reached the large, black, glossy double doors. The baroness opened one of them and natural light poured into the entry hall of the house. A breeze met them and, at that very moment, a purple butterfly fluttered into the hall and then drifted outside again. The baroness smiled.

'You see. They like the biscuits we made for them,' said the baroness happily.

Poppy smiled.

Eight years later, Poppy's grandmother, the wife of the 11th Baron, passed away in her sleep while Poppy was at All Saints. The news of her grandmother's death had devastated her. Gemma, Violet, and Gula all stayed up late into the night attempting to console the inconsolable Poppy.

The next morning, Poppy, wearing her school uniform, boarded a train for the Lake District. The Inseparables had walked with her to the train station. Gemma had carried her leather box suitcase for her. The uniformed school girls all took turns hugging the crying Poppy on the platform of the train station.

Poppy boarded the train, still sobbing. She didn't look back. If she had, she would have noticed that the girls were all waiting quietly on the platform for her train to leave. All of them had tears in their eyes. Gemma cried openly.

As the train prepared to pull out out of the station, a butterfly fluttered into the train carriage through an open window where Poppy was seated. It landed on one of the arm rests in the carriage. A gentle breeze then entered through the open window and the purple butterfly fluttered out. At that moment, Poppy knew. Poppy knew that her grandmother was alright. She was safe. The fairies wanted her to know that. Poppy then leaned back into the upholstered seat, and through tears, the young Poppy smiled.

5 ARCADIA

Gemma—England—The Blue Bristol

MARBLE ARCH

Photos can evoke memories. So can objects. A simple ring of Welsh gold can evoke memories of love, of a special day in June, of a bond. A simple coat formerly worn by a loved one found while cleaning out a room can also evoke memories, both happy and sad.

An object need not be expensive to have value. Someone's most valuable and prized possession may have little or no intrinsic value at all. Yet, because it had once been owned by someone who was loved, it is priceless to some. Thus it was with a car that sat in a garage in Marble Arch.

The blue 1977 Bristol 603S had been purchased by Külli's father in the mid 1980s when the leather footwear company he had founded in the 1960s had seen its profitability skyrocket. Külli's father, an Estonian refugee, had finally become successful.

He wanted his tiny family in Surrey to be truly British. He sent his only child, Külli, to a posh all-girl boarding school in Sussex favoured by the daughters of the nobility. He bought a relatively small and dilapidated Edwardian country house in Surrey and had it restored. He wore Savile Row suits, English cut ties, and black morning coats and striped black trousers when the occasion called for it.

Külli's father, a war orphan, had learned how to play cricket as a teenage refugee in a second tier boarding school in the north of England; the tuition had been paid by an Estonian refugee committee. He had received an excellent English education. He had desperately wanted to become an English gentleman, and in many ways he was, except for his mild Estonian accent.

Külli's father had been handsome. He had had brown hair and brown eyes. Külli had inherited them. She had also inherited her father's intellect, ethical code of behaviour, and business acumen. While her father had been relatively short at 5' 7", Külli would grow to be nearly six feet tall. Yes, as her mother was also fairly short, Gula's height was a bit of a mystery.

Külli's father was almost fifty when Külli was born; her mother had been in her late thirties. Külli's father knew that his time with his daughter would be limited. He was determined to make the most of it and insure that his only child had a happy childhood. He also wanted to insure that she receive the best education possible. He knew that Külli would find herself bereft of parents at a young age. That both of Külli's parents had arrived in England as war orphans also meant that their only child would be alone in the world when they had both passed away. He wanted Külli to be able to take care of herself. He wanted Külli, his beloved 'Gula', to have a network of golden friends. The kind of friends one could only make at a posh boarding school in England.

It had worked. All of her father's careful plans would eventually reach fruition. Only, sadly, he had not lived to see it. He would pass away in a hospital room in the early morning hours on a day in July—all alone—when Külli was only 25. It had all happened so quickly. Külli had received a telephone call late one night while on a business trip from one of her father's employees. Gula was devastated. She sat in her white walled hotel room in Tokyo and sobbed—all alone.

Külli's mother, grief stricken, passed away three months later.

Now, alone in the world, Külli knew she could move in only one direction: upwards.

THE CAR
Külli had been given the Bristol 603S as a reward for winning a place at

Oxford University. Her father had purchased this most British of cars for Gula, who was part of a 'new' British family. He had paid the Bristol car company to completely restore and upgrade the car, upgrades which included a new Connolly leather interior, modern air conditioning, and a new V-8 engine. Gula loved the car. It was beautiful, well engineered, and most importantly to Gula, fast. It also represented her father's unconditional love for her.

Külli, known to the former roommates at All Saints as 'Gula', had kept the car in near mint condition. She still drove the 603S regularly. And she always drove it when she went to visit her parents' graves in the small Anglican cemetery in the Cotswolds.

Yes, objects can evoke memories, and this midsize blue car definitely did. It was one of Gula's most prized possessions. A foreign billionaire industrialist had once tried to purchase the 603S from her for an obscene amount of money, but Külli politely and determinedly, had refused.

Gemma—England—Lucy and Henry

THE DRAWING ROOM
Lucy and Henry were both sweet and good-hearted children. They were also very cute. And, as if continuing a family tradition, Lucy was 'dangerously cute'. The twins were also very close and enjoyed playing together. They never argued and shared everything.

The twins loved their aunts Poppy and Gemma. And they were looking forward to seeing Freya and Louise again. The girls all loved the twins. The summer was shaping up nicely.

THE BARONESS
The baroness, in blue cotton trousers and a white cotton blouse, sat in one of the large Art Deco purple upholstered chairs in the drawing room. The cold air of the central air system was quite soothing after spending a hot afternoon waiting for the train to arrive at the small and unair-conditioned rural station.

The baroness looked remarkable for her age. She had largely avoided the sun and had used expensive Japanese cold creams for most of her life. She neither drank nor smoked. She had also maintained a strict diet. She rode horses and hunted for exercise. She was a crack shot and often practiced at the family's makeshift shooting range on the property.

The baroness was from a noble English family; her father had been a viscount. She had attended excellent schools and graduated from Oxford University, where she had met her future husband, the 12th Baron.

The baroness was also a good mother. She had raised James and Poppy to be kind, considerate, unselfish, and brave. Coupled with her husband, the children couldn't have had a better upbringing.

Now, with her entire family around her, the baroness felt serene, complete. That Gemma, Freya, and Louise had joined them had made everything that much better. Gemma was like a daughter to her.

The only other person outside of the family that she regarded as one of her own children was Mars. Mars, the former hedge fund manager and now London real estate developer, had been close to her heart since they had met when he was a young teenager. Mars had been crushed by his mother's death, and it was to James' family that he had turned to for solace. The family had been protective and caring. The family loved Mars. And Mars loved them.

Which reminds me: Where is Mars? Oh, yes. Mars was planning to join the family that summer, too, as soon as he had completed overseeing renovations of a building in North London that was being converted into offices.

'It's good to have all of you here with us in The Lake District,' said the baroness.

The very pregnant Poppy sat next to Gemma and Helen on the purple Art Deco sofa. James sat in one of the large chairs next it, and the twins sat together on another Art Deco chair next to James.

'It's good to be back, Mummy,' replied James.

James was wearing khaki cotton trousers, a brown leather belt, and a white button down Oxford dress shirt over a white undershirt. A silver Omega watch on a tan leather strap adorned his wrist. His blond hair had been cut the day before. James had a surprisingly crisp appearance, considering the temperature outside. The svelte James was strikingly handsome, even pretty. Poppy bore some resemblance to him. He smiled.

'The children haven't stopped talking about their summer plans with you, Mummy,' said James happily.

'Yes, Granny, we want to look for fairies and hobgoblins with you this summer,' said Henry excitedly.

'Yes, I want to finally meet a fairy,' said Lucy happily.

'I'm sure the summer will be filled with adventures,' replied the baroness, and she smiled.

Her grandchildren were finally back with her, and in the countryside. Yes, it was better here.

Poppy smiled and said, 'We will have to leave small gifts for the sprites and fairies, if you want to see them.'

'You mean biscuits?' asked Lucy.

'Yes,' replied Poppy. Poppy then looked around rather melodramatically and said, 'There is a large number of them living in the castle. The fairy queen also lives there. She loves biscuits, especially raspberry and chocolate ones.' And Poppy smiled.

The black-uniformed Croatian maids entered the drawing room. One of them carried a large silver pitcher filled with ice water; the other a silver tray with tall glasses. One of the maids poured icy water into a glass held by the other and then the maid politely served each guest, starting with the baroness.

'Thank you, girls,' replied the baroness. 'This is just what we all needed.' The baroness smiled.

Everyone sipped their drinks and for a moment the room was silent. Lucy was the first to speak after drinking cold water from her glass.

'Aunt Gemma. Will you come with us when we look for the fairies?' asked Lucy.

'Of course,' replied Gemma, and she smiled.

'Where are Freya and Louise?' asked Helen.

Helen, wearing (quite uncharacteristically) faded blue jeans and a blue and white striped top, was seated next to Gemma, her dark sunglasses in one of her hands.

'Oh, they went to the local village. They decided to visit St George's. Louise and Freya wanted to tour the church and meet the vicar and his wife,' replied Poppy.

'Well, that means they'll be staying for lunch,' said James happily.

And everybody laughed.

ST GEORGE

After a pleasant lunch filled with interesting conversation and delicious food, the vicar and his wife took Freya and Louise on a tour of the small medieval stone church. The girls were especially impressed with the stonework inside the building.

'Yes, those are angels,' said the white- haired vicar as he motioned towards the ceiling. 'They were carved by stonemasons hundreds of years ago. They survived The Reformation because the barons never allowed the church to be defaced or damaged by the misguided. It was quite brave of the family to protect the church. But, I am glad they did,' said the vicar, and he smiled.

The vicar, in his Anglican collar, walked to the altar and stopped. 'If you look carefully at the top of the altar, you will notice that the stone is somewhat different from the rest of the stone in the church. That's because this altar top was brought from Jerusalem. One of Poppy's ancestors transported the stone from the Holy Land just for this exact purpose. The stone was part of the walls that protected the city. This piece of stone was dislodged during the siege, and he kept it.'

Freya and Louise looked carefully at the altar. Yes, it was quite different from the rest of the grey stone church. The pale dolomitic limestone appeared to be heavily weathered, but also quite dense. Engraved along the edges of the altar top were five small crosses. Freya nodded in understanding.

'They represent the five wounds of Christ,' said Louise.

'Yes, that's right,' replied the vicar.

'The altar at All Saints has the same engravings,' said Freya.

The upper edges of the stone walled church had had Latin letters carved into them. Freya and Louise both stopped to read the inscriptions.

The vicar and his wife then led the girls outside to the cemetery. It was filled with tomb stones, tall lush green grass, and shaded by large leafy trees. Most of the tombstones were hundreds of years old. Some of the tombstones had human skulls carved into them.

Freya and Louise walked among them. Several of Poppy's ancestors were buried in this graveyard. They stopped in front of one of the newer tombstones. Louise studied it for a moment and then said, 'It belongs to Poppy's great uncle Howard. We stayed in his bedroom on our first visit,' said Louise quietly.

Freya walked towards Louise and looked at the cut stone that stood before her. Yes, 1915. That must have been when he was killed. Freya felt a wave of sadness wash over her, and she really didn't understand why. It was almost as if she could sense the loss emanating from the stone itself. Freya sighed.

'How sad. How tragic. Poppy said the family had never really recovered from his death,' said Freya.

'Yes, and that's why Jane was forbidden from marrying her Prussian fiancé. Oh, what was his name again?' asked Louise.

'Eugen,' answered Freya.

'Yes, that was it,' replied Louise sadly.

Freya then noticed another tombstone a few meters away from Howard's. It was Jane's. The girls walked over to it and studied it carefully. Engraved on the stone was her full name: JANE MORGAN DEVEREUX.

Gemma—England—The Trenches

THE WESTERN FRONT
Autumn 1915
The Honourable Howard Arthur Devereux peered at the enemy position through a pair of field glasses. It was cold and an icy wind lashed at him as he adjusted the magnification on the binoculars. Ah, that's better. There they are: the Germans.

The Hon Major H. A. Devereux DSO had been fighting on the Western front for eleven months. He had been stationed abroad, patrolling the Indian highlands, when his regiment had been transferred to Europe. His hussar regiment had suffered horrendous losses. Most of the men who had served with him in India had been killed. The replacements sent from England were often killed in the fighting so quickly that sometimes he never even learned their names.

It was here, in one of the most active sectors of the front, that Howard Arthur Devereux found himself leading the remnants of one of the British Empire's most formidable combat units. Howard's hussar regiment, otherwise known as The Bright Seraphims, had long ago been deprived of their horses and sent into the trenches. The regiment had proven itself in engagement after engagement. The ferocity of The Bright Seraphims was well known to the Germans, especially the Prussians.

The Honourable Howard Arthur Devereux was now the acting commander of this regiment of hussars, the two previous commanding officers having been killed in action the month before. Howard was exhausted and near physical collapse, but so was everyone else in the regiment. The Hon Major H. A. Devereux had to lead by example. He could not appear tired. He could not show fear. He must smile in the face of adversity. His men needed reassurance and it was Howard's duty to instill confidence in his young hussars. He had never failed in that regard. However, Howard was human, and he wondered if he had already reached the limits of his endurance.

The trenches could be muddy in the spring and summer, icy in the fall and winter, but never comfortable. Today, on this gloomy, overcast, and bitterly cold grey day, the trenches were as hard as stone. The position, though heavily fortified, had been badly damaged by heavy artillery barrages in the days before. The exhausted hussars, when not attacking or counter-attacking, worked endlessly to repair and reinforce the fortified positions that had been allotted to them.

It was windy and cold and the front was relatively quiet. The orange light of dawn was breaking over the horizon and that gave Howard just enough natural light to see the Germans moving down through their trenches.

It was a rotation. Exhausted Saxons were being rotated out and replaced with well rested and relatively fresh troops. Only, unbeknownst to the middle-aged hussar officer, the replacements were an elite unit of Prussians. There assignment: Take Howard's position and hold it at all costs.

Major Devereux lowered the field glasses and then stepped down from the earth-filled wooden ammunition boxes he had been standing on to peer over the top of the trenches. He put the binoculars into the tan leather case that hung from a worn leather strap and then his gloved hands took out a folded paper map. It had been heavily marked with colored pencils.

Major Devereux was wearing thick soled leather shoes with leather gaiters, khaki jodhpurs, and over the rest of his uniform a thick wool coat, the stiff wool collar, which had been lined with fur, was flipped up to protect him from the icy winds. His cap rested securely on his head, its leather visor partially covering his eyes. Brown leather straps crisscrossed his body: one holding his Webley revolver, another held a leather case containing a pair of field glasses, and another a square map case, and yet another, a gas mask. All of this may sound cluttered, but it had been carefully arranged in full accordance with army regulations and was worn without any undue encumbrance.

Howard walked ramrod straight and in sharp movements. He was a natural soldier. The Hon Major H. A. Devereux was a highly capable, tough, and exceedingly brave English officer.

Howard turned to the young platoon leader standing next to him in the trench and said, 'Mr Acton. Take the platoon to the 3rd sector. There seems to be a lot of German activity there this morning. I think it's best we reinforce the men there as soon as possible.'

The teenage blonde subaltern, an Old Etonian, snapped to attention and nodded. Without a word, the exhausted young officer from Surrey made his way down the frozen trench. That was the last time they would ever see each other again.

THE HUSSAR

Howard was now forty-one. He was alone in the world. He had devoted his life to England, his homeland. He had spent half his life in India, protecting the Raj. Had it been worth it? Howard had never really pondered that. He had joined the army and been assigned to a regiment in India. It was his sacred duty—yes, sacred—to protect England and by extension, the British Empire. For King-Emperor and country!

Howard's life had been an endless cycle of parades, patrols, parties, tiger hunts, and meals in the officer's mess. When not attired in khaki and in the field, he was resplendent in his full dress hussar's uniform. On some occasions he wore white tie and tails, and on others, cricket whites.

Howard lived in a beautiful bungalow located in a hill station nestled among green trees and even greener lawns. It was a white washed Victorian structure. The house would have been quite out of place in the tiny hillside Indian hamlet, had it not been surrounded by dozens of other houses similar to it, all filled with English colonials. The only Indian thing about them was the servants.

The stone house, assigned to him by his regiment, came with no less than five servants. The servants all wore white jackets and turbans of various colors; the colors determined by the religious or ethnic background of the wearers.

Howard's bedroom was on the second floor and had a magnificent view of the valley below. He would usually awaken to cold misty mornings in this quaint and isolated station in the Indian highlands. The pyjama clad Howard would pull on a blue silk cord next to his mahogany framed bed and downstairs a small brass bell would ring. That bell summoned another one of his servants, a young man whose job it was to boil water and fill Howard's white enameled iron clawed bathtub, which was located in the white tiled bathroom at the end of the hall.

While Howard immersed himself in the hot bath, another white jacketed servant would be carefully preparing his hussar's uniform for him. Usually this meant Howard's light weight khaki uniform and polished brown leather boots. The servant would have carefully ironed the jacket, jodhpurs, and shirt the night before. The servant would have also carefully cleaned the leather webbing, pouches, and holster. Everything in the house revolved around the middle-aged English officer who resided in it, like planets orbiting a sun.

The servants had titles like khitmagar, khansama, mali, pani-wallah, and doodh-wallah. There had once been a female servant, an ayah. She was an Indian nanny. Yes, once Howard had had need for one.

AMELIA
When Howard was twenty-five, he married a fresh faced and lively flaxen haired girl from Manchester. Amelia was the youngest daughter of an English family involved in the textile trade. She was tall, slim, beautiful, and **talkative**. She was hardly a wallflower; she was extremely outgoing. She was boisterous when she should have been demure. She was anything but prim and proper. She was completely out of place in Edwardian society. And Howard loved her for it.

Howard's father, the 10th Baron, had met Amelia's parents and been left deeply unimpressed by the wealthy parvenus. He had tried to talk Howard out of marrying Amelia, but Howard refused to listen. Amelia was not only beautiful and sweet, she was a free spirit. Amelia's free spirited nature had left the 10th Baron a bit ruffled. Surely a girl like Amelia was not an appropriate choice for a 'Hon' like Howard. Howard privately agreed. However, Howard loved Amelia. She brought happiness into his otherwise harsh, rigid, and highly regimented life.

Howard and Amelia married at the small stone Anglican church in the village next to the family's ruined castle in the Lake District. By the time the young couple had disembarked from the steamship in India, Amelia was pregnant.

Less than a year after their marriage, Amelia gave birth to a daughter they named Audrey.

Howard's life for the next three years was one of uncomplicated happiness. Howard now fulfilled his military duties with a new found energy and discipline. Howard now had a stake in life.

Howard had used some of the money left to him by his grandfather, the 9th Baron, to start the construction of a cottage on the family lands within walking distance of the ruined castle. He wanted his family to have a home of their own. And he wanted Audrey to explore the castle and look for fairies and sprites like he had with his siblings. Yes, the castle ruins were home to a mystical array of woodland creatures, and he wanted his daughter to look for them with him. Audrey could also walk to the village with her parents to attend church services and shop at the local market. Yes, family holidays in England would be happy ones.

And then one day a tropical fever took both Amelia and Audrey away from him. It had all happened in less than a week. There was nothing the doctor could do. Howard could only sit at their bedsides and cool his wife and young daughter's fevers with a damp towel. The medicine administered by the regimental doctor had failed. Little Audrey passed away first, and then a few hours later Amelia followed her. Howard was devastated. How could this have happened? Why had it happened? Was it necessary for God to take both of them from him? How cruel and inexplicable.

Howard, now bereft of family, devoted himself to military service and the defense of the empire. There was nothing else left for him to do. The void left in him would never be filled. Howard's life became one of motions, empty motions.

THE FRONT LINE
The exhausted hussars, cold and hungry, emerged one by one from the bunkers which lined the trenches of this bitterly contested sector of the front. The khaki-clad hussars stood in the earthen trenches well kitted it out and carrying their Lee-Enfield rifles. The trenches with were soon a stream of steel helmeted hussars.

As Howard made his way down the line, the battle weary hussars all snapped to attention one by one. The smartly attired major radiated strength and confidence. It was contagious.

THE END OF THE BRIGHT SERAPHIMS
The Prussian attack on that grey morning, through a thick cloud of poison gas, had been a lighting advance across No-Man's Land, rapidly cutting through the barbed wire and moving over the cratered earth so quickly that the exhausted hussars had not even been able to radio HQ and inform them of it. The Bright Seraphims all perished to a man that morning.

Their commander, The Honourable H. A. Devereux, had died as he had hoped: fighting.

The glass lenses of Howard's gas mask had been shattered when a young Prussian soldier bashed him in the face with his rifle. Howard's final thoughts had not been of himself and his fate, but of his wife Amelia and his young daughter Audrey. The last sensation he felt was the terrible pain of breathing in poison gas.

Gemma—England—Arcadia

THE DINING ROOM
The black-uniformed Marija and Kata, the Croatian servants, moved carefully around the long, polished burl wood table. Kata and Marija carefully placed a white table cloth over the entire length of the table.

A rolling metal trolley sat near one end of the room. The chrome cart held a stack of white gold-edged bone china plates, sterling silverware, and and an assortment of Edinburgh Crystal.

Both young women, wearing white cotton gloves, moved adeptly around the table, placing the plates, silverware, and glasses at perfect intervals on the table. Occasionally one of the servants would stop and with a small wooden ruler, measure the distance between the plates, sterling silver utensils, and glasses. Everything had to be spaced correctly. That was very important.

In less than an hour, the table had been set, and the girls disappeared into the kitchen.

UPSTAIRS

The 12th Baron stood in front of the mirror. He was wearing a pair of grey trousers, a black leather belt with a silver buckle, and a white dress shirt. He was also wearing black leather shoes. It was summer, and this was meant to be a fairly informal dinner, but informality was not easy for the baron.

He was clean shaven and his snow white hair was cut like a British army officer's. He was still slim and naturally stood ramrod straight. He was still quite handsome. His hair had once been blond, but that time had long past.

The baron, approaching seventy, paused for a moment and stared at his reflection in the narrow gilt framed mirror. Now retired after a short career in the army, and a long career in banking, the baron, for the first time in his life, found himself with very little to do. Hector ran the estate quite efficiently; his tenant farmers were productive and paid their rents on time. With the exception of the agricultural events at the local village and church attendance, the 12th Baron found himself idle most of the time.

He was happy to finally be out of London. The city was no longer the place he had known when much younger. London had changed so much that it seemed to be a foreign city in a foreign country, not his own. It was no longer safe. It was also no longer British. The baron shook his head.

Irresponsible leaders had failed to protect the country. These people had failed Queen and country. They had failed on every level. What kind of England would his children and grandchildren inherit? The baron sighed. He had to put together some kind of escape plan for his family; something that could even be activated after he had passed away.

'It's so good to have everyone here. It's especially nice to have Poppy spending the next year with us. I was worried that Poppy would never marry or have a baby. I'm so glad she has finally found someone as perfect as Brian,' said the baroness as she exited the bathroom.

She was wearing a pair of navy blue cotton trousers and a pale blue cotton blouse with an open collar. Her long white and grey hair was pinned up with silver pins. The baroness smiled.

'What are you thinking about?'

'The future,' replied the baron, and he sighed.

'You worry too much, darling. Now, let's just enjoy the summer with everyone here.'

'Yes. Of course. You are right.'

Future plans could be put off, at least for tonight. He would meet privately with James and Poppy later and talk about his plans with them.

THE HUSSAR'S ROOM
Freya had decided to wear a tea length cotton dress to dinner. She had purchased the pale blue dress in London in June and had not yet had a chance to wear it. The rather simple dress had a white collar and it looked really nice on her. She would wear it with a pair of dark blue patent leather flats.

Freya's long glossy blonde hair was still divided into two large pony tails, each resting on either shoulder.

Freya looked into the bathroom mirror and adjusted the dress. Alright. She was ready.

Freya entered the bedroom and found Louise brushing her strawberry blonde hair. Little Louise was so cute, even angelic. And in a few weeks, they would be separated and head off to different universities. It was awful to even contemplate life without Louise at her side.

'You look really nice, Freya.'

'Thank you,' replied Freya. 'You look *rather* nice too. I'm glad you decided to wear the skirt you bought last weekend,' replied Freya.

Louise was wearing a red and blue tartan skirt and white cotton top with an open collar. She was also wearing a silver cross on a necklace. Louise had developed her own fashion style. It was quite posh really. Louise radiated confidence. Her brown eyes darted around the room.

'Ah, here it is,' said Louise happily. Louise walked over to the wooden dresser and took a small box off of it and then turned around. She looked at Freya and smiled.

'Freya, I have something for you,' said Louise quietly. She walked forward and held out the small box. It was wrapped in purple gift wrap and a small purple bow. It was from Asprey.

How could Louise afford that? Freya was a bit worried that Louise had spent her entire summer allowance on a gift for her. Freya smiled anyway and said, 'Thank you, Louise. But what is this for?'

'For being so dear to me,' replied Louise, her voice starting to break with emotion.

Freya took the small box and sat down on the white duvet which was on the unmade bed. She looked up at Louise for a moment and then unwrapped the box carefully. She lifted the lid. Inside was a polished silver ring.

Freya took it out and examined it carefully. Inside the glossy silver band was engraved: **'F and L undaunted'**. Freya smiled. She stood up and then embraced the diminutive Louise.

'Thank you, Louise. What would I have done without you?'

'We would both have been lost without each other,' replied Louise in voice that was barely above a whisper.

THE EGYPTIAN ART DECO CHAMBER

Gemma carefully helped Poppy put on her skirt and blouse. The bespoke outfit, stitched together by a well regarded London seamstress, fit quite well. The pleated blue wool skirt had an elastic waist band that would fit Poppy comfortably even as she continued to gain weight during her pregnancy. The white blouse was loose fitting and had open cuffs and an open collar.

 It was one of a half dozen white cotton tops that James had brought with him on the train that afternoon. Poppy looked quite nice and rather stylish. Yes, stylish. The seamstress had done well.

Gemma then carefully helped Poppy tie her silky blonde hair back with a white ribbon. She made a few adjustments to Poppy's blouse and then stepped back. Perfect.

'Thank you, Gem.'

Gemma smiled.

'Poppy, any surprise guests I should know about tonight?'

'None that I know of, Gemmy. But, with Mummy, you never know,' answered Poppy, and she laughed.

Gemma was wearing a pair of narrow leg khaki trousers and a white cotton top with a large collar. Gemma's slim and slinky figure moved across the room towards the door as if it was floating. She opened the door and smiled.

'The world awaits you, Mrs Poppy Atherton,' said Gemma with a rather melodramatic flourish. And Gemma smiled.

THE DINING ROOM

James, Helen, and the twins were all standing in the polished burl wood walled dining room and looking out the window together when the baron and baroness entered. The small family, unaware of their presence, continued to look.

The sunset was beautiful. Rays of orange, red, magenta, and then blue filled the sky. Then the orange and red disappeared and there were only wisps of blue and purple light on the horizon. The fading light illuminated the faces of the family as they watch the sun slowly disappear beneath the horizon until it was gone and only darkness was left behind.

'Yes, the sunsets here are unlike anywhere else in the world,' said the baron.

All at once, the family became aware of the two people standing behind them and turned around.

'Yes, it is *rather* amazing, isn't it,' replied Helen in her Sloaney intonation.

'I have been able to secure a full three weeks of vacation this summer, Father. I'm looking forward to doing very little,' said James.

The baron and baroness both smiled. 'James, that is fantastic. You, of all people, need a vacation,' said the baroness.

The single glossy white door to the dining room opened and Poppy entered. Gemma entered behind her and gently closed the door. Poppy looked really nice in her new outfit.

'It's so good to see you out of your pyjamas and bathrobe,' said the baron happily.

'Yes, I had almost forgotten what you looked like in regular clothes,' said James, and he smiled.

His younger sister did look nice, and most importantly, happy. Poppy was alone now; Brian had not yet been able to join her. James knew that it must have disappointed Poppy to find herself alone at the house. James was glad that he could deliver something to her that would cheer her up.

The diminutive Gemma stood next to Poppy. Gemma, attractive and poised, smiled. Age had been gentle with her. She nodded slightly to Poppy's parents and the others assembled next to the large set of sash windows that lined the wall of the room.

'How are the renovations coming along, Gemma?' asked the baron.

'*Splendidly*,' replied Gemma. 'I am planning to add a few Art Deco touches to the decor later this year. My country house will then be complete.'

The final guests to arrive were the Happy Girls formerly of Sussex, Freya and Louise. The strawberry blonde Louise entered first, as cute as ever. Or should we now say as 'dangerously cute' as Poppy had ever been?

And then Freya walked into the room. She was starkly beautiful. Perhaps it was how the dress clung to her every curve? Or maybe it was the way her blonde hair, parted into two glossy ponytails, framed her face? Whatever it was, Freya was continuing to mature into an alluringly beautiful young woman. Everyone noticed.

Freya rarely wore any makeup. It wasn't necessary. Her skin was clear and translucent. Freya usually wore faded blue jeans, white collared tops, blue blazers, and dark or mirrored sunglasses now. They almost concealed her true beauty. Now, wearing little more than a slip of pale blue cotton cloth, Freya's unbridled beauty was apparent to all. Freya flashed her healthy white smile. Yes, Freya had arrived.

THE STAFF

Meals at the family pile with close friends were rarely ever formal occasions. The family, while dressing up somewhat, was happiest in comfortable clothing and relaxing amongst themselves and their closest friends.

The dining room, with its polished burl wood panelled and stone walls, crystal chandeliers, and glossy Edwardian furniture made every occasion formal whether intended or not. The long polished table was covered with an ivory white table cloth, bone china, Edinburgh Crystal and silver cutlery.

The well-trained and highly attentive staff also made every meal into an occasion.

Edward, long employed by the family, had been become a top notch chef. In the past, when the entire family decamped to London, Edward would work at London's finest hotels and restaurants. It was in these establishments that he was able to hone his culinary skills and gain invaluable experience.

The Croatian house maids cleaned the house efficiently and methodically. They had a set routine when the family was away. They would start in the bedrooms on the second floor, gently mopping the hardwood floors, dusting, changing the bedding and making sure all of the lights and appliances worked properly. They would then clean the bathrooms carefully, launder the towels, fold them, and place them in one of the four different linen closets on the second floor of the house.

The first floor was the most difficult part of the house to clean, and impossible to complete in just one day. Instead the servants would focus on one room a day. The kitchen and dining room were priorities. The library was the most onerous. Cleaning the two storey library's ornate plaster ceiling was left to a professional crew that would arrive with scaffolding, ladders, and work lamps three times a year. The drawing room was the most frequented room in the house, and great care was taken to gently clean the Art Deco velvet upholstered furniture and clean underneath all of the furniture and polish the burl wood panelled walls as well as the sterling silver clock on the mantle. There was so much to do.

The girls would have their meals in the kitchen. If Edward was at the house, he would prepare their meals himself. If he wasn't, the two young Croatians would prepare Croatian dishes that always involved having a jar of avjar, a roasted red pepper sauce, on the table. The girls would make the avjar themselves when alone in the house in their spare time.

The girls lived rent-free in a small stone cottage a short distance from the main house that was hidden in heavily wooded part of the estate. Hector, the estate manager, had a cottage and office only a few meters away from them.

Hector, rarely spent the night in the cottage provided by the baron. He owned a house in a village a short distance from the family pile and would usually drive home in his 1995 yellow (yes, yellow) Defender after work.

Hector was a tall and powerfully built Englishman who had served in the Life Guards. A retired NCO, he had once served under the 12th Baron. They had remained in touch, and when Hector retired in the early 1990s, the baron had hired him to manage the estate. Hector was quiet, and though his appearance could be intimidating, he was actually kind. He worked hard and was always willing to assist the family or staff.

Hector kept most of his work clothes in the cottage, along with an extra tweed suit. Hector kept a double barrel shotgun and three boxes of extra shells by the bed. The three room cottage consisted of a bedroom, bathroom and on the other side of the bedroom, a small front room with a fireplace. Outside the backdoor of the small cottage were three pairs of black rubber boots.

A small wooden desk had been placed in the front room, and it was here that Hector would do routine paperwork, meet tenants, and have tea. The hardwood floors creaked as the giant and ramrod straight Hector strode across the floor and out the door every morning to make the rounds.

The baron still owned almost a thousand acres of land. Most of it had been leased to tenants who farmed and raised livestock. Maintaining an estate this size was daunting and very expensive. The baron couldn't afford permanent full-time employees beyond Hector and the small household staff, so Hector hired locals as needed. Though expensive, the family felt that holding on to what remained of their lands was an ancestral duty. The family had been given these lands by the crown over 900 years ago, and it was their sacred obligation to protect them. Of course, the costs had been high.

The family had been forced by financial hardship to first sell off most of the family art collection after the war to pay the savage tax imposed by successive Labour governments. After the art collection had been largely depleted, the family was forced to sell off thousands of acres of land. It had been an extremely bitter blow for the family. Now, the family waged a daily struggle to hold on to what remained.

DINNER

The dinner party was relaxing and pleasant. A calm evening that James appreciated more than anyone after his retreat from the tumult of modern London. James, at 47, felt he was too young to retire. He had two young children and a wife to take care of, not to mention the family pile. Poppy and Brian, James knew, would always help financially when necessary. But ultimately, as the future 13th Baron, it would fall to James to bear the financial brunt of holding onto the ancestral home.

Helen was relieved to be out of London too. She wished, more than even James, that they would never have to return to the city. She could place the children in the village school and then send them off to boarding schools in a few years. The children would be safe and happy among the trees and green fields of the country. London had lost much of its charm over the last decade. Helen doubted it would ever return. Perhaps the family should consider looking for a new home even farther afield?

And for Gemma, a special treat: steak. Yes, steak had always been Gemma's favorite; everyone knew that. Poppy had asked that it be served tonight for Gemma and the visiting girls. Besides, Poppy liked steak almost as much as Gemma.

That evening, with so many of her closest friends in attendance, Gemma could not help but think back to the previous winter, when her life and future were so uncertain. Gemma had survived. Poppy had saved her, but Poppy always saved her. And now Gemma had found love. Finally. Oh, please, God, please, make this love true.

Gemma, seated next to Poppy, reached over during dinner and gently squeezed Poppy's small soft hand. Poppy smiled. Yes, I'm here, Gemmy. Always.

Freya, seated next to Helen, enjoyed talking with her about her life in the City and her brief spell in Tokyo. Helen had always been nice, but Freya had really never spoken to her until that night. Freya, Helen quickly realized, was very intelligent and surprisingly ambitious. Freya wanted to do *something* with her life, but, like many young people, she didn't quite know what. Freya had an edge. Helen had detected that quickly. She was indomitable. Under all of that stark beauty was a young woman of iron.

Helen really didn't know Violet, Freya's mother, that well, but she knew that Violet, 'Vava' to her closest friends, was also an intelligent and determined woman. Freya, at eighteen, had her entire life before her. What direction she would take was anyone's guess.

Louise found herself, surprisingly, seated next to James. She had barely said a word to him the previous winter. She had spent the evening having a deeply rewarding and even healing conversation with Mars. Yes, Mars understood her. Mars had lost his own mother at a young age. Mars had been deeply wounded by it, and so he understood Louise. And not only that, Mars was kind and insightful. Louise had reflected on that conversation many times since. Mars' words, while not a cure all, had been extremely helpful to her. Yes, Mars would always be one of her favourites.

Louise had been happy to see him at Poppy's wedding. Mars, in his mid-forties and with a few silver and grey hairs now peppering his brown hair, had looked dashing in his black morning coat that day. He had sat with her and Freya at the reception. The reunion had been a happy one for both of them.

Louise had sincerely hoped that Mars would have arrived at the house by now; she wanted to see him again. Soon, though, Mars would be here. Louise didn't want to lose that connection.

James was attractive, kind, smart, financially savvy, and interesting. He was also a good listener. He had asked Louise about her writing. Louise enjoyed telling him about the novel she had started writing in Mayfair a few hours after she left All Saints for the final time.

'What will the theme of your novel be, Louise?' asked James.

'Loss,' replied Louise.

James nodded a little, perhaps regretting that he might have brought up something uncomfortable for Louise. Louise noticed.

'I hope that my novel will help others deal with their own loss. So many kind people have helped me. I would like to return the favour.' And Louise smiled gently.

James nodded again and said, 'I believe that is what great writers do; they help their readers understand things and heal.'

Louise and James then talked about James' time in the Life Guards as a young officer. Louise enjoyed hearing about the life of a young subaltern protecting the sovereign. Also, the information James provided could be used in a future novel.

Gemma was happy to talk with Henry. Gemma truly loved little blond Henry. He was sweet and polite. He was also shy. Gemma was able to bring him out of his shell easily. Henry spent the entire evening talking about dragons and knights like St George.

Lucy was happy to talk with Poppy and her grandparents about the coming cricket match and the fairies and sprites that lived in the castle ruins. Poppy told her what hobgoblins (usually) looked like. Lucy listened intensely and questioned Poppy and her grandparents about the frequency of their appearance in the area.

Dinner was a rather long affair that evening. Everyone was happy to relax, ensconced in the baronial manor, safe from the dangerous world that existed just beyond the horizon.

Edward and the housemaids were busy in the large kitchen. The girls would bring in empty white plates and sterling silver trays and white bone china bowls and place them on one of the large wooden tables.

Edward was carefully preparing the dessert. Tonight, at Poppy's request, raspberry ice cream and chocolate cake. Why? Because that's what the fairies liked the most.

Gemma—England—Icarus

LONDON

Mars leaned forward at his desk and looked at the architectural drawings in front of him. The large blueprints were marked in yellow highlighter and black ink. Yes, the renovations were going well. The renovated factory would soon be ready to show to perspective clients; some of who had already expressed a willingness to sign leases before the renovations had even been completed.

Mars took off his black-framed eyeglasses and placed them on the desk. He looked out the large window of his office in North London. It was a rare sunny day in London. It was also rather hot. The air conditioning, installed a month earlier, cooled the office. Mars liked the room to be kept very cool, almost cold.

Mars stood up and walked to the window. The real estate development company was headquartered in a former metal works. This red brick building had once had a forge and had manufactured, among other things, bronze bells, iron railings, and ornate metal gates. The company, family owned for over 151 years, had gone bankrupt in the late 1990s. Now, with the exception of the large bronze double doors and the ornate bronze lamps which hung from either side of the entrance, there was nothing else to remind people of the buildings former purpose. The bronze had been heavily patinaed by air pollution. The patina effect was rather interesting. The bronze seemed ancient, like the entrance to the lost civilization of Atlantis.

Mars' life had changed beyond recognition in the last three years. The heady days as a financial titan seemed like the memories of a stranger, not his own. Mars had lost everything. Those three days of miscalculation and disaster had ruined his life. Now he was divorced, childless, and alone. His parents and only sibling, a brother, had all passed away. The family pile had been lost to his brother's massive debts. He had inherited a noble title: He was now the 13th Baron. But nothing else.

How, at 47, would Mars rebuild his life? Mars sighed.

Mars was luckier than most. An Oxford classmate had given him a job at his real estate development company in London. He was paid a good wage. It allowed Mars to live a middle-class life. Well, the life middle-class people lived in London.

He lived in a tiny flat in North London with barely enough room for his bed and a small desk that he had purchased online and assembled himself. He hung his clothes in the closet that took up half of one wall. All of his suits, shirts, and shoes were of the highest quality, remnants of his former life. He had also managed to keep his silver Omega watch. A small victory, he supposed.

Mars walked across the hardwood floor of the office and opened the door to the small white tiled private bathroom. He turned on the light and looked into the mirror which was over the small white porcelain sink. There he stood. He was wearing a white cotton dress shirt, a blue and red striped tartan neck tie, and dark grey trousers. He was relatively slender. His brown hair, cut like a City banker's, almost sparkled with the odd silver and grey hair. He was clean shaven. Did he look old? Mars studied his appearance carefully, looking for wrinkles and any other telltale signs of age. Mars couldn't decide. He didn't feel old.

Mars had never been handsome. He knew that. But he had also never been considered ugly either. Mars had always been rather plain. It was his posh mannerisms and the way he spoke that had attracted people. That he was a member of the nobility had also, undoubtedly, added to whatever attraction he held for women. Well, at least when he was younger.

Why had Mars married *that woman?* Why had he not listened to his inner voice warning him? She was beautiful. Mars still remembered the first time he had caught sight of her when she entered the club's main dining room in Mayfair. It had been as if a bolt from the Heavens had struck him. He stared; what else could he do? Such a woman would never be his. She was way out of his league. But, as fate would have it, they were seated at the same table. Mars had surprised himself by striking up a conversation with her. What did they talk about? Oh, yes. Horses. Mars had been stunned when she agreed to go on a foxhunt with him in the Cotswolds. Now Mars wished she hadn't. The brief spell of happiness his ex-wife had given him had been just that: brief.

POLLY
There had been another girl. A girl he had met at Oxford and dated for a year: Polly. But Polly would never do. Polly was a commoner. Not just a commoner, but a very common one.

Polly, the daughter of a bricklayer father and a mother who worked part-time as a secretary at a paint factory, had earned a scholarship to Oxford University. She was studying history, but had a talent for painting. She had wanted to attend an art school, but her parents insisted she attend Oxford. She was, after all, the first member of her family to even attend a university.

Polly was slender and had light brown hair. Her teeth were a little crooked. Mars' arrogant and boorish older brother, also studying at Oxford, had given Polly the cruel nickname of 'Tory Teeth'. He had said that at least she looked like 'one of us, *even if she wasn't'.*

Mars hated hearing his older brother make fun of Polly behind her back. At

187

least, thought Mars, he wasn't openly rude to Polly. He generally avoided being around her. The future 12th Baron thought Mars was just embarrassing himself and the family dating a girl *like that.*

'Please warn me when Polly is going to meet you, Mars, so that I can depart before "Tory Teeth" arrives,' his brother had once said to him.

Polly was cute, not beautiful, but definitely attractive. She was almost the same height as Mars. She dressed well, and was well-spoken. She wasn't posh, but she could certainly **pass** as someone of a **much** higher social class than she actually was.

OXFORD UNIVERSITY
Autumn 1993

Polly made her way down the ancient alleyway quickly. She was running late. She had to meet Mars and his father for dinner. It was cold. As she emerged from the alley and passed through a medieval arch; she faced a burst of red, gold and yellow colors from the changing leaves of the tall trees that lined the street. She stopped and took in the scenery. It was beautiful. Not even the grey, overcast sky could dampen it.

Polly, wearing a long pleated beige wool skirt, white blouse, and a blue blazer, looked at her small inexpensive wristwatch. If she hurried, she still might make it on time.

Oxford was beautiful and so was her life. She was in love. Mars was so kind and handsome. Yes, handsome. At least Polly thought so. A couple of Polly's friends had thought Mars rather bland looking. Love has a way of making one attractive, even beautiful.

Mars had told Polly that she was beautiful on so many occasions the she had started to believe she was. It had filled her with confidence. Polly now walked in a different way; her demeanor had changed considerably. She was now mimicking the way the smart set that passed by her in the cloisters of Oxford University walked, dressed, and even talked. And she had decided not to cut her hair, but let it continue to grow out. Mars liked long hair. Polly tied it back with a blue ribbon. Polly wasn't happy with her teeth, but

Mars had assured her that he liked her smile. It made her even cuter. Mars had told her that, and he had meant it.

Polly, the bricklayer's daughter, was about to marry into the nobility. She could barely believe it. But, why not believe it? Polly was intelligent and accomplished. She was a first rate student. She had a brilliant future ahead of her. Of course, Mars wanted children; so did she. She wanted to have a little girl. Polly knew she would be a good mother. And she was sure that Mars would be a kind and devoted father and husband. Polly was lucky. Polly had been blessed.

At her dreary and rundown state school in Cardiff, she had never dreamed that her life would be like this. **Like this.** No, she had never dreamed that she would attend Oxford and meet such a good-hearted, intelligent, handsome young man. That Mars was the son of a baron really meant nothing to Polly. She would have loved Mars even if his father had dug ditches. Polly's love for Mars was pure, true. True love, that rarest of love. And Mars had found it with Polly.

Polly turned and was walking down the narrow street, leaves crunching underfoot, when she spotted Mars standing in front of the post office. Mars was skinny and at only 5'7", a bit shorter than her roommate would have looked for in a potential husband, but Polly thought Mars was the *perfect* height. Mars was wearing a pair of grey wool trousers, white dress shirt, and a navy blue duffle coat. He looked nice. Polly smiled. She crossed the street and approached him.

'Mars. Sorry I'm late. Have you been waiting long? I'm sorry,' said Polly apologetically. 'Well, let's hurry to the restaurant, shall we? I don't want to make a bad first impression on your father,' said Polly, and she smiled with her crooked white teeth.

Mars nodded, but he didn't smile. He took Polly by her soft hand and walked with her down the street. They reached the bottom of a set of stone steps, turned, and started to walk up them.

It was cold and windy. The temperature seemed to be dropping as they made their way up the stairs. They were alone. Mars stopped. He let go of her hand and sighed heavily. Something was wrong.

'Polly. I'm sorry.'

'I'm the one who was late. I'm the one who should apologize, Mars.'

No. I mean. My father isn't going to have dinner with us tonight.'

'Well. That's alright,' smiled Polly. 'We can meet him for dinner another night.'

'No, Polly. You don't understand. My father will never meet you.'

Polly felt her feet freeze.

'Polly. I'm sorry. I am so sorry.'

Polly's felt her heart breaking. She knew. It wasn't necessary for Mars to say anything else. But, since Mars was being a coward and breaking her heart, she wanted to hear him say it. She looked at him. Mars looked away. He couldn't even look her in the eye? The Honourable Mars Rupert Arthur Noel wasn't even brave enough to do that?

Mars stared at the grey stone wall for a few moments. He said nothing.

'Mars. I'm not going to make this easy for you,' said Polly quietly, her voice breaking with emotion. 'If you are going to drop me, then I want you to tell me why. I want you to tell me.'

Mars felt like he would shatter. He wished that he would. Why couldn't he be strong? Why couldn't he defy his cold and distant father and arrogant older brother? This was his life, not theirs. He had found someone that truly loved him, and now he was going to break up with her? He was going to break the heart of the sweetest girl he had ever known? Mars. You are truly a coward.

'Polly. We are different. We are from two different worlds. It would never work. I'm sorry. This is for your own good. It is.'

Polly said nothing. Tears welled up in her eyes, and then tears started to roll down her face. Mars finally looked up into Polly's eyes and when he saw that she was crying, he started to cry too.

'I'm sorry, Polly. I'm sorry.'

Polly's world had suddenly stopped. Her happiness had been snatched away from her in an instant, and by the last person in the world she ever thought would do it. The two of them stood half way up the stone steps in the cold afternoon air and cried quietly. After a couple of minutes Mars started to walk up the stairs alone. He turned his back on Polly and walked up the stairs. He stopped, turned around and spoke. 'Polly, I know this seems cruel, but one day you will realize that this is for the best. For both of us.' Mars then turned back around and walked up the stone steps until he reached the street above. He turned left and kept walking. Mars was gone.

Polly had watched through tears as Mars had walked away. She had wanted to run up the stairs, grab him, tell Mars she truly loved him, and not to leave her. Instead, she had said nothing. Now, alone on the stairs, Polly started to speak, in barely a whisper. 'Please come back. Please, Mars. Please come back. I love you. I need you. Without you my heart will break.'

After waiting for an hour in the cold for Mars to return, Polly finally turned and made her way down the stairs, all alone.

Polly never came to the realization that Mars was right. She could never accept that their marriage would never have worked. They might not have ever been accepted by Mars' family, but Polly could have lived with that. Mars couldn't.

Polly graduated with honours a year later. Mars never heard from her again. But, then again, why would she bother Mars, the God of War? Mars had never searched for information on Polly. Had she married? Did she have children? Was Polly happy? Mars was afraid to find out. What if Polly had ended up alone and broken? What if she had died alone? It would have been too much for him to bear. Mars, you coward.

Mars became a highly successful hedge fund manager in Asia. Polly had probably figured that Mars had forgotten all about her. The miserable truth was that Mars had put Polly largely out of his mind while in Hong Kong. He was too busy being rich and successful to think much about her. It wasn't until his traumatic downfall many years later that Mars had realized what he had lost. No, not lost. What he had thrown away.

Gemma—England—A Touch of Art Deco

THE LAKE DISTRICT
The renovations to the former classroom building were almost complete. Almost. The building now consisted of a large drawing room with a vaulted ceiling, two small, white-walled bedrooms, a long and narrow tiled kitchen, and a large white tiled bathroom.

The drawing room had once been the main classroom. The furniture manufacturer had taken out the chalkboards decades ago and turned the room into a workshop. When his daughter had vacated the premises, all she had left behind was a heavily worn hardwood floor and four walls. Gemma had the floors redone by local workmen and the walls repaired and repainted white. She had also had bookcases installed along with new sash windows. She was happy with the results. The polished hardwood floor gleamed and the white walls reflected and re-directed the natural light which flooded into the cavernous room. Only one detail remained: What to do with the ceiling?

ART DECO
Gemma had acquired a love for Art Deco from Poppy. Poppy had acquired a love for it from Jane. Gemma had decided that her new house wouldn't be a home until it had a few touches of Art Deco. The Egyptian Art Deco ceiling in Jane's former room—now Poppy's—had inspired Gemma to create an Art Deco ceiling of her own. Gemma spent most of her free time pouring over books on interior design. She decided that a plaster ceiling and surrounding crown mold would work best.

Poppy contacted the highly skilled plasterer that the family had awarded several projects to and asked him to meet with Gemma at the family pile. The plasterer sat with Gemma and Poppy in the drawing room of Poppy's country house.

Gemma, armed with dozens of photos on her smartphone and a tablet computer, explained to the man what she wanted. And what did Gemma want? A white Egyptian Art Deco ceiling filled with hieroglyphics and a crown molding made up of ancient hieroglyphics and ancient Greek letters. Yes, really. As Gemma explained it, she liked Poppy's ceiling. She had found comfort in it and wanted to replicate it in her drawing room. Could the plasterer recreate the lighting effect? Having light bulbs placed behind the plaster hieroglyphics that would cast beautiful shadows?

Gemma had selected a set of ancient Ptolemaic Egyptian glyphs and ancient Greek letters and asked that they be used. The highly skilled plasterer agreed. The price: rather steep. But Gemma had readily agreed. It would be worth it to have such a soothing detail as a Ptolemaic ceiling like this. The ceiling installed in Gemma's house would not be Ancient Egyptian, it would be Ptolemaic.

Gemma had another reason for insisting on having a ceiling like this: It would remind her of the play that she had acted in with Enoch. Yes, all things Ptolemaic now reminded her of him.

Yes, of course. It could be done. The plasterer would start on the project immediately. Work on the ceiling would commence in a couple of days. The ceiling would be completed in less than a fortnight. Gemma was thrilled.

POPPY'S ART DECO CHAMBER

Poppy sat at the highly polished burl wood table near the window. She was holding a soft pale blue cloth and her sterling silver Egyptian Art Deco bracelet in her hands; an open jar of metal polish was on the table next to her. Poppy carefully polished the tarnished metal bracelet.

After fifteen minutes, the bracelet reflected the sunlight beautifully. The bracelet was stunning to behold. The ancient Egyptian hieroglyphics engraved in the long silver pieces which made up the bracelet almost glowed in the bright natural summer sunlight.

Poppy slipped the bracelet onto her wrist and gazed at it. Yes, it was beautiful. Eugen had given it to Jane because he had truly loved her. This bracelet had meant the world to Jane. She had worn it almost every day since Eugen had given it to her in 1925. Poppy always felt a tinge of sadness whenever she thought of Jane. Happiness had eluded Jane.

Happiness had almost eluded Poppy, but fate had given her Brian. Poppy loved Brian more than words could describe. Poppy, at forty-one, was married and pregnant. She was finally a wife and would soon be a mother. Jane had wanted something as simple as that and yet it had been cruelly denied her. Jane had died of a broken heart. Fate, kismet, had spared Poppy that. Why had Poppy been saved? Poppy didn't have an answer. Poppy could only feel gratitude. Deus vult.

THE DINING ROOM

Poppy, Gemma, Freya, and Louise sat at one end of the dining room table. A white table cloth covered the entire length of it, but only one end had been set for lunch that day. The rest of the family had travelled in the Range Rover and the silver Bristol 411 to explore the Lake District.

The large windows had all been closed and the room was filled with cool air provided by the air conditioning system. Natural light filled the room and the silverware on the table glinted in the sunlight.

Poppy sat at the head of the table. She was wearing a white cotton top with an open collar and long sleeves. She was also wearing a knee-length, bluish-grey, pleated skirt, and a pair of soft white slippers. Poppy was also wearing the sterling silver bracelet. Poppy smiled. She happily showed everyone at the table her Egyptian Art Deco bracelet. Everyone was deeply impressed.

'The bracelet is unlike anything I have ever seen,' said Freya. 'And I have seen a lot of jewelry.'

Freya was clad in faded blue jeans that afternoon. So were Gemma and Louise. Freya was slowly coming to terms with the idea of attending a different university than Louise. It wasn't easy for either girl. The future held uncertainty for them both. Would they drift apart? No. That was unthinkable.

Freya leaned back in her chair and looked out the large sash windows on the other side of the dining room. It was a warm, sunny day. Freya then gazed at Louise who was sitting opposite of her next to Poppy. Louise smiled as she listened to Poppy talk about the silver bracelet. Yes, they were both about to enter adulthood—away from each other. Freya could only feel immense sadness at that moment. She sank down into the chair.

Gemma, seated next to Freya, could sense something was wrong. And Gemma could guess what. Gemma reached over and held Freya's hand. Freya looked in her direction and Gemma smiled slightly.

'Lunch today will be something rather nutritious,' said Poppy to the girls. She smiled. 'Do you like spaghetti? Edward prepared spaghetti with garlic, lemon, and chili especially for us. It's fantastic,' said Poppy happily.

'I haven't had spaghetti since All Saints,' said Louise.

'The food at All Saints was always good,' sighed Freya.

'Yes, I do miss the meals at All Saints,' said Gemma.

'Then you will love lunch,' replied Poppy to the assembled All Saints alumni, and she smiled.

Gemma—England—Summer Holiday

THE COTSWOLDS
July 2019
The glossy blue Bristol 603S automobile glided off the motorway and onto the narrow country road. The car decelerated as it made its way down the tree lined approach to the village.

195

The village, where Octavia had grown up, though much like an Edwardian postcard, appeared to be quite tiny, perhaps a couple dozen structures surrounded by farm land, large leafy trees, and lush green fields ablaze with Cotswold lavenders and other wild flowers.

Octavia, in faded blue jeans and a navy blue, white edged v-neck, cotton top, was excited. Külli wasn't. She was nervous. Let's see: Octavia was 29; Külli was 41. And they were a couple. Octavia had assured Külli that her parents and grandparents were kind and accepting.

Octavia's paternal grandparents had come to terms with her sexuality much faster than her father. Both her father and grandfather were retired army majors.

Her grandfather, almost 94, had been born in India during The Raj, had fought against the Japanese in Burma during the Second World War, and witnessed the Independence and violent breakup of India. He had also fought in the Malayan Emergency. Her grandfather had experienced the collapse of the British Empire and the the loss of his family's tea plantation. The family had also once had a grand house in Calcutta (now known as Kolkata). His aged body had been left heavily scarred by hard fighting during the retreat from England's colonial outposts, and now the slender old man walked with a pronounced limp and the aid of a cane.

Her white-haired grandmother, the daughter of a village pharmacist, had always been supportive and kind to Octavia. It was her grandmother that a twenty-year old Octavia had confided to during a Christmas holiday. Her grandmother's only response had been to smile and embrace her. She told Octavia that it was no matter to her and that she loved her no matter what.

Octavia's mother had been a bit of harder sell than even her father. The news that her only child was gay had left her deeply disappointed. She had wanted grandchildren and a son-in-law, a regular family. Now, with Octavia's professed homosexuality, that dream had been shattered. It wasn't that Octavia was gay that really bothered her, it was that she was an only child. If there had been a sibling then the family line could have continued.

Octavia had broken the line...

Her father, formerly of the Gurkhas, had been left speechless by the news. He had never suspected it. Octavia, beautiful, poised, intelligent, and well-educated, had always been the object of considerable male attention, and had even had a boyfriend (of sorts) at Oxford. And now this?

While Octavia's mother sobbed quietly in the drawing room, her father had gone for a walk that cold afternoon with his elderly father. They discussed it and after an hour returned home. Octavia, said her father, was still his beloved daughter. He wanted her in his life, and her orientation would not change that. Her grandfather was surprisingly accepting. He had only commented that he hoped she find someone good-hearted and intelligent to spend her life with.

Christmas was a bit strained that year, but before the holiday was over, Octavia's mother had come to terms with it.

Now, at 29, the family was looking forward to meeting Külli. The only issue they really had was the age difference.

THE OLD RECTORY

The family home was the former village rectory. The family had purchased it for a song in the early 1980s. The building hadn't been lived in since the early 1970s. The structure had been relegated to a storage facility. The small building had been filled with stacks of cardboard boxes.

The building was in fairly good condition when they bought it. A couple dozen buckets of white paint and plumbing upgrades were all that had been required to make it liveable. The one-storey structure had provided Octavia with a happy and safe environment to grow up in.

The house was surrounded by trees that had been planted in the 1890s, when they structure was built. Now tall and strong, the long branches shaded the house from the summer heat and the sun's intense glare. Behind the rectory was a green house of red brick, iron, and glass. Octavia's entire family enjoyed gardening, especially growing exotic fruit from India and Malaysia.

Octavia had attended the village school until she was sent away to an all-girl boarding school in Surrey. She played field hockey at school in Surrey and was happy to play it with the local children on the village green while on summer holiday. All of her childhood friends had remained friends. Octavia appreciated every one of them. Octavia, beautiful, intelligent, and good-hearted had grown up surrounded by kind and loyal friends. Octavia had had something that many children could only dream of: a happy childhood.

THE VISIT
The glossy blue car motored slowly through the small village, past the tree-lined village square with its statue of King Edward VII, and the small grey stone Anglican church. There were several automobiles parked in the village, most of them small hatchbacks. There were also a couple of Range Rovers from the 1980s. A few residents were about, many of them quite young.

'The village grandchildren flood in every summer and winter break,' said Octavia happily. 'The village green hosts cricket matches constantly these days. It's *terribly* fun, *rather*,' said Octavia in her posh intonation. And Octavia smiled.

Külli slowed and then stopped the car of front of the rectory. Yes, just the like photos she had been shown. Külli glanced at Octavia.

'Don't worry. My parents know all about you. They want to meet you. Everything will be alright.'

Külli smiled. 'I'm looking forward to meeting them too.'

Gemma—England—A Private Bank

THE CITY
The tall narrow window allowed a bright shaft of sunlight to illuminate the small office on the top floor of a Portland stone building in the City. The hardwood floors gleamed in the natural light. The polished panelled wooden walls absorbed most of the sunlight which reflected off of the polished, if a bit worn, hardwood floor of the office. There were heavy dark

blue curtains tied back with heavy gold tassels shrouding the lone window. The office was not a modern one; that was obvious to anyone entering it. The effect was intentional.

The private bank, founded in 1877, was yet another curious remnant of the British Empire. The bank had been founded the same year Queen Victoria had been crowned Empress of India. The founder, a former officer in the Bengal Native Infantry (when it was still part of the East India Company) and the son of a former high ranking official of the once wealthy and powerful East India Company, had founded the bank to preserve the wealth of the empire. Or, maybe it would be more accurate to say, the wealth of individual British colonists.

Now the British Empire was no more, but this stone building in the City was still here. Its primary purpose had not really changed in the decades since the Raj had come to its ignominious end in 1947. That purpose? The preservation of wealth. Well, that is, the wealth of its clients. The bank was strictly above board. That is, it obeyed all the laws and regulations of the City. Such as they were.

The bank's clients were as rich as they were powerful. They were also secretive. They were not shadowy figures, but were in fact quite well known in many circles. The true extent of their wealth was not. Only parvenus bragged of their true wealth. The truly wealthy knew better than to draw too much attention to themselves.

The bank's clients were not gangsters or oligarchs with coffers overflowing with stolen gold from The East. No, these were men of ability and means. These were men who had made money through (relatively) legitimate means. Their goal was to maintain as much of their wealth as possible. That is, to shield as much of it as possible from taxation. After all, what was the point of making money if it would all end up being taken away? No, the means had to be found to invest it in ways that not only avoided its expropriation by Her Majesty's Revenue and Customs but also making even more money with it.

Brian was good with money. Brian had always been good with numbers. He also had a keen understanding of banking regulations and laws. Brian knew how to make and protect money legally. He had never broken any banking regulations or laws. Brian was an honest man. And, to the best of his knowledge, this private bank in the heart of London was the domain of honest men. Brian felt that it was a citizen's duty to pay tax and support his country's public services. Not everyone in the City felt that way. Brian knew who many of these people were, and he avoided them. Brian was loyal to Queen and Country.

Brian had been employed by the bank for almost two decades. Every client he had been given had made large returns on their money. Brian had connections all over the world. He knew where to invest money, and most importantly, he knew when to divest it.

Brian now held a senior position in the bank. He controlled the portfolios of dozens of fantastically wealthy clients. They rarely, if ever, visited the bank. Brian would go to them.

Brian's life in the City had been a good one. He had an interesting life. He did not find the pressures of financial crisis harsh, but exciting and opportunistic. The last two decades had been tumultuous. Brian, ever cool under fire, had weathered the financial storms which had destroyed so many around him. Brian's abilities were recognized, greatly appreciated, and richly rewarded. Brian had long been a success in the City. Now, with his wife Poppy pregnant, Brian felt his life was almost complete.

The City was a veritable rogues gallery. Some good, some bad, and many somewhere in between had made huge fortunes in it. Some of them were men and women of great ability, and some were just shameless thieves. Some of the denizens of the City were unknown quantities, which made them far more dangerous than any of the notorious financiers which prowled the cobblestone streets of the financial district. To Brian and Poppy, the notorious ones were nothing but vicious cut throats and traitors. They were just looting England. Brian and Poppy both despised these people.

One of the biggest unknown quantities of the City was Enoch Tara. Little was known about him. Brian had been thunderstruck to meet him, and with Gemma, of all people. Enoch didn't seem to be bad at all. He seemed to be rather kind and good-hearted. He seemed to be…

Brian had been too in awe of him to speak with him at Gemma's flat. He had spent the entire evening stealing glances at him and listening to Violet talk with him as if he were the local milkman. Really, Vava wasn't easily impressed. She would have been with Enoch, if she had been aware of his true reputation.

The mysterious Mr Tara had remained as mysterious as ever.

Gemma never spoke about any of Enoch's financial dealings. She seemed completely unaware and uninterested. Gemma wasn't the kind of person to pursue anyone for wealth. While Gemma was reluctant to speak to Brian about their relationship, Poppy had told him that it was Enoch that was pursuing Gemma and not the other way around.

Gemma, ironically, was quite uninformed on the sometimes strange and pernicious going-ons of the City and the world of finance. **Irony** was becoming more and more common place in the world of global finance and the City. That was hardly a good sign.

Brian tapped out a quick email on his encrypted laptop and then sent it off to a client in Hong Kong. He opened a file and scanned through it. The truly secret documents were never downloaded into a computer at the bank, only paper copies were made and access to them was carefully controlled. They were kept in a separate vault which had been constructed strictly to hold financial documents.

Brian noticed something. He stopped and then turned back to the previous page. What was this? Something was amiss. Brian laid the file down on his desk and started to lay the documents out one by one of the desk top. **There was a problem.**

As the City sweltered in the heat of the summer, a huge financial storm was brewing. Few had any notion of it. Brian certainly didn't. At the epicenter of that storm: Carter Holland.

6 THE GOLEMS OF ALBION

Gemma—England—Yellow Umbrellas

THE FORMER CROWN COLONY
The conference had been planned late last year. Alexa still had large investments in Asia, it was only natural she attend this one. Of course, in 2018, few would predict the tumult that was approaching, at least those outside of Hong Kong.

THE HOTEL
July 2019
Gemma, wearing light weight cotton khaki trousers, a white cotton blouse with a large collar, and tortoise shell sunglasses, walked into the hotel lobby. She checked in at the front desk, received her room key, and made her way to the elevator.

THE REFURBISHMENT
The relatively small hotel, built in the 1920s, had been recently refurbished and restored to its *former colonial glory*. Yes, the current owner, a native Hong Kong Chinese, had decided not to modernize the hotel. He had purchased the shabby and faded hotel with the intention of turning it into apartments, but after touring it one day, he had a change of heart.

Mr George Chang OBE, a graduate of Balliol College, Oxford, decided that having been a crown colony of England had not been such a bad thing after all. The elderly millionaire and his Surrey born blonde English wife both decided restoring the hotel was a fantastic idea.

He went into the backrooms of the hotel and found all of the original architectural plans as well as numerous brochures and even a few magazine articles with an extensive number of both black and white and color photos which he could use in his restoration efforts. His daughter, an interior designer and an enthusiastic supporter of his ideas, agreed to return to Hong Kong from London to supervise the restoration of the interior.

After more than a year and millions in Hong Kong dollars, the hotel was reopened with great fanfare. The hotel was an immediate success. The Jubilee Bar and Restaurant were also wildly popular and barely a week passed when the private room, its large windows overlooking the harbour, were not booked for posh events.

There was a problem, however. The decor seemed a little too celebratory of British Rule. The former British Hong Kong flags, hung decoratively over the bar, were also noted by a bespectacled government official. The Hong Kong government sent the official who politely asked Mr Change OBE to tone it down. He refused—politely.

THE CONFERENCE
Alexa had selected the smaller hotel, which was farther away from the International Finance Centre than the hotel she usually stayed at, in order to avoid the large protests which were now surging through the city.

The IFC, while still the site of the conference, was not easy to get to because of the mass protests which now engulfed the center of Hong Kong. Alexa, Jemima, Tarquin, and Gemma would have to hoof it and try to navigate through the umbrella wielding protesters, who, fortunately, who were usually quite polite and helpful to visiting foreigners.

TEAR GAS AND UMBRELLAS
It was hot that day, and Gemma, wearing a surgical mask, was lucky enough to make it through the protesters, tear gas, and riot police that encircled the IFC.

She entered the cavernous marble floored atrium of the modern skyscraper and promptly made her way to the restroom, where she was able to wash her face.

The sting of tear gas still filled her eyes as she made her way up the steps to the conference, dressed in a light grey pencil skirt, white blouse, and black high heels. Carrying her laptop in a black leather shoulder bag, she met Alexa and the others at the entrance of the conference room.

Alright. We're ready.

The presentation had gone extremely well. Alexa, as smooth and polished as ever, had impressed everyone. Investors lined up.

After the conference, they all had dinner in one of the IFC's restaurants. Gemma, tired, but at the same time, exhilarated to be in Hong Kong, excused herself from the table. She wanted to walk back to the hotel, exploring the city while she did so. Alexa warned her to avoid the protests as Gemma departed the restaurant.

Gemma left the IFC through a side entrance. She noticed a column of riot police in heavy gear and carrying large shields standing at the corner of a side street, their helmets and riot gear glinting in the illumination of the street lamps.

THE YELLOW UMBRELLA

She walked past the platoon of riot police and slowly made her way up a long set of cement steps to a paved street lined with closed shops.

Near one of the street lamps, she noticed a discarded yellow umbrella. She approached it and picked it up. It was slightly bent and broken. She examined it under the light.

'Miss. You should be careful. If the police spot you holding that, you could be arrested,' said a young voice in the darkness. Gemma looked around, but saw no one. Still holding the broken yellow umbrella, Gemma walked forward and looked in the direction she believed the voice had come from.

'Please. Put it down and go,' said the young voice again.

'Who are you? Where are you?' asked a perplexed and slightly nervous Gemma.

'I'm close. Please listen to me. Drop the umbrella and go. I say this as a friend,' the young voice said from the darkness.

Gemma looked in the general direction of the young voice. It had no discernible accent. It was spoken in very clear English, the speaker's ethnic or national origin indeterminable.

Gemma peered carefully into the darkened alleyway. She could see a shape, a human outline. It was slender and about her height. She supposed it belonged to a young girl.

'Please; the police are coming; drop the umbrella and go,' said the young voice.

'Okay. Thank you,' said Gemma. She dropped the umbrella and then started to walk in the opposite direction.

'Please, hurry. The police are almost here. Go,' said the young voice.

Gemma stopped, turned, and then peering back into the darkness said, 'Good luck, my friend.'

'Thank you,' replied the young voice.

Gemma then moved away quickly from the broken yellow umbrella and the young voice.

The police patrol, a collection of flashlights and radio static, arrived just two minutes later. They found the broken umbrella, collected it, and then continued their patrol after finding no one nearby.

Gemma—England—The Hyena

THE CITY

There are several attributes a man—yes, a man—must possess to be successful in finance. The most important is greed. What drives a man to make money varies drastically. Money, it must be remembered, is a means to an end. The way one makes money is really unimportant. What matters is that you make enough money to attain whatever you want. And one must do whatever is necessary to make money if one is to attain what they *really want*.

Carter Ajax Holland was one of the most successful financiers in the world. And, he was virtually unknown. That was by design.

Carter's father had been a career army officer in the British armed forces. He had not been a warrior. He attended a mediocre third tier boarding school outside of London, a third tier university in London, and finally, the Royal Military Academy at Sandhurst—but just barely. His time at Sandhurst had been a disappointment. Actually, every school Carter's father had ever attended had been disappointing. His father had wanted so much to be good at something, anything, but all of is endeavours had ended in failure.

He had wanted to be an infantry officer; instead he ended up in logistics. He was privately miserable. He worked hard at his job, only to be overlooked for decorations and promotions. It was only longevity that allowed him to retire as a major. His nearly ribbonless uniform now hung in the closet of Carter's house in London. He saw it every morning when he opened the door to the walk in closet lined with Savile Row suits. It reminded him of what he didn't want to be: a failure.

It was forward or death. Like a brave hoplite, Carter would press the attack until his enemies were vanquished. Carter rarely took prisoners. They would always end up rising up against him later, if he allowed them to escape. No, it was best to utterly destroy his rivals financially and professionally in the City.

Carter could have said it was 'nothing personal', but he never did, because

207

in fact, it always was. It was not so much that Carter was trying to avenge his father; a man's mistakes are his own. But a rival, no matter how unthreatening or indifferent they appeared, **must be destroyed** if Carter were to protect his wealth and status.

A powerful rival was like a fleet-in-being. The mere existence of such a person prevented freedom of movement. It could dissuade him from attack. Carter was doing everything he could to avoid becoming a failure just like his father had been. Well, at least in business—which is all that mattered to Carter.

Carter was divorced. His wife had been a blonde South African supermodel—but of course she had been a supermodel—Carter would never have accepted anything less. A supermodel wife was but another symbol of success.

She had given him twins: a son and a daughter; neither of whom had spoken to him in over a decade. Had Carter ever loved his ex-wife? No. Easily no. Had he ever loved his children? Hard to say, really. They had never loved him. Why should they have? He had barely been around them as children, and when he was, he treated them all as nothing but a terrible nuisance, which they had been. Did he miss them? Yes. Why? Because almost everyone in his circle had glitteringly successful children, and his refused to even speak to him.

The twins spoke of him as if he were the reincarnation of the 9th Marquess of Queensberry. Hardly. He had never been violent towards either of them. He had simple ignored them, and occasionally ~~scolded them~~ shouted at them.

His long suffering wife had finally called it quits ten years into the marriage, not because of Carter's constant philandering and psychological abuse of her, but for the sake of ~~their~~ her children.

Carter had paid for the twins to attend posh boarding schools, the kind he wished he had been able to attend, and they were now attending universities at his expense. But did they appreciate their father? No.

Truth be told, it was part of the miserly divorce settlement. She got very little out of the divorce, the only demand she had was that Carter pay for their children's education. Carter had resisted even that much, but the attention the case was starting to get from the press had forced him to quickly sign the agreement.

His wife had been left with virtually nothing. She returned to modeling and even had supporting roles on television and in films, that had kept the small family afloat financially. The children would never forgive him. Not for what he had done to them, but for what he had inflicted on their mother.

Carter had not attended a glorious English public school like Eton or Harrow. He had attended local state schools with lower middle class and working class children. Carter's father could not afford to send him to an English public school, so Carter had been condemned to a substandard and dilapidated school filled with substandard teachers, yellowed and torn textbooks, and hollow shells called students.

Carter hated it. He knew he deserved better. Academically he excelled. He was a hardworking student. Well, perhaps not that hardworking. He was naturally intelligent and he easily passed his exams with little more than a cursory review of what few notes he had taken in class. He rarely ever missed class. He also rarely took notes. He had a cast iron memory. His memory was his strength. And with this ability came another equally valuable and necessary ability: **analysis**.

Carter did not like team sports. He joined the debate club and the fencing team. He was good at fighting. He wasn't physically tough, but he was highly skilled at avoiding physical altercations, unless they were on his own terms. He carried a pocket knife. He had used it to slash more than one boy who thought the slim, smartly dressed, and flaxen haired, school boy an easy target. He preferred to slash his attackers across the eyes, to blind them. Yes, that was best. He didn't really want to kill his attackers. He wanted them to suffer. Maiming them was the best way to do it. Carter's young face was the last they would ever see. He had never been arrested. The police had never been able to locate him. Eventually a strangely intimidating aura radiated from him, and young school boy from the local rundown state school was left alone.

Oh, I almost forgot to mention: Carter was extremely attractive. He possessed the epicene beauty and posh mannerisms of a public school boy. Only he wasn't one. And it bothered him a lot.

Carter was determined to better himself. His middle class background wasn't a bad one. His father was a retired army major. When anyone asked him what (light infantry, Para, or Guards) regiment his father had (undoubtedly) served in, the smartly dressed, attractive, and posh Carter would reply nonchalantly, 'What does it matter?' And often yawn. Yes. Keeping secrets was necessary for Carter.

His intellect had allowed him to attend the London School of Economics (LSE). Carter was proud to be admitted into LSE, but he found his instructors dull and uninspiring. He attended all of his classes, and occasionally took notes—after all, he would have to pass *their* exams. But Carter knew that his education and thus his future, **were in his own hands**. It was in the cavernous library of LSE that Carter Ajax Holland had educated himself.

He graduated and ignored his father's recommendation to pursue a military career. What was the point of all that? England was now in steep decline. The British Empire was, save for a few tiny enclaves, gone. There was no empire to attain glory serving. No way to earn a peerage in Her Majesty's Armed Forces now. The way to recognition now lay with the new adventurers of the former empire: The financiers of the City. Or were they more like pirates? Pirates. Yes. Pirates.

No, Carter had never failed at anything, except his private life. But, what did that really matter? Carter often wondered why he had even bothered to marry and have children. They were just an unnecessary expense and took away from his other pursuits—his other pursuits being a myriad of sins.

He stood 5'10" and was slim. Carter felt that the overweight were spiritually lazy and he (privately) refused to hire them. He didn't like any male who grew facial hair or allowed their hair to grow long, that, to Carter, was a sign of vulgarity. And facial hair was unhygienic. Most of Carter's body was naturally hairless. He did, however, have a beautiful full head of glossy blond (but now greying) hair and a clear glowing complexion.

Carter exercised daily, even on the weekends. He rode horses, attended foxhunts, shooting parties, and gala events. Sometimes he even attended fashion shows.

Carter crackled with energy. He was extremely intelligent and highly cunning. He also exuded an air of violence. He was widely feared and disliked, even hated, in financial circles. Stories of Carter's violent outbursts were whispered of in London. Carter was good at intimidating people. He enjoyed it. He reveled in it. Yes, Carter was still willing to resort to physical violence when he felt the occasion called for it—which had never been necessary in the City. However, there were places beyond the glass and wood panelled walls of the conference rooms and offices of the City that were an entirely different matter.

Carter was not only rich, he was extremely rich. He had worked with clients from all over the world. While Westerners, especially Americans, generally grew to hate and distrust him, the warlords, oligarchs, gangsters, dictators, war criminals, and rogues of Africa, Latin America, the Middle East, Eastern Europe and Northern, Central and Southeast Asia, truly liked him. Carter was a man of real talent, true ability. Why the financiers of the City and Wall Street couldn't see that was a bit of a mystery to the creatures that prowled around Moscow, Belgrade, Harare, Lagos, Beijing, Jeddah, Tehran, Mexico City, Damascus, and other points farther east and south.

Carter knew that the oligarchs of the outer world and near abroad were a different breed all together. As much as they liked Carter, Carter despised them. He knew they weren't really beings of real talent or intellect. They were just thugs who had gotten lucky and cashed in. Carter didn't mind helping them launder their money, few financiers did. And besides, why should he care if these creatures were looting their own countries? They had no loyalty to anyone, despite their professed ~~patriotism~~ nationalism and love of country. But, come to think of it, Carter had no loyalty to his own country.

QUADRIGA INVESTMENTS

Carter's investment company **did not produce anything**, that is, no tangible products. It didn't own any factories, build automobiles or airplanes, own farm land or mines, or even have that many employees. It was a company that made money through 'financial instruments' such as derivatives, ETFs, and an array of other things that were usually beyond the average person's ability to even comprehend. But, Carter's company did make money. And it made a lot of it.

Quadriga investments was housed in a Grade II listed building in the City. It had once housed a colonial merchant bank. Carter had purchased it in the early 90s and promptly had it gutted. While the exterior of the Portland stone Edwardian building remained preserved (by law), the interiors were savagely modern. Carter hated the old. It represented **rot**. Past glories were just that: in the past. Modernity required a clean slate.

The interior of the three storey building was a collection of sterile, unadorned, white walls. The hardwood floors had been preserved, but the decorative plaster crown and ceiling moldings had been scraped away and replaced by smooth white surfaces.

The ornate hand carved wooden doors had all been discarded and replaced with doors covered in smooth burl wood laminate with chrome door handles. The swirling patterns in the burl were pleasing to the eye. Well, that's what Carter believed and what he believed is all that mattered. And burl wood laminate was cheap, not just cheaper than real burl wood doors, but dirt cheap. And it was easy to install and virtually maintenance free.

And Carter felt that the stark white interiors made him stand out in his dark suits when meeting with clients. The overall effect was quite intimidating, which is exactly the effect Carter liked to have on people, especially potential clients.

The furniture was another stroke of genius by Carter. All of it had been bespoke. It was all lightweight. The desks were simple aluminum structures consisting of a smooth desktop and four drawers. The chairs were simple chrome metal frames covered with black synthetic leather. The synthetic leather wasn't very expensive, and it was durable, lasted much longer than real leather, and required zero maintenance. Also, the chairs were antibacterial, somehow. Carter didn't really understand how, but he didn't care. They looked quite modern, and modernity is now.

The company letterhead was an ancient and armored warrior driving a horse driven quadriga; the image was stamped in silver surrounded by the words: Quadriga Investments. All of the company's business cards were also adorned with the same glittering image. Carter's enemies (and he had plenty) would tell each other that a more appropriate logo would have been a cut throat razor and a pair brass knuckles.

Carter had dozens of employees (officially) and a few others that were paid off the books.

THE HYENA

England was a rotting carcass. A once majestic and ferocious animal that had died, not killed in glorious battle, but had instead chosen to just lay down and die one day. It had been left to rot. This once mighty and proud creature had ruled an empire that stretched across the globe, and now it was nothing. How can any true man respect that?

Carter was a vulture (or a hyena) among a horde of vultures (or were they hyenas?) that was tearing off pieces of flesh from the rotting carcass once known as England. No, England was finished. **The colossus was dead.**

Carter had to make—**no take**—as much money as he could from the dying system, and then flee this sinking, rotting, ship. Oh, and he wouldn't be alone. There were *many* in the City who felt just the same.

Carter had homes—and women—in London, Hong Kong, Moscow, Belgrade, Mexico City, and New York.

He only drove German and Japanese cars, but only because the British couldn't be bothered anymore to build automobiles worth buying.

Carter, at fifty-one, was a financial deity. He was virtually unrivaled in the City. Few could match him. Very few.

One of the men who could: **Enoch Tara.**

Gemma—England—The Office

THE CITY

Enoch sifted through the documents on his desk carefully. So much work to do. Enoch didn't mind hard work; he enjoyed it. His true love was theatre, but the stage seemed a distant memory now. Enoch was now involved in finance. His life had taken an unexpected turn almost two decades ago, and now he found himself sitting at a desk in one of his offices in the City.

He had several offices across the globe, but this white walled office in a Grade II listed Edwardian bank with a Portland stone facade in the City was his favorite. Well, it was now. Why? Because Gemma worked in an office nearby. Enoch had never used the office which had been set aside for him when he had purchased the bank. But now, with Gemma a short distance away, Enoch had shifted a large part of his organization into it.

The staff of the small merchant bank had witnessed a veritable tsunami of workman, painters, electricians, and movers, all under the guidance of one of an interior decorator favoured by many financiers in the City. Well, that is the financiers who liked classic English interiors. Enoch, like Gemma, loved the traditional.

The white walls were repainted and the plaster moldings repaired, if repairs had been needed. The light fixtures were replaced, and a mostly red and blue Persian rug had been run down the center stairway in the main lobby of the bank. The office furniture, mostly pre-war, had been left alone.

Enoch's office was on the fourth (and top) floor. Its large sash windows looked out on the financial district. The Gherkin could be clearly seen just a few blocks away. Gemma worked on the 12th floor of the building. He

214

found that very notion somehow reassuring and calming. Enoch would often stop what he was doing at gaze at the glassy skyscraper while seated behind his desk. He had had the desk moved in front of the windows for just that purpose.

Enoch's office was huge. It stretched nearly the entire length of the top floor. The worn hardwood floors stretched away from his desk in all directions like ocean waves. At one end of the room was a glossy white panelled door which led to a white walled waiting room and four secretaries. There were also two smartly attired and very alert bodyguards who stood in front of silver elevator doors that were just beyond the secretaries work stations.

At the other end of the long office were a set of silver metal elevator doors and another glossy white panelled office door. The elevator was private and could only be accessed by someone with a metal key, a digital card, and the security code. It had access to all four floors and the sub basement parking garage. Enoch rarely ever entered the bank through the main entrance. He instead would park his car and take the elevator directly to his office.

The glossy white panelled door opened into a private white tiled room. The center room contained two different sinks and mirrors. The door to one side led to a small bathroom, while the opposite door led to an Edwardian claw footed white enamelled bathtub that had been there as long as the bank.

There was also a wooden wardrobe that held three business suits, a winter coat, and a built–in set of drawers that held carefully pressed white and light blue dress shirts.

There was a large wooden conference table in the middle of the expansive office. Wooden high backed chairs were placed at exact intervals along each side. Enoch's chair was at one end.

Enoch's large desk top included a leather blotter and four laptops and two tablet computers—all which were encrypted. There were also several smart phones sitting on the desk. The desk was Edwardian and made of maple.

THE KING OF THE GODS

The white crown molding that hovered above and encircled him was made up of ornate patterns. Enoch would sometimes stare at the patterns when lost in thought.

Enoch moved through the world of finance with **Jupiterian discernment**. The financial world, yes, the entire financial world, looked upon Enoch Tara with dread and awe. Many doubted the Enoch Tara was even real. That is, he was merely part of a hidden cabal. Enoch acted as the brain trust's spokesman, nothing more. Yes, it was all a ruse. No one person could be so able. The markets were too difficult to navigate alone. Enoch must be part of a much larger team.

Nothing could be further from the truth. No, the truth of the matter was that **Enoch operated alone**. Enoch's mind was like no other. It was infinite. Boundless. Enoch had always possessed this ability; an unwanted ability, but nonetheless, the ability.

He had only ever wanted to be a stage actor. Film had never really interested him. He had supposed, while at Oxford, that he could act in films to pay the bills, but that would be enough to live on. Enoch's heart belonged to two entities; one was the stage. He had planned everything out while studying at Oxford. He would do his time in the smaller regional theatres and eventually make his way to London. He would get better and better roles; he would win awards and prizes; he would be recognized as a great actor. He would be happy. His life would have purpose.

He had realized that night on stage in Oxford that he would never have the one thing he really wanted: Gemma's love. Gemma had been in love with someone else. Enoch would not interfere. Enoch's heart had broken that night on a stage filled with golden and glittering Ptolemaic backdrops of canvas and wood. He had retreated backstage, his face wet and tear streaked in black from the heavy kohl eye makeup that had been carefully applied just two hours before. Enoch, at nineteen, had lost the love of his life. Gemma would never be his.

Enoch had devoted his life to the theatre, a second love, but that too had been taken from him.

Fate had been cruel to Enoch. Though unrivaled in finance, Enoch had been left adrift. Enoch was good at making money, better than anyone else. Enoch's life had been filled with gilded triumphs, but little else.

He had nice homes and a few automobiles. He collected art, but nothing expensive. Not really. Art was not an investment for Enoch. He bought what he liked. Enoch was in love with gentle beauty. And who or what was more gentle or beautiful than Gemma? No one or nothing.

Gemma had reappeared in his life. He couldn't believe it. **Gemma**. When Gemma had emerged from the offices of Millennium Investments that morning at the Gherkin, he had wondered if she were a mirage. Could this really be her? After two decades—a lifetime—Gemma was standing before him. And when she spoke to the young woman at the front desk, he had been instantly transported back to the stage that autumn night in Oxford. Yes. Gemma was unlike any other.

Enoch had moved slowly. Gemma was like a small pond. Any sharp or sudden movements would cause ripples. Gemma was fragile. Enoch could sense that. He didn't want to cause her any harm. He loved her and Enoch's love for Gemma could not have been more pure.

Enoch had failed to come to Gemma's assistance when she had most needed it, and he couldn't understand why he hadn't. He had simply watched as Gemma had been destroyed in the press. What was it that had kept him away? Enoch couldn't answer. It had left him a bottomless well of grief and regrets. Is this how one treated someone they really loved? Enoch had abandoned Gemma when she had needed him most.

Now Gemma's heart had been won. Well, perhaps. Gemma had feelings for him. The kiss delivered in a tousle of brown hair and a cool summer breeze had made all of that very clear. But what next? Enoch was filled with doubt.

Doubt never held any sway with him in finance, why had it with Gemma? Enoch knew why: Gemma's love had to be won; earned. One had to be worthy of it. Enoch wanted to be worthy of it. Now, the like a fading dream, Gemma was within his grasp. But for some reason, Enoch could sense that this window was closing. Gemma was fading away.

Fate had granted Enoch ability, and like Heaven's Mandate, it could take it all away from him.

Enoch looked out the window of his fourth floor office. It was late in the evening. Twilight. **The Gherkin** appeared before him in silhouette. The sky was layered in rays of orange, magenta, blue, and purple light. The Gherkin had come to symbolize so much to Enoch. So much.

Gemma was on summer holiday in the Lake District. She was spending it with Poppy and her family. Gemma was also working on her small country house. Enoch was happy that Gemma had been able to purchase the small structure because it had made her so happy. And more than anything else, Enoch wanted Gemma to be happy.

Enoch sighed. He had so much work to do. Gemma had telephoned him the day before and invited him to come up and see her. His first impulse had been to attach his private railway car to the first train moving north, but he had had to refrain.

There was work to be done. Even Enoch Tara had to pay attention. He was almost done. A few more minutes and the project would be complete. He could then pass it on to the staff waiting for the file on the third floor.

The final glowing rays of purple, blue, and orange light illuminated Enoch's face as he typed out the instructions to his staff. Yes, the hand of Jupiter moved adeptly and quickly with the fading of the light. Now the light that caressed his face was purple and blue. Now blue. Now purple. Enoch completed his report and the sky finally went black.

Gemma—England—Mars Ascendant

THE LAKE DISTRICT
Louise and Freya were flat on their backs and staring at the ceiling of Gemma's drawing room when Louise's smartphone pinged. Louise hesitated to pick up the phone and look at it. The white plaster ceiling was infinitely more interesting to her at that moment. The ancient Egyptian hieroglyphics ran parallel to the ancient Greek letters. Yes, quite Ptolemaic.

The workmen had completed the ceiling in only a week. Gemma was thrilled with the results. When the second button on the light panel was pushed, lamps behind the white plaster hieroglyphics and Greek letters cast long shadows across the domed white ceiling. It was all so fantastic. Yes, Gemma's drawing room had been transformed into something Ptolemaic.

Louise and Freya now lay on the large red and purple Persian rug that covered the center of the drawing room. The rug was brand new and not quite Persian. It had been made in a factory in Holland owned by an Albanian entrepreneur. It was not only beautiful but quite affordable. And it was partly purple. It was also comfortable.

'So, what do you think, girls?' asked Gemma as she entered the drawing room. She was wearing light weight khaki trousers and a white open collared cotton top.

'Fantastic, Godmother,' replied Freya. Freya's eyes remained decidedly fixed on the ceiling above.

'Yes, Gemma. It's *marvellous*,' said Louise.

Both girls, clad in faded denim jeans, continued to stare at the domed plaster work above when Louise's smartphone pinged (again). Louise rolled over onto her stomach and looked at her phone.

'It's Mars!' said Louise happily. 'He's has just arrived at Poppy's. He says that he will be staying for the next week. That's great!' chirped Louise happily.

'It will be good to have Mars with us again,' said Gemma. 'When I visited the house on summer holidays while at All Saints, Mars, James, and some of their classmates from Eton and Oxford would play cricket in the castle grounds. It was so much fun. The boys were all dressed in beautiful cricket whites. Mars liked to wear the felt Eton cricket cap. James was going through his floppy hair phase and had a beautiful shock of glossy blonde hair. James was so handsome. He still is,' said Gemma.

She paused, stared up at the plaster ceiling for a moment, and then directed her gaze at the girls and continued.

'I would go up to the top of the tower with the other girls and watch the matches. We were a collection of sunglasses, straw hats with blue and white ribbons, and cotton skirts and white blouses. Oh, Poppy's hat usually had a purple ribbon. We would always carry a wicker basket of sandwiches and cold bottled drinks with us. Kulli would wear one of James' cricket blazers and we would all clap during the match. We would then sit on some wooden folding chairs and talk about, well, everything. We would usually watch the sunset with James and his friends from the tower.'

Gemma sighed and said, 'Mars was so young. We were all so young. Mars was always really nice to us. He taught Poppy about the constellations and how to identify them.'

Freya sat up and looked at Gemma. 'Is Enoch going to vacation in the Lake District this summer?'

'Yes. He said he would be arriving tomorrow. He has a house somewhere around here.'

'Really? That's interesting. He seems to have a house wherever you happen to be at the moment,' replied Freya with a mischievous grin.

'Freya. Stop,' replied Gemma, and she smiled.

'I bet if you were sunning yourself on the deck of a sailboat in the Atlantic, Enoch would show up on a battleship,' said Freya and she laughed.

Gemma and Louise both burst out laughing.

'Freya, stop it,' said Gemma.

'It will be nice to see Enoch again. I didn't really get to speak with him that much at the wedding. Enoch is really cute, Gemma. He seems really sweet,' said Louise.

'Where did you two disappear to during the reception? Yes. I noticed,' said Freya.

Gemma smiled and then laughed. 'Freya, when you find a boyfriend, I'm going to be merciless with you.'

Louise tapped out something on her phone and then smiled. 'Mars is having cold pepperoni pizza for dinner. He says that everyone but James is asleep. He says that it is good to be back at the castle.'

'Poppy's baby never seems to tire of pizza,' said Freya and she smiled.

Louise's phone pinged again and Louise laughed. 'That's what James just said to Mars.'

Gemma then looked at her silver Cartier watch: 10: 53pm. 'Girls, let's sleep on cots in the drawing room tonight.

'Sounds great, Gem. I haven't camped out in *yonks*,' said Freya in her now effortless Sloane intonation. Yes. Freya, under her mother's tutelage, had graduated into the ranks of the Sloane Rangers.

The girls all then walked into the back room to collect the camping cots and bedding. It was time to go to bed.

THE DRAWING ROOM
Mars, wearing khaki moleskin trousers, a white cotton dress shirt with a St James collar, and brown leather Oxfords, sat on one of the purple velvet

Art Deco chairs. Here, at the stately pile in the Lake District, Mars could relax. He was away from London, a city that now seemed to be in constant turmoil. He was glad to get away. These days, he was always glad to leave London.

His employer and former Oxford classmate had agreed to sell him a small cottage in Cumbria. It needed work, but nothing too extensive. The stone house needed to repainted, but the structure was sound. The cottage had been left unfurnished. No worries. Mars preferred to buy new furniture. He had already ordered a new bed frame and mattress. The house was only a half an hour away from the 12th Baron's castle. Mars wanted to be close to the family. His only neighbours were local farmers. The cottage was surrounded by farmland. That was perfect for Mars. After London, Mars preferred the relative isolation of the house.

Mars shipped what few belongings he had out to the house the week before. Everything Mars owned now fit into the back of a small white moving van. A few cardboard boxes of books, some school uniforms, classic tweeds, hunt coats, jodhpurs, leather riding boots, an old cricket bat of English willow he had had since Eton, and a box of photos. He also had a red leather case that held his baronial coronet and an old leather box suitcase that contained his baronial robes. Mars, once one of Hong Kong's most successful hedge fund managers, had been reduced to a few boxes of belongings and a four room cottage.

Mars wasn't depressed by the situation. He was actually quite happy. Like Gemma, Mars was now a homeowner again. Yes, he now lived in much reduced circumstances, but Mars felt he had regained his footing. He was doing well at work and rapidly building up his savings. He was also making investments that he hoped would allow him to leave London permanently. He was also in the process of buying a home overseas. Mars had found his way again.

Mars, the 13th Baron, leaned back in the Art Deco chair and looked at his silver Omega watch. It was almost noon. The cricket match would start soon. It was time to change into his cricket whites.

Gemma—England—Cricket among the Ruins

THE CASTLE RUINS

James, clad in crisp classic cricket whites, stood on the lush green lawn at the center of the castle grounds. The lawn had been carefully mowed the day before by a local landscaping company. The sun peaked out from behind giant white clouds that moved slowly across the blue sky gently propelled by the summer breeze. The weather that day alternated rapidly from warm, to cool, to cold, and back to warm again.

James had decided to teach his flaxen haired eight year-old twins how to play cricket. He had purchased them classic cricket whites the week before in London. He already had all the equipment he needed at the house. Well, that is, scattered all over the house. Ash and English willow cricket bats stood in several corners of several rooms of the house. There were cricket bags filled with equipment from his days at Eton and Oxford. Oh, and there were several cricket blazers from Eton and Oxford too. Felt caps hung from the backs of doors and were rolled up in dresser drawers. Cork cored cricket balls were easily found everywhere throughout the house, that is, **easily found when you weren't looking for them**. Yes, it was best for James to purchase more equipment while in London.

The girls, that is Poppy, Gemma, Freya and Louise, had been told of his plans and had all brought their uniforms with them or purchased cricket whites for the summer matches. Poppy, unable to play while pregnant, had purchased a white cricket outfit anyway, just to watch, and, if necessary, umpire some of the matches.

Louise and Freya had both played cricket while at All Saints. Freya was actually quite good at it; Louise, not so much.

Freya and Louise stood to one side of the smooth, shimmering, green cricket field in all the majestic trappings of the All Saints tri-color. Both wore blindingly white uniforms, but Louise had insisted tying her off-white All Saints cricket sweater around her tiny waist; the v- neck and cuffs bore the red, blue, and purple bands of the school. The strawberry blonde Louise also wore the purple (with blue and red stripes) felt cap of All Saints. Louise had insisted on wearing that too. Freya was content to wear mirrored Gentle Monster sunglasses and occasionally the All Saints cricket cap. Her blonde hair was still worn in two pony tails. Freya, resplendent in her cricket whites, stood like a white obelisk in the summer breeze.

Gemma had never really liked sports very much, but was happy to play it with the twins. She wore cricket whites and the traditional dark blue felt England cricket cap; her blue eyes were hidden behind her tortoise shell sunglasses.

Helen knew how to play cricket, and while not very good at it, was enthusiastic about teaching her children to play it. Helen, always stylish, had opted to tie her off white cricket sweater around her shoulders. Her long blonde hair had been tied back with a white ribbon.

The twins, Henry and Lucy, stood next to their mother in cricket whites. Both wore dark blue felt cricket caps. The eight year-old twins were excited; they had never played cricket before. They were about to become part of a long held family tradition. The blonde twins spoke to each other excitedly about the coming match. Henry insisted on giving his sister Lucy advice on how to play.

MORE THAN JUST A GAME

Cricket was important to the family. Members of the family had been positively devoted to the game since the 19th Century. The 12th Baron had been an excellent cricketer as had James. Cricket matches had been played on the castle grounds by successive generations of the family. James had hosted matches for his Eton classmates while on school holidays. The grounds had not hosted any matches since the 1990s. There had been only two male family members left to play and James did have children until he was almost 40. Poppy hadn't had any yet. Yes, the family line had been facing extinction. Now with two children of his own, and a party of willing house guests, James had enough people to play.

The weather that day in July was perfect. A gentle breeze cooled the group as they gathered in the Medieval grey stone ruins in their classic cricket whites.

The servants had set up a large off white canvas tent that was normally used during foxhunts. The sides had been rolled up to allow the wind to blow through it. A long, wooden, folding-table had been set up under it and a dozen folding wooden chairs were placed around it. There were several glasses set on a white cloth. A large blue plastic cooler with a white lid filled with ice and bottled water was on the grass next to the table.

Poppy, the baron and baroness, and Kata, one of the Croatian servants, took their places under the tent. The baron and baroness both wore cricket whites, but only the baron intended to play that afternoon. Kata, was wearing a light weight cotton version of her black uniform and dark sunglasses. Sometimes the young Kata let her sunglasses rest on her head of thick light brown hair.

Then, making a grand entrance, Mars, the God of War, appeared. In cricket whites and wearing a blue blazer, he made his way towards the cricket field. He was also carrying an English willow cricket bat. The God of War's brown hair, with a liberal sprinkling of grey, white, and silver, blew in the gentle breeze as he approached. Mars, resplendent in his cricket whites and blue blazer, was quite handsome.

'Sorry I'm late. I had to show one of the house guests where he could change into his whites,' said Mars as he stopped in front of the canvas tent.

Poppy arched an eyebrow. 'What other house guest?' asked a clearly perplexed Poppy.

'I found him walking up the drive with his cricket bag when I stepped out the front door. He said he was here for the cricket match and that he was a guest. I'd never seen him before. Marija seemed to be expecting him.'

James, standing next to the wicket, smiled. 'That's Gemma's friend from the City. Gemma asked if she could invite a friend to the match. Father agreed with me that we could use another bowler.'

Poppy tilted her head to one side and then another. *Enoch Tara is going to play cricket at my ancestral home? The mysterious Mr Tara is here?*

'Well, this *is* a surprise,' said Poppy, and she smiled. Gemma had drawn the elusive and highly secretive Enoch Tara to the Lake District. He must really love her. *I hope he really does.*

'Why wasn't I informed? Doesn't anyone ever tell me anything anymore?' asked Poppy laughingly.

Gemma couldn't hear what was being said across the green, but she could guess that Enoch must have arrived after all. Gemma had doubts that he would be able to make it. He had so much work to do in the City. But, she was happy that he was here. Yes, Enoch truly loved her. For sure.

A cool breeze raced across the castle grounds and ruffled the canvas tent a little, and then Louise turned her head and said happily, 'It's Enoch. He's here, Gemma.' And Louise smiled.

Gemma and Freya both looked in the direction of the castle gate. Enoch, in classic cricket whites and wearing the blue (with white piping trim) Harrow blazer, was carrying his cricket bag as he exited the gatehouse and made his way towards the large canvas tent. He slowed down a little as he noticed Gemma standing on the other side of the cricket field. Enoch smiled and nodded slightly in acknowledgment as he continued towards the baron and baroness. Courtesy demanded that he present himself to them first.

Enoch was so youthful and cute. No, not cute. Handsome. Gemma smiled.

The baron and baroness stood up and waited to receive their guest. Poppy, with a little help from Kata, did the same. James and Mars stood under the tent with the others. Helen and the twins walked up to the edge of the tent and waited under the shade of a large leafy tree. Gemma, Freya, and Louise walked across the cricket field to join the rest of the group.

Enoch reached the edge of the large off white canvas tent, hesitated for a moment, and then stepped into the tent. Enoch smiled.

'Welcome to my home, Mr Tara,' said the baron. 'I have heard quite a bit about you, from so many. It's nice to finally meet you,' said the baron, and he smiled.

'Thank you for allowing me to visit, your lordship.'

'This is my wife, and I believe you have already been met my son James and my daughter Poppy.'

'Yes, I have, sir. It's nice to meet you, ma'am. I met James at the wedding and Poppy at a Hungarian restaurant with Brian.' And Enoch smiled.

'Oh, and this is Mars, a member of the family too.' Upon hearing the 12th Baron's kind words, Mars, the 13th Baron, smiled.

'It's nice to meet you, again, Mars.'

'It's nice to meet you, Enoch. Again.' And Mars smiled.

Enoch, new to the circle of friends which surround Gemma, had been too shy to introduce himself to many of the guests at the wedding the month before. Now, with Gemma more firmly in his life, Enoch's confidence had returned.

Gemma, Freya, and Poppy then stepped into the tent. They stood to one side and listened to the conversation.

James and Mars started speaking quietly to each other a few feet from the group. James then walked back to the group with Mars and arched an eyebrow. 'Enoch, did you attend Harrow?'

'Yes, I did.'

James sighed and shook his head. 'You know, Poppy, we let one Old Harrovian into the family, and now more are starting to show up.'

Mars shook his head in agreement.

Enoch tilted his head and looked at the Old Etonians.

Poppy smiled and then burst out laughing. 'Welcome to the castle, Enoch!'

And everybody laughed.

'You had me going there for a moment,' said a relieved Enoch and he smiled. He then turned his attentions to Gemma. He approached her and smiled. 'It's good to see you, Gemmy.'

Gemma smiled. 'I wasn't sure if you would be able to escape the City. I'm glad you did.'

Gemma's words made Enoch melt. At that moment he felt that, yes, this would work out. They would be together. They would finally be a couple. Now and forever.

'Enoch, Freya and Louise have been looking forward to your visit too.'

'It's nice to see you again,' said Enoch to the young bowlers.

'You look really nice, Enoch,' said Louise happily. 'Are all Old Harrovians as handsome as you?'

Enoch smiled and was momentarily speechless; Poppy rescued him. 'Yes, probably. Mine is,' said the very pregnant Poppy who was wearing Brian's Harrovian blue blazer with her classic cricket whites. And Poppy flashed an impish smile.

Enoch turned slowly to face the diminutive Poppy, and said, 'Thank you, Poppy.' Enoch then turned around and his confidence restored once again replied, 'Poppy's right, Louise.'

And Enoch smiled.

THE CRICKET MATCH
The white clad bowlers, batsman, wicket-keepers, fieldsmen, and umpires thoroughly enjoyed themselves on the smooth, green, and lush cricket field on that warm (and sometimes cool) and breezy day in July.

The willow trees on the edges of the castles grounds swayed in the breeze and the children enjoyed looking for wayward cricket balls among the lavenders and tall grass that grew on the outer edges of the cricket green.

And yes, Gemma and Enoch slipped away after lunch.

And everyone noticed.

Gemma—England—Albion

THE HOUSE
Gemma's white Peugeot hatchback crested the hill and the sight that

awaited her and Enoch was breathtaking. It seemed the entire Lake District had suddenly appeared before them. Lush greens and silvery lakes seemed to envelop them as they moved along the road. The sky was a mixture of blue and white. The clouds were majestic. The swirling disc of fiery heat hovered in the distance.

Gemma, wearing her tortoise shell sunglasses, slowed as the small white automobile made its way down the hill.

THE MATCH

After the cricket match, the guests, still in their cricket whites, and the odd blue blazer, felt cap, and v-neck cable knit sweater, made their way into the large tent. Three of the sides had now been let down, though carefully placed vents in the canvas allowed for breezes to move through it. Piles of cricket equipment had been placed next to the large tent.

The house guests, tired and hungry, took their places around the long wooden table. This was meant to be an informal occasion, but Edward, the family chef, and the Croatian staff had seen to it that lunch was a rather posh affair. A white table cloth topped with white bone china, sterling silver silverware, and glassware had been carefully placed on the table. The wooden table was foldable and was usually kept in a stone shed with the canvas tent and folding wooden chairs behind the castle for just such occasions.

A late lunch (or was it an early dinner?) of braised beef and mash was served. There was also a selection of fresh bread, cold pasta salad, and fresh fruit, most of which had all been picked from bushes and trees around the castle. White ceramic bowls of cherries, strawberries, and raspberries had been placed in the middle of the table. Cold drinks were served by the staff.

The black-uniformed Croat housemaids moved adeptly between the tent in the castle grounds and the 12th Baron's blue Range Rover which Edward had used to ferry the food from the main house. The blue behemoth had been parked just outside the main gate.

Poppy's father had had an enjoyable day watching the makeshift cricket match. Poppy had occasionally donned a felt All Saints cap and umpired. Most of the time, it was Freya, quite the bowler in her own right, that did it.

The twins had had a great time. Each of them had done very well. Well, that's what everyone had told them. Really, that was as it should have been. The match was really for the children. Everyone made sure they had a fantastic time.

Louise, clad in cricket whites, had enjoyed the day as well. She looked quite nice in her cricket whites and felt cricket cap, and she knew it. Gemma and Poppy both had noticed how attractive the diminutive Louise had become. And confident. Yes, Louise had flourished at All Saints and now was about to enter university. Gemma and Poppy were happy. Louise had survived a very difficult childhood. Gemma and Mars both had gone through similar experiences and were happy for her.

Mars, James, and Enoch had enjoyed the cricket match too. A sort of light-hearted rivalry had developed between them. Enoch found himself captaining a team consisting of the twins, Gemma, and Helen. James, Mars, Freya, and Louise made up the rival team. James captained the rival team.

The cork cored cricket balls sang like partridges as they flew through the air.

Enoch seemed to spend a lot of time watching Gemma. He was quite pleased at her appearance in classic cricket whites. Eventually Gemma retrieved her cream colored cable knit All Saints cricket sweater from the backseat of her hatchback and tied it around her shoulders. The red, blue, and purple bands around the neck and cuffs shimmered around her. Enoch quite liked that small detail.

Gemma, for her part, loved the twins and was happy to have the opportunity to play cricket with them. She hugged them when they managed to hit the gentle pitches thrown by James, Mars, the 12th Baron, and Freya. When the twins smiled and laughed, so did Gemma. Yes, Gemma had been unable to have children of her own, but her friends had been kind enough to entrust their own children with her. For Gemma, this had been enough.

Freya had impressed *everyone* with her athletic ability. She had only started playing cricket because Louise had wanted to play, but she had discovered one of her hidden talents. Louise was not jealous; she was proud to have a friend like Freya. Freya, as Louise would often tell others, was not only beautiful, but highly intelligent and a skilled cricketer. Freya and Louise had never been rivals in any way, shape, or form. They were devoted friends and allies. This leisurely paced game of cricket had been but one more happy memory for them both.

Now, at lunch, the happy band of cricketers could relax, have a delicious meal, cold refreshments, and listen to the twins happily and excitedly tell everyone about their glorious exploits on the field. Yes, here amongst the castle ruins, the cricket party could find happiness, peace, and calm. Here, ensconced in the ancestral family lands, they were safe and away from the turmoil of the cities which now blighted their native land.

THE ESCAPE
Eventually the party started to drift away from the tent. Poppy's parents were the first to return to the main house, followed by Poppy, Helen and the twins. James, Mars, Freya, and Louise headed up the tower to enjoy the view. That left Enoch and Gemma walking around the castle grounds.

It was now evening; however, the days were quite long in the summer, so plenty of sunshine awaited them. What to do with it?

Enoch wanted to take Gemma away. He wanted to be alone with her. Their relationship had taken a much hoped for turn. Gemma consumed his thoughts. Enoch was living an impossible dream. Gemma was never meant to be his. But now, she was. Gemma walked alongside him. She loved him. Did she really? Of course she did; otherwise, she would not have kissed him. Gemma would never have done that unless she had loved him. Enoch smiled.

'Gem. Would you mind if we went off on our own? I mean. I would like to spend the rest of the day with you, if that would be alright with you.'

Gemma stopped walking and glanced at Enoch. The cream cable knit sweater was still wrapped around her shoulders. Her tortoise shell sunglasses were resting on her silky head of brown hair. She looked at him for a moment. Enoch started to wonder if he had said the wrong thing. Was he taking Gemma away from her surrogate family? Was if wrong of him to have asked? Enoch stood and waited for her response. It didn't take long.

'Yes. I would like that, Enoch. Where would you like to go?' Gemma then arched an eyebrow and smiled.

Enoch exhaled.

'Well, how about your country house? I have heard so much about it. I would love to see it.'

Gemma tilted her head back and thought carefully for a moment.

'Alright. I'd love to show you the house. My car is parked in the main garage. We can walk to it.'

'What about the others. Shouldn't we tell them we are leaving?'

'No. I think everyone is fully expecting us to slip away unannounced. It's what we do when we are together at gatherings, isn't it?' And Gemma smiled mischievously.

Enoch thought about what Gemma had said for a moment and then smiled. 'You're right, Gemma. We do tend to slip away from events together. It's practically a tradition now.'

'Alright then. Let's go.'

The departure through the gatehouse by the couple had been noticed immediately by the small party on the battlements. No one said a word. None of them even seemed to be surprised. All of them assumed that this would happen and so they returned to discussing the history of the castle with James.

THE COUNTRY HOUSE
Gemma drove slowly down the tree lined road and stopped in front of her country house. Well, the former Royal Air Force building that she described as her 'country house'. She unbuckled her seatbelt and looked at her silver Cartier watch: 9:10pm. It was late. The Sun would soon begin its slow descent.

'Welcome to the country pile,' said Gemma and she smiled.

They both exited the small white hatchback and Gemma led Enoch to the front entrance. She turned and said, 'Enoch, you are about to enter Cleopatra's throne room. Are you fully prepared for what awaits?'

'Yes. I am. I hope so.'

THE PTOLEMAIC ART DECO CHAMBER
The couple, still wearing cricket whites, entered the large red brick structure. Enoch, in classic cricket whites and blue blazer, entered the large drawing room. Obviously Gemma had some kind of surprise planned for him.

Gemma walked in front and then stopped and turned around. Gemma was standing on the large red and purple Persian rug in the center of the nearly empty room next to a wooden coffee table. She smiled. The fading summer daylight filled the white walled room.

Gemma smiled. She then walked over to one of the large sash windows and closed the white curtains. The room grew darker. She then went window to window closing each curtain until the room was almost completely dark. Only a few rays of sunshine entered the room thrown then gaps in the drawn curtains.

Enoch was now standing at the entrance to the drawing room. Enoch and Gemma were now both appeared as shadowy figures.

Enoch watched Gemma walk across the room and then stop at the wall. Gemma pushed a button on a small white panel and a set of dim lights came on.

Enoch's gaze could not help but notice the white plaster ceiling that hovered over them both. It was stamped with all kinds of intricate patterns. Art Deco? No. Enoch's eyes adjusted and refocused on the glyphs and ancient letters that had been stamped in the ceiling: Egyptian hieroglyphics and ancient Greek letters covered the entire ceiling. The crown molding consisted of white plaster hieroglyphics cut outs. Suddenly the lights came on and even in the dwindling light of the late summer day Enoch could see the lights behind the plaster glyphs casting elongated shadows across the ceiling. The effect was amazing. The outlined shadows of the hieroglyphics arched up and across the domed ceiling.

Gemma clicked another button on the light panel and then the light intensified. She then pushed the third button and the lights went off. Now only natural light filled the room.

'Fantastic, Gem!' said Enoch. 'The ceiling is spectacular. It makes the house, Gemmy.'

Gemma, illuminated in electric light cast by the wall lamps, then stretched her arms towards the ceiling and said, Welcome to Alexandria.' And Gemma smiled.

Yes. Quite dramatic.

'Quite impressive, Gemma. Quite imaginative.'

'Actually. I got the idea from the design of Poppy's bedroom at the family pile. Her great aunt Jane designed something like it in the 1920s. I added the ancient Greek letters because I wanted something Ptolemaic, not solely Egyptian. That detail was mine.'

Enoch smiled. Suddenly a wave of emotion swept over him. Enoch was standing with Gemma in her small house in the country. She was showing him this decorated room because she wanted him to see it. She wanted him to be there with her. Three months ago, Enoch would have thought all this impossible, and now it was happening. Enoch inhaled and then exhaled. He felt lightheaded. Was this really happening? Yes. Why had he waited so long? Why had he failed Gemma? He should have come to her rescue years ago. He hadn't. Was he worthy of her? No. He didn't deserve her. Gemma needed someone who would always be there for her. That someone was not him. Enoch felt his throat tighten. He sighed.

'What's wrong?' asked Gemma. The concern in her face was apparent.

Enoch was rooted to the ground. He felt himself go cold. Panic filled his eyes. **He was losing her.**

Gemma, now distressed, approached him and stopped. She looked into his eyes. What was wrong?

'Gem. I failed you. When you needed me most, I failed you. I don't deserve you, Gem,' said Enoch, his voice choked with emotion. 'You deserve better. I'm sorry.'

'Enoch, what is wrong?'

'Gemma, during the trial, I didn't help you. I watched you being destroyed and did nothing.'

Gemma exhaled. She now understood. Enoch, sensitive soul. Gentle soul. He was grief stricken. Gemma looked into Enoch's eyes and said softly, 'Enoch. Please. Don't leave me. I need you. If you leave, you will hurt both of us. You will destroy both of us. We have a chance, Enoch. God has given us this chance. Don't you see that? Enoch, you have to forgive yourself. I have made mistakes and it took me a long time to forgive myself. Enoch, you are not responsible for what happened to me.'

Enoch, trembling, remained unconvinced.

'Gemma, if I had come to your aid immediately, you would not have suffered all that you have.'

Gemma shook her head. 'Enoch, who is to say it wouldn't have happened anyway? Maybe something even worse would have happened if you had intervened? You don't know. We will never know. What I do know is that I love you, and I need you. I need you.'

Enoch now stood motionless. Another wave, like iron slammed into him. Yes, it was all clear now. Enoch was sure. Alright. Everything will be alright. Courage, Enoch. Courage.

And then the world stood still.

'Gemma. I have to ask you now,' said Enoch and he took a breath.'Gemma. I love and need you more than anyone. Please. Stay with me. Gemma. Will you marry me?' asked Enoch.

Gemma wrapped her arms around Enoch, looked into his eyes and said softly, 'Of course.'

www.ingramcontent.com/pod-product-compliance
Lightning Source LLC
Chambersburg PA
CBHW05073818180626
46814CB00002B/814